THE TIES THAT BIND

An Amish Romance

Seekers
Book Two

Linda Byler

New York, New York

The characters and events in this book are the creation of the author, and any resemblance to actual persons or events is coincidental.

THE TIES THAT BIND

Good Books books may be purchased in bulk at special discounts for sales promotion, corporate gifts, fund-raising, or educational purposes. Special editions can also be created to specifications. For details, contact the Special Sales Department, Good Books, 307 Fifth Avenue, 4th Floor, New York, NY 10016 or info@skyhorsepublishing.com.

Good Books is an imprint of Skyhorse Publishing, Inc.®, a Delaware corporation.

Visit our website at www.goodbooks.com.

10 9 8 7 6 5 4 3 2 1

Library of Congress Cataloging-in-Publication Data is available on file.

Print ISBN: 978-1-964219-18-9
Ebook ISBN: 978-1-964219-39-4

Cover design by Jon Godfredson Design

Printed in the United States of America

Chapter 1

In late January there was an unexpected thaw. An array of icicles dripped from Raymond Beiler's barn roof as he stood in the doorway contemplating the beauty of the setting sun reflected on the drops of water that suspended for a split second before they fell.

A quiet man in his upper forties, his smooth face unlined, his felt hat sitting low on his forehead, his eyes were unclouded with the anxieties many men would have experienced at this stage in his life.

A toothpick in his teeth, his hands in the pockets of his broadfall trousers, he shook his head very slightly, shuffled his feet in the melting snow, and turned to open the barn door. He nodded in answer to the low nicker from his driving horse. His thoughts were miles from the task at hand, so he shoved the feed scoop into the bag of turkey feed and watched it flow into the feedbox. Only when the horse snorted and stamped one foot in confusion did he catch on to the mistake, then proceeded to dip it out with his bare hands.

The male turkey let out one of his rusty gobbles, a sound delighting his senses. Taking up the feed scoop, he unlatched the door on the turkey pen and scattered the cracked corn into the low plastic dish, leaning an elbow on the wooden post to watch the gobbler and four hens walk on their skinny legs to reach it.

A bevy of brown and white quail darted between the heavy turkeys for their share. From the rafters, the low, contented cooing of homing pigeons gave him a sense of well-being, an aura of peace.

He'd just come through another tumultuous evening meal with his beloved, if troubled, wife of over twenty-five years. The only child remaining at home was their daughter Cathy, the oldest of only three children, a contentious young woman given to a petulant nature and an almost total disregard of her upbringing.

Raymond winced, drew a hand across his stomach as it rumbled painfully, a normal occurrence and one he kept largely to himself. His wife, Lydia, had more than she could handle these days, so he certainly meant to make life easier for her in every way possible. He belched and felt relief, turned away to refill the scoop for the driving horse, then took up a few blocks of hay and threw them in the wooden hay trough. Taking down the broom, he swept halfheartedly at the few wisps of hay on the cement floor, hung it on the nails provided for that purpose, and stood quietly in the middle of the barn floor, biding his time.

Reality seeped in slowly, as if a small crack in his reserve allowed troubled water to ripple his quiet peace of mind. What was this? What was happening to his beloved children, his beloved wife? For they were beloved, by him, surely. Had always been, although it seemed as if all the love in his heart could not stem the flow of tainted waters threatening to create turmoil in his existence.

He did not want this. None of it. So he exchanged troubled thoughts for a childlike optimism, one that carried him above the turbulent events surrounding him. He did not want to go back into the house at all, but he believed this was his duty—to spread love and cheer to his wife and daughter, to smooth out the wrinkles of their contention, always clinging to the idea of a love that never failed.

He avoided confrontation at all costs, believing the Christian way of peace and love was his calling, and he was meant to create a quiet atmosphere in spite of adversity. He felt a physical pain in his chest, remembering the exchange at the supper table, the hurled accusation of turning a blind eye. In retrospect, perhaps he had done just that, but he couldn't help but feel a raw pity for his youngest daughter, a pity hurting him as if his own skin was scraped by knives.

Two months, give or take a few days, since she'd left, creating a whole new level of chaos in a house often brimming with ill feelings.

Lavina had her father's quiet nature and had suffered through days of tense conversation, dire predictions spouting like loosened openings on a fire hydrant. For years, Lavina had done well, thriving in her own world of spreading love, placating ill tempers through acts of kindness, soothing frazzled nerves, a heroine to Raymond, a shining star.

And then one night she was gone.

Raymond shook off the memories, took a deep breath, and turned his face to the rafters of the barn, the cobwebs and old barn swallow nests both a serious offense to his wife. She detested the barn swallows making a mess on the barn floor. Why in the world would he allow it?

And how often did he sweep cobwebs? Her own father would never have allowed an accumulation of them the way he did. Well, she wasn't about to start cleaning his barn. She kept everything else spotless and had enough to worry about.

But somewhere above the rafters, there was God, whose face shone through—the patient, ever-loving, and benevolent Father of Lights who gave his children all gifts to enjoy. Raymond truly believed He was a God of love and well wishes, sending trials from time to time, no doubt, but it was all a chastening out of love.

He closed his eyes and spoke to his Father, asking for the safety of Lavina, peace for Cathy, and to please help Lydia carry the burden of real and imagined anxieties.

The air had turned colder as the sun slid behind the mountain, but he took a deep breath of the invigorating air and stopped to admire the twilight through the trees before making his way to the house.

The flowering quince bush was alive with the frantic twitters of the purple house finches, a common little bird Lydia disliked, calling them hogs at the feeder. He found them fascinating, these tiny, dull birds with oversized beaks, so skilled at extracting sunflower seeds from their shells.

They reminded him of his aunt Barb, the way she chewed so fast and furious, never opening her small mouth before she swallowed.

He smiled to himself.

He couldn't remember the last time he'd seen Barb. A single maiden lady, she was quite confident in her preferences to live life on her own terms without the inconvenience of having to cater to a needy husband. In her settled opinion, a good man was rare—they all needed to grow up.

He smiled again, then let himself into the kitchen, where he bent to remove his boots, setting them side-by-side on the clean plastic tray provided for them. The house was quiet, and for this he was grateful.

No one called his name. He saw the washed dishes stacked in the drainer, the spotless countertop and floor, heard the shower upstairs, and felt a distant sense of relief. He padded across the kitchen in his stocking feet, dropped into his gray La-Z-Boy and put up the footrest, then reached for the daily paper.

He was thankful for the rest after the evening meal in winter, felt the length of his body relax into the comfort of a good chair, and sighed. Yes, there was always, always something to be thankful for, just the way the plaque on the wall said.

"There you are, Raymond. What took you so long?" His wife came through the basement door carrying two jars of home-canned grape juice.

"I didn't realize it took longer than usual."

"Well, I need you to look at the spigot upstairs in Cathy's bathroom. She says it drips and it's annoying when she lies awake at night."

"Okay, but it sounds like she's in the shower now."

"I didn't say now."

She lifted a jar of grape juice, frowned, and clucked.

"Does this stuff look right to you?"

She brought it over and held it below the battery lamp.

He felt her nearness, saw the color of her sleeve, the smooth hands with the clipped nails clutching the jar, and the slight pucker above her nose, her forehead pinched the way it always was when she concentrated. She smelled of soap and fresh air, with the slight scent of food from the kitchen, a familiar scent. A great love welled up in his heart. His own dear wife, in spite of everything.

He put his glasses on his nose, peered through the bifocals.

"Looks alright to me."

He found her eyes and let his love shine through, but she turned away and told him he just wasn't concentrating on the color.

"That's the thing about buying this New York grape juice instead of juicing your own grapes. You really don't know what goes into this stuff. They could add leaves and insects, anything. I'm making grape mush to take to Susan's quilting tomorrow, and you know how she is."

"No, I don't know how she is," Raymond said, smiling a little.

Lydia wave a hand. "You know, everything has to be right."

Raymond thought better of answering and instead lifted his paper and perused the front page. As he read, he heard cupboard doors, a kettle lifted, put on the stove, and felt a small whirl of joy for no reason.

Upstairs, the shower stopped, and before long Cathy came pounding down the stairs, dressed in a brilliant red dress, carrying a hooded fur coat, her eyes alight with excitement. Raymond folded the paper and laid it aside, apprehension mounting in his chest, watching for Lydia's reaction from the stove.

There was a sense of time being suspended and a sharp intake of breath.

"Cathy!"

Lydia's voice was thick with despair and disappointment.

"What?" The insolence in her tone was palpable, and the stone in Raymond's chest threatened to stop his breathing.

"I told you no. Raymond, help me here," Lydia pleaded.

"Where are you going, Cathy?" he asked, keeping his voice mild.

"Out."

Lydia's strident voice broke through the atmosphere so tense with the very thing Raymond avoided at all costs. Lydia wailed, pleaded, and threatened, but when the headlights came up the drive, Cathy threw on the coat and tossed her head, slammed the door vigorously, and disappeared.

The only sound was Lydia's breathing, a car door slamming before pulling away.

The usual tirade followed, Lydia's voice rising and falling as she unloaded blame and guilt, piling it on his shoulders until the weight threatened to crush his spirit. He took up the paper, pretended to read, but could not tune out the strident accusations. Finally, he got up and went to the basement to remove himself from the harried attack.

The basement was his refuge, the place of warmth and solitude, where no voice or prying eyes could follow. The wood stove with its constant heat was the heart of the home, his old chair beside it like a true friend.

He folded himself into it, looked around at the paneled walls, the neat pine trim, and was doubly thankful for the previous owner's skilled workmanship.

A few guns on the wall, his fishing rods and tackle box. There was never extra money to buy the things he would have loved to own, but that was the sacrifice a man made for his family. He had no desire for the headache of owning his own business, but rather chose to live on a budget, faithfully paying his mortgage and real estate taxes, a sense of gratitude his guiding star.

Like the ping-pong table bought at an estate auction for twenty dollars, in perfect condition. He was so proud of that deal. He brought it home to Lydia who lifted her hands, her eyes wide with amazement. That was what really brought him happiness, for sure.

The couch on the far wall, the two chairs and coffee table had all been purchased at yard sales. Good furniture, although Lydia had frowned and dismissed his love of a good bargain before paying ten times the amount to have a steam cleaning company come in to disinfect it, which seemed wasteful to his way of thinking.

There was a bookshelf, an old sideboard, a child's kitchen set, and the small table and chairs the children used when they were small.

He could hardly wait for grandchildren, the crowning glory of every parent, but the way things were now, he could hardly see it happening.

Where was Cathy going? He couldn't remember all the yelling at the supper table, just bits and pieces. It wasn't really yelling, just strong conversation, and there was nothing wrong with that.

Did it matter so much where Cathy went? To his way of thinking, Cathy was old enough to make her own choices, but he would never stand up and say that, afraid of the disagreeable torrent of words following.

If a child was strong-willed, determined to go their own way, he couldn't see there was much to be done. All the discipline in the world would only create a heart of stone, and one power struggle after another. But this conviction he kept to himself as well.

And so he holed up in the basement until he heard the shower and footsteps, waited till there was blessed silence before heaving more wood on the fire and closing the draft for the night. He made his way up the stairs heavily, a certain sadness riding on his shoulders as he entered the kitchen. He should read in the Scriptures, but didn't have the heart for it just now, so he poured a glass of water, took a shower, and climbed into bed. He touched Lydia's shoulder tentatively and asked quietly if she was asleep. When there was no response, he turned on his side and began to pray, remembering his son, Amos, and Lavina who had gone to make a home with him.

Lydia, however, was far from sleep, lying awake with her heart pounding in fear, her thoughts racing headlong into the dark void of worry, self-blame, and the helplessness she felt so often at night. She longed to talk to Raymond about all of the family's problems but knew he would not say much of anything. He did not think it was necessary to discuss thoughts and feelings. They never really had, so why start now? She knew how he was. Sweep it under the rug, act like everything's fine.

She seethed quietly before tears slid from beneath her lashes and across the bridge of her nose, saturating her pillow as she began to heave. What was wrong with her children? Why couldn't they listen the way other people's children did?

Look at Amos Fisher's and Ben Lapp's children. All Amish, all keeping the *ordnung* (Amish rules), *gehorsam* (obedient), upstanding members of the Amish church who truly believed and respected the rules. Oh, she was a failure at parenting. A total failure. Shame and guilt suffocated her as her thoughts continued their wild leap from one shortcoming to another. It was like being a mouse trapped in a five-gallon bucket, a plastic one with smooth sides you could not scale, so around and around you went, wearing yourself out and still clueless.

She heard the grandfather's clock chime out the hour, then another, and still Cathy did not return. Suddenly furious, she reached for the small flashlight on her nightstand, threw back the covers, and made her way across the floor to the clock. She yanked the door open and stopped the pendulum, muttering to herself about her lack of sleep, raising children, and getting married in the first place.

Plus, she had to go to work in the morning, cleaning Viola Cleason's house, the worst one of all. Five hours of cat hair, cat litter, and cat food. She could absolutely throw up. She tried to stop her thoughts, tried to pray, but was immediately distracted by a rush of anxiety about that grape mush. It was the cheapest, most common dessert to take to Susan's quilting, but the truth of the matter was astounding—her checkbook was empty, and she only had a few dollars cash in her wallet. She was low on groceries and didn't have Cool Whip or Oreo cookies or any of the ingredients for a nice dessert. She couldn't believe how her money disappeared. The price of groceries was atrocious, especially eggs and milk. She'd have to see about getting chickens, maybe a nice little Guernsey cow.

She used to milk at home, thought she was quite capable, until her mother complained about the straw, or the bits of dirt in the fresh bucket of milk. She couldn't do anything right for her mother.

And so her thoughts tumbled and roiled. Her feet felt as if they were buzzing, such an absolute misery, so she rolled on her back, shoved one foot out into the cold air, then the other. That brought relief, but then goose bumps chased each other up and down her spine.

She felt chilled, so she tucked her feet back under the covers.

Raymond made a funny noise in his throat, then began a full repertoire of snoring, a loud rumbling, wheezing sound that set her teeth on edge. She could not believe this.

"Raymond," she hissed, hitting the middle of his back with her elbow.

"Hm? What?" he mumbled, turning on his side. Blessedly, he stopped snoring.

Lydia practiced deep breathing, began to yawn, tipped the alarm clock and pressed the button. One-twenty. *You have got to be kidding,* she thought wildly.

Where was Cathy?

She actually thought of calling her, but she hated the fact that Cathy owned a cellphone—and not a flip-phone, either. One of those dreadful smart phones where she had access to all kinds of evil, worldly things. She would never call her. If she did, it meant she was accepting that horrible device.

Finally, a pair of headlights wound its way up the drive, casting a brilliant white light on the ceiling, then down the walls. Oh, wonderful relief, these lights. Cathy was home. She waited for the door to open, familiar footsteps, but there were none. Now the lights had vanished.

Lydia crept to the window, parted the blinds, and stared out at two orange parking lights like malevolent eyes staring back at her.

What were they doing parked in the driveway like that?

She thought of Raymond and herself, tying the horse at the hitching rack, dating so sweetly and innocently. A hot anger tore through her.

Well, she wasn't getting away with this.

She pulled on her ratty old housecoat, thrust her feet into house slippers, threw on a sweater, and used her trusty flashlight to make her way between banks of melting snow. She walked up to the white vehicle and rapped sharply on the window. When there was no response, she did it again, her heart pounding almost painfully.

She stepped back when the door hit her stomach.

"What do you want?" Cathy hissed.

"I want you out of that vehicle and in the house. Now."

Cathy pulled on the door handle. Lydia pulled it open. Cathy yanked it shut and locked it, leaving Lydia pounding on the window.

In the morning, Lydia had two hours of sleep behind her, a roaring headache, and a sour stomach, but she packed Raymond's lunch, made his breakfast, and didn't say a word. She had absolutely no idea how she was ever getting through the day, but she was not telling Raymond, not now.

She knew Cathy would pout for days, but she carried a sense of victory, a bolster of self-worth taking her through the day.

Viola Cleason was in her mid-eighties, a wealthy eccentric living on the first floor of a huge Victorian house on Chicago Street in Rochester. She drove an immaculate Cadillac from the seventies, a long, sleek fire engine-red monstrosity she wobbled along in, narrowly escaping mishaps as she clutched the steering wheel with knobby, arthritic fingers and liver-spotted blue-veined hands. Lydia always wore her seat belt and hoped for the best as they wound along country roads.

In the house, Viola liked for Lydia to use undue amounts of Scott's Liquid Gold on her furniture, vinegar water and crumpled newspaper on windows, Glade air freshener on ancient chairs and sofas, powdered Comet for bathrooms.

Six immense felines ruled the house, and Lydia gritted her teeth and smiled as they rubbed against her skirt, chased the old Hoover vacuum, and pounced silently on countertops and doily-laden dressers. They regularly knocked over lamps and figurines and threw up on vintage rugs. They were all named, of course, but Lydia could never keep them straight.

"Lydia," she heard in Viola's quavering voice.

"Yes?"

"Come. I have something for you."

She put down the dust rag to find Viola seated at the kitchen table, a cup of steaming tea and a slice of pie before her.

"One for you," she beamed, pointing to the opposite side.

"Thank you, Viola. This is surely a treat."

She scalded her tongue on what she could only guess was tea made from catnip—just awful. The pie appeared to be mincemeat, that gruesome mixture of ground meat, raisins, and spices that tasted and smelled like cat food.

She vowed she would tell Viola she was quitting, give her two weeks' notice. Still, she felt obligated to keep forking up small pits of pie, thinking self-pitying thoughts as she listened to Viola's accounts of raising her darling children, both through college, with children of their own, good marriages, such a blessing the Lord had provided.

"That's wonderful," she said, scraping her rough tongue over her teeth, feeling the heat in her face as she glanced at the thermostat on the wall. Seriously. Seventy-eight degrees.

But when Viola counted out six twenty-dollar bills and thanked her so profusely, she was not in a state of mind to disappoint the old friend and agreed on a date two weeks later.

RAYMOND WHISTLED AND hummed his way through the day, working in the large and well-ventilated shop, doing what he loved, creating furniture and spindles for railing, the scent of sawdust and shavings reminding him he was exactly where he wanted to be. Lydia had packed him a wonderful sandwich, cold meatloaf with ketchup and pickles on homemade bread, and a jar of golden sliced peaches, plus peanut butter crackers with marshmallow cream. She had surely gone to a lot of trouble.

He had a good wife in so many ways and he felt the familiar rush of gratitude. A blessing, a virtuous woman.

One of the young men who worked in the paint room stopped to watch him at the lathe, peered into his face expectantly, so Raymond shut down the machine, lifted his safety goggles, and raised an eyebrow.

"Are you always happy?"

"Oh, I wouldn't say that. I can be grouchy."

"I don't think you know how to be grouchy."

Raymond laughed, shook his head, couldn't think of anything to say. The young man clapped a hand on his shoulder.

"You're the best, Raymond."

He watched the youth move away, felt his eyes fill for a moment. Who could deserve that now? Not him.

He bent over, started the lathe, and whistled on, a nameless tune that spoke of his inner joy.

THEIR EVENING MEAL was sullen, a silent display of ill feelings between Cathy and her mother, but nothing was said about the previous evening's theatrics. Raymond complimented the chicken soup, ate his hot dog on white bread and said he'd never had a better one.

Cathy glared at him, and Lydia shrugged, so he quit trying to lighten the atmosphere and went out to feed the horse and his flock of turkeys.

He often thought of Amos and Lavina, wondered sadly if they got along together, and how soon she would be back. He certainly hoped they would not both stay with the English people in the future—it was hard enough losing Amos to the English. He would have to call Amos again, try and keep him from forgetting his Amish background, bring him back to the fold, if such a thing was possible.

Why was it Amish parents of children who decided to leave the faith were counted as Class-A failures? Successful parenting was measured by adherence to the rules, every child meekly following in the forefather's footsteps. But shouldn't people let God be the ultimate judge? What human could really know another human's heart, whether Amish or English? He chewed on a long piece of hay, ran a hand along the silky neck of his driving horse, and wondered these things. He knew Lydia well, and she would think he was a heretic with such thoughts. Amish was the right way, and English the wrong way.

Well, Raymond figured he was on a journey till the day he died, and he only had to allow the Holy Spirit to guide him. He knew he must remain teachable, not set in all his own ways.

Chapter 2

The large yellow house, its tall windows framed by black louvered shutters, with a deep porch wrapping around two sides and broad steps leading to the massive front door, glowed in the sunlight as the sun slipped toward the mountain.

The barberry bushes glistened with melting ice and the white pines were alive with a small flock of black-eyed juncos creating a rollicking little fuss with their incessant twittering. The grounds surrounding the house were immaculate. Even in winter, the pruning and fertilizing was apparent in the way boxwoods were trimmed, lilac and forsythia bushes in neat little groves. Rose bushes were protected by stakes wrapped with burlap, the garden down by the shed a lovely green sea of tillage radishes beneath the layers of snow.

Great white and red oak trees, spruce and maples, sycamores in their loose white bark by the creek created a picturesque scene waiting to be photographed by some traveling journalist, though most folks never saw past the small gatehouse down by the end of the drive.

This was where Amos Beiler made his home when he answered an advertisement in his father's newspaper when he was seventeen. Obese, skin like punched bread dough, painful acne and small brown eyes hidden in puffy folds, he had lumbered through his years in an Amish parochial school, often mocked and belittled, even by his own sister Cathy. His mother, Lydia Beiler, sewed larger and larger trousers, bought husky shirts in extra large that popped buttons across his stomach. At sixteen, a job in a bulk food store went south when he was accused of touching a girl inappropriately, and he walked away, accused unfairly, roiling in shame and terrible humiliation.

The best thing he'd done was to answer that ad. He met Joseph and Lila Smith and learned what love actually was. It was acceptance, praise, a sense of having done something right for the first time in his life, and he fully devoted himself as a groundskeeper to the old couple.

He missed his parents and Lavina sometimes, and would return to visit, but he was always met with stiff opposition by his mother, his father passive and bowing to her wishes.

So he left the Amish way of life, eventually got a license and his own truck, saw a dermatologist for his skin, and joined a gym and made friends there, especially the owner named Scott.

Now in his mid-twenties, his sister Lavina, tired of the never-ending dramatics at home, had asked to live with him, was introduced to Joseph and Lila, and a new chapter began. Amos was grateful for Lavina's company, especially after his beloved dog Fred got hit by a truck and passed away. The loss had broken his heart.

Amos had been dating an Amish girl named Anna Riehl, but they decided to take a break because of their differences, although she still came to the house each spring to do a thorough cleaning.

Amos and Lavina had both been invited to dinner soon after she arrived, which was actually supper to Amos and Lavina's way of thinking, and they sloshed up the long winding driveway as the sun spread liquid gold on the beautiful old house.

"You know, this place is breathtaking," Lavina commented. Amos nodded.

"Some days I still can't believe I get to live here. At the same time, it's hard to imagine ever living anywhere else."

Lavina nodded, her large, round eyes on his face. She was a very attractive girl, same as Cathy, but with a sweet, sunny disposition and a soft heart, like her father, Raymond. When she'd explained her reasons for leaving home in pleading tones it had sent her mother into hysterics, her father into himself, retreating to the basement with sadness.

They were welcomed into the house, seated by the fireplace, and given warm drinks till Nancy had dinner on the table.

"I'll help," Lavina offered, and went to find Nancy, who was swinging cupboard doors, kicking refrigerator doors closed, and taking out a great roaster of pot roast and potatoes.

"Can I help you with anything?" Lavina volunteered timidly.

"No, of course not. You go sit down."

Lavina felt a bit embarrassed, but Lila laughed, said she might as well get used to Nancy. She didn't want help in the kitchen, in spite of having to work the way she did.

From their place at the massive dining room table, Amos and Lavina learned the ways of the English well-to-dos. There were two forks, a soup spoon, and a dessert spoon, goblets and water glasses. They learned never to place elbows on the table, to always say please and thank you. Joseph said good etiquette was being forgotten by too many.

"There are old traditions among our people, same as yours," Lila remarked. "Joseph and I strictly adhere to good manners at dinner."

She watched Lavina put her napkin beside her plate and gently reminded her to place it on her lap. Lavina opened her eyes wide and asked why, which made Joseph laugh louder than Amos had ever heard.

"What good does a napkin do on your lap?" she repeated.

Lavina became a fast favorite that evening and was soon a fixture at the big house. She cleaned and learned how to do laundry Lila's way, which included ironing sheets, pillowcases, all Joseph's shirts, and quite a few of Lila's dresses.

Their evenings were spent quietly in the gatehouse, often watching television, which Lavina wasn't sure was a good thing.

"You know, Amos, our parents wouldn't approve."

"It seemed wrong for me, too, in the beginning, it really did. But I don't know. It's like choosing reading material. There's decent stuff and stuff you shouldn't waste time watching. I don't really see a problem with watching the decent stuff."

Lavina nodded, then looked up at him.

"Do you hate the Amish? Our people?"

"Of course not. There are many good Amish people."

There was a long silence between them as they became lost in their own thoughts. Finally, Lavina asked what he thought the problem was at home.

Amos looked up, raised one eyebrow comically. "There's a problem?"

"Come on, Amos. Why are we here?"

Amos sighed, and the silence stretched like a taut string.

"It's hard to talk about."

"It's hard to admit your own mother is a mess. And even harder to admit your father is unrealistic and has absolutely no spine."

"Did you just say that, Lavina? Wow. Honestly? You want to know the truth? Our house was a battleground and Cathy was the queen. She ruled, no doubt about it."

After they advanced into forbidden territory, there was no holding back. Everything, every dysfunctional working of their home, was dissected, examined, and discussed. There were tears, sometimes rage, and often an underlying sadness they could not deny, much less know how to deal with.

When they checked the time, it was after twelve, and they laughed with a self-consciousness of having overstepped certain bounds.

"But we were taught to present a certain air of perfection, to act like everything was OK."

"Lavina, you know what? I'm going to check into online classes."

"For what?"

She was yawning now, blinking tired eyes.

"Human relations. Analyzing human behavior."

"You mean, that psychiatry stuff? You're crazy."

"We may be," he said, smiling.

"You, maybe."

But they both went to bed with lighter hearts and minds, the result of carrying a burden together rather than alone.

During the night, the moon rose full and majestic, creating an almost magical scene, the big house whitewashed by the moon, the snow with splashes of shadow and light, great winged owls gliding hungrily in search of prey, while inside the small gatehouse two young people lay wide awake with the newfound discovery of a bond of unity.

WINTER WAS AMOS's quiet time, so he enrolled in a course in human relations through a Christian college in Vermont called North Academy. He spent hours on the computer in the evenings, then spent his mornings at the gym working out. He would always have to be aware of weight creeping back, his constant hunger and love of food his adversity.

Over the years, he'd worked hard with the owner's guidance, lifting weights, doing cardio, stretches, leg lifts, which had increased his strength and honed his muscles. His appearance had been altered completely, his height now an advantage, his bulk now an appearance of strength. His dark hair was cut neatly, and a trimmed beard hid most of the deep acne scars.

In his own mind, he was still humble, not aware of the fact he was changed quite as much, still carrying a sense of failure wherever he went, which created a quiet voice, a shy demeanor which endeared him to most of the people he met.

He would have had plenty of opportunity to engage in the local bar scene, to drink alcohol and join the popular crowd in town, but he had never been tempted. It simply wasn't his thing. Loud music mocked him, alcohol had a venomous taste, and he was afraid of scantily clad girls. Many rebellious youths had taken that route, but he simply had no interest and told himself he was no better than anyone else.

He made friends easily, but it never amounted to more than casual acquaintance after an invitation to a bar. The owner of the gym, Scott, invited him to his church, which he attended almost every Sunday. He missed the in-between Sundays, a tradition of his upbringing where church services are held in the homes every other week. Some of his best memories of home were on those Sundays, when both parents had slept late, then there'd been a big breakfast with bacon or sausage and pancakes, everyone in good humor most of the time.

Sometimes they'd hitch up the driving horse and visit the grandparents or aunts and uncles, which Amos always enjoyed in spite of being stuffed in the back seat with Cathy and Lavina, trying to make himself as small as possible. At Dawdy Beiler's there were always cans of Mountain Dew and he loved the delightful taste, the fizz and the sweetness of it.

His mother thought it abominable, these old people drinking that stuff, the sugar and carbonation a death trap for both of them. They should know better. Amos told her it was delicious and was hushed immediately. Raymond smiled to himself, thinking about his one Coke every day on his lunch break from the machine in the corner, something his wife did not need to know about.

After years of attending an English church, Amos was accustomed to the new and modern rituals, carrying his own Bible and highlighting passages, the new way of worshipping with music, giving money when the collection plate was passed—all new and very different from the way he experienced church as a child.

He was an "*opp-gangana mensch,*" one who deserts the faith. A heretic, in some ways of thinking. But was he really? He didn't feel like one, didn't feel condemned and lost, miserably wandering in a barren no-man's-land without God.

He never doubted God was his God as well as all the Amish people's God, or *Gott* in German. *Der Herr.* My Lord. Since leaving his Amish home, Amos had discovered that God was much greater than he'd previously thought. God was God of the whole world, not just God of the Amish in the way he'd imagined as a boy.

He'd wrestled with the term *ungehorsam* many times as he began to dress as an English person, learned to drive. Yes, he was disobedient to his parents, he could not get around that, ever. They wanted him to be a member of the Amish church, to dress the way they did, to drive a horse and buggy, to marry an Amish girl and raise a family in the old tradition.

But he had not always been treated with fairness, not in his home, in school, or at his jobs. He had been slow, untalented, fat, and cumbersome, and was often told so. He'd never measured up to anyone's expectations. The only person who could have stood up for him was his father, who seemingly never understood the role of leadership in a family.

It was through Joseph and Lila he'd learned about the fullness of God's love, and the fact that God loved him exactly the way he was, which brought him to his knees in true worship. His mother had railed against this, telling him he was terribly misled, he could not believe this love was for him, an *ungehorsama mensch* (disobedient one). His father remained silent, stuffed into his usual corner by the strident voice of his wife.

So it had been up to him to figure things out for himself, to navigate a confusing labyrinth of doubts and fears, old myths of misfortune raining down on anyone who left the Amish way of life.

He was still searching, still seeking for truth in a world he could not always understand. He was *in die velt*, yes, he was in the world, away from the safe confines of Amish *ordnung*. This he fully understood. To remain within the church, to accept the rules, was a protection from worldly practices like driving a car, owning a phone or a television, using electricity, all deemed sinful by the elders.

And here was Lavina, sweet and mild-natured, entirely perplexed with the nuances of their Amish life, afraid of everything leading her into the world, yet suspended on the tightrope between the appearance of right and what that word actually meant.

His days in January took on new meaning, his enrollment in college courses keeping him occupied much of the time.

He often went to the big house for lunch with Nancy Farmer and Lavina and they were the best hours of his day. He enjoyed listening to Nancy's widespread and scrappy view of her life with Tom, the craziness of her kids, the skyrocketing price of everything, the incompetence of doctors, dentists, banks, and everyone who worked for the government, including the mailman.

She lived in a double-wide mobile home, the yard dotted with vehicles, some of them repaired into use, others disabled and sitting in a bed of untrimmed weeds. Amos had been to their house, where alcohol had flowed freely, and that experience had confirmed his position that he would stick to soft drinks. But this was Nancy's way of life, and he had no right to judge.

He sat at the huge kitchen island, with his roast beef wrap and protein shake, with Lavina beside him, and felt grateful. So much in his life was good.

"You going to eat all that?" Nancy called over her shoulder as she filled a cup at the coffeemaker.

"Of course. I could eat two or three," Amos answered.

"Want me to fix you another one?"

"No. I sat most of the morning."

"Didn't go to the gym?"

"No. Too cold."

"Ah-hah. You're slacking, Amos. Now what's Anna gonna say about that? I haven't seen her. Where's she been?"

"Home, I guess."

"Aren't you two seeing each other?"

"Not for a while. Her parents have a problem with me not being Amish. It's complicated."

He waved a hand in dismissal.

Nancy looked disappointed. "That's a shame, she's a nice girl."

Amos nodded, suddenly feeling unsure of every decision he'd made.

"Should I go back?" he asked suddenly.

"Don't ask me. I don't understand that religion stuff. Ain't up to me."

"I know." He sighed. "We decided to take a break for a while, to figure out which direction we need to go."

Nancy sipped her coffee, watched him over the rim of her cup.

"Ah. I don't know," she said, setting down her cup, placing both hands palms down on the countertop, lifting her shoulders. "Religion complicates everything. It ain't necessary. Me, I just wing it. Just go with my gut. Figure the Man upstairs don't mind."

Amos caught her eye, shook his head and grinned, "You're doing alright, Nancy. I like you just the way you are."

"See? We get along." She slapped his arm, then laid hers across his shoulder, squeezed, and smiled.

Amos responded in the same way he always did, a gentle smile, a small shake of his head. Nancy was a puzzle. She was, by all accounts, a woman of the world—her lifestyle, her attitude, everything. But why did she often bring him to tears with a slap on the shoulder? Her praise was rough around the edges, but it was praise, nevertheless.

If his mother had praised him once . . . Even the words, "We get along," would have been music to his ears. Would that have been enough to keep him from leaving home?

Sometimes he wondered about Nancy. Under all that rough exterior, there was a heart of gold. Was she seeking the spirit of God, and just didn't know it?

He searched Scripture for truth, grappled with the intricate knots of right and wrong, and now he was studying the ways of a counselor. A person who counseled.

He had no idea where this would go, and why he had found this deep-seated interest in what made people tick, but there it was.

Amos called to Lavina to come see the sunset. The sky was an amazing display of pinks and purples. As she stood beside him, her arms crossed around her waist, he realized he had never felt closer to his sister.

She had been a gift, a soothing presence in his loneliness.

Later in the evening, there was a firm rapping on the door, a sound that startled both of them. Lavina wiped her hands on the dishtowel as Amos got to his feet and went to the door.

There were a few seconds of total silence before he stepped back and welcomed his parents into the house. His father shook his hand but would not meet his eyes. He swept off the broad-brimmed hat and shifted his weight uncomfortably.

He greeted his mother, took her hand in his, but she, too, would not meet his eyes.

"Lavina," she said, going to her, with no handshake or hug, only a taking in of her youngest daughter's presence.

"Mom, how are you?" Lavina responded.

There was a sharp intake of breath, her plump shoulders heaving as their mother burst into loud, wailing sobs. Raymond shifted his weight, his hands turning the brim of his hat. Amos stood, waiting, but Lavina laid a hand on her arm, said, "Mam."

Amos went to the side table by the couch, brought her a few Kleenexes, which she used to stem the copious flow of tears. Her face turned blotchy, her eyes swollen to red puffs, and still she wailed on as Raymond fumbled with his hat and turned a beseeching face to Amos.

Amos went to his mother, put a hand to her back, and guided her gently to the recliner. The television showed the news anchors from CBS, casting a blue light across her black coat and bonnet.

As her sobs subsided, she looked up at Amos and removed her bonnet.

"Turn that thing off," she said, then blew her nose.

Amos obeyed, asking his father to sit down, which drew Lavina to greet him as he moved to the couch.

There was a torrent of words then, from their mother, who seemingly had regained her composure.

"We came tonight to bring Lavina home with us. My nerves are shot, Amos, shot."

She glared at him, the dark eyes accusing.

"If you would have been obedient in the first place, Lavina would never have left. You are the one to blame, and it's time you search your soul."

She blew her nose again, dabbed at her eyes, sniffed.

Amos stood, swallowed, and said quietly, "I have done that many times."

"Not enough. The fruits of repentance are plainly seen, and here you are, blending into the world as if your upbringing meant absolutely nothing. You are throwing away everything we taught you, living the life of the *ungehorsam*."

She sat forward, her hands pressed onto her knees, her arms braced.

"You have to listen to me, Amos. God warned the wicked kings and the false prophets in the Bible, as I am warning you. You will bear many hurtful things in your life if you harden your heart against me."

Amos sighed, then turned to meet her eyes, and found them.

The same dark, accusing gaze, the look of disappointment, only now he was even lower in her esteem—disobedient, worldly, locked away from the grace of God.

"Mom, we've been through this before. I have searched the Bible and have found what I believe is the truth. I go to church, Mom. I do, and I have found forgiveness, acceptance, and love."

"I don't believe any of it," his mother said, shaking her head as if to dispel a clinging demon. "You know better. It's all *falshheit* (lies)."

Raymond cleared his throat. "Lydia, perhaps you should consider that English people go to English churches and it is good and right for them."

"See? There you go again, your liberal thinking is what's wrong here. You never helped me discipline these children. You always support them instead of me."

A toxic silence, the churning of minds brewing.

His mother looked directly at Lavina.

"You are coming home with us."

The inner conflict Lavina was experiencing was like a dagger in Amos's heart. He could not contain his pity.

"Mom, don't you think it would be best to allow her to make her own choices? You know our home is not . . ."

He stopped, unable to express the atmosphere of the home in which he was raised. The turbulence his mother created, the whimpering silence of his father, Cathy and her own strident determination.

"Amos, shut your mouth. Keep it shut."

Shocked, he retreated into silence.

And her voice went on and on, harsh opinions hurled at them all, finally clumsily portraying her own martyred state, that of a good Christian enduring the ravages of a husband and children lusting after worldly things, keeping her head above water financially and spiritually.

Amos felt suffocated, as if her words were a blanket of wool, heavy and uncomfortable. He felt united with his father, and then suddenly saw that he would turn into him if he did not find the courage this situation required.

He spoke in turn, gently, but reminded her of the ways in which he had never measured up to her expectations, which had been devastating, crippling.

"Well. You were awful big," she said defensively.

Amos knew then that there would be no reconciliation. She would never see her own shortcomings, and he would never be able to make her.

"Lavina?" his mother asked sharply.

"Mom, I want to stay." She began to weep softly, her hands to her face. "But I feel I should go home."

Excited now, his mother rose to her feet, her hands outstretched.

"Come home with us, Lavina, please. To a good Amish home where you are taught to be a conservative Christian. Things will be better. Right, Raymond?"

Raymond nodded, sensing his wife's nervous condition would soon be at an end, meaning he would be back in her good graces.

How many nights had she turned her back, refused him, counting him among the disobedient children, a burr of resentment, a crust of self-righteousness creating the wall between them?

Chapter 3

That night, Lavina packed her things, tears streaming down her face. But deep down inside of her, she felt clear and peaceful. Someone had to try to mend the division in the family. Someone had to be willing, teachable.

She heard the words, "Lord, make me an instrument of thy peace." Astounded, she stopped, held her breath. Chills washed over her as she wiped her tears, and she knew she had been given a message from God.

Her face was without expression as she emerged from the small room she had come to love, the space so tiny and cozy, engulfed in peace.

To wake up in the morning to an expression of love, the warmth of Amos's approval, his happiness like a stray sunbeam, had been all she ever wanted in life. But now she knew her leaving home had been selfish.

The stakes were too high. Her family needed help.

She clung to Amos, whispered "Pray for me," and he nodded, gave her a reassuring pat on her back. She did not look at her mother's face, knowing the victory she would see there would fuel bitterness. Instead, she followed her father's bowed head out the door of the beloved cottage, the haven for her embattled spirit.

She sat beside her mother as the driver guided the vehicle over icy patches, snowbanks rising on either side like ghostly rails.

They turned right, toward the town of Rochester, which brought her mother's voice, immediately.

"Well, Amos didn't offer us coffee or a snack, and we didn't have supper. Let's stop at the McDonald's on Lincoln Way."

"Sure. Do you have the time, Richard?" Raymond asked the driver.

"I could use a cheeseburger."

Raymond smiled, nodded.

And when they were seated, the food before them, her mother turned into an ebullient person, teasing her husband, batting her hand at the driver, her nervous breakdown evaporated.

"Lavina, aren't you happy to be coming home? Oh, I knew it. I knew we could persuade you. You didn't feel right with that television blaring, driving with Amos in his truck."

She had gone to battle, had conquered, her cheeseburger and fries the reward for her Christian leadership. And Raymond was relieved of the burden he felt for his wife, would be able to show his love, and things would surely return to normal again.

Lavina picked at her fries, saying nothing.

THAT FEBRUARY, THE days were dark, overcast, with intermittent snow squalls or a cold, driving rain. Amos had too much time on his hands and found himself losing heart for the online classes. He struggled to understand the endless and mystifying words. He kept his phone handy, googled everything, heard the pronunciation, but it was a painstaking process.

He'd never been good in school, his report card a testimony to his *dummheet* (stupidity). He left it in his lunchbox, where his mother would find it without him. If nothing else, it delayed the uncomfortable encounter that would surely come.

"Why, Amos?"

He remembered the stab of rebellion. Why indeed? He couldn't understand the words then, and struggled now. To raise his hand meant drawing attention to his large, ungainly, stupid self. If the teacher hovered over him, a finger on the page, his mind lost all direction, knowing he was being observed by his classmates.

Meanwhile, his mother glowed with approval of Cathy's straight A's.

He would always fight his past, the black tide of his own stupidity. Still, there was the landscaping now, the pruning and planting, the mowing and cutting precise borders. He had learned to accept the approval of Joseph and Lila, praise he did not know what to do with. He would always bend his head, shuffle his feet uncomfortably, then murmur some absurd answer, hating himself.

What Joseph said wasn't true. English people flung praise around easily, as foreign to him as another language.

His phone pinged. He reached for it, read the text. His heart beat heavily in his chest and he swallowed.

"How's everything with you?"

Why did she care? He found himself not wanting to return the text. He knew the ropes. If someone said they needed time to think things through, it was a kindness, a gentle maneuver to get out of a relationship.

Anna was gentle, without a mean thought in her head.

No, better to let sleeping dogs lie. He wasn't ready to face the cold hard truth, the long bleak days without her.

He pushed back his chair, got to his feet, and turned to the comforting thought of food, the single thing in life that never let him down.

He stopped with his hand on the refrigerator door. His lack of exercise, his penchant for sliding back into the old habit of filling the void with high-calorie food.

He pushed his arms into his coat, took up his keys, and turned off the lights. A gray February drizzle, starlings perched on the wires, dirty snow like discarded laundry.

At the gym, lights blazed, machines whirred. He hung up his coat and found Scott, buff, good looking, his handsome face alight with welcome.

"Hey there. Where have you been?"

Amos shrugged. "Backsliding."

"Come on, man. We've missed you at church."

"I didn't mean church."

Scott waved an arm, beckoned him to his office. Amos shook his head.

"What is it?"

Seeing Scott's genuine concern, Amos felt the childish lump form in his throat. Better to stay out of that office where his hidden emotions might come spilling out.

He shook his head, walked away.

He lifted weights with a vengeance, worked his body into dripping sweat and aching muscles, focused now, sure of every maneuver.

If he did nothing right, here was his redemption: sheer brute force. He felt adrenaline pour through his veins, felt power and a sense of well-being.

He looked up to find Scott resting one shoulder against the wall, a foot hooked over the other, a smile on his face.

"You're a tiger today, Amos."

Amos straightened, lifted his T-shirt to wipe his streaming face, reached for his water bottle, then met Scott's eyes, shrugged, and grinned.

"Anything you want to talk about?"

Amos shrugged again.

"Come on."

He followed Scott, sat with his elbows on his knees, his head in his hands. Scott waited. When Amos lifted his face, Scott was appalled to see the misery stamped on his features.

"I don't know," Amos ground out, like rusty gears loosening.

Scott said nothing, and Amos began to talk. He shared the story of his parents' visit, the accompanying doubts and fears, the realization he might actually be what his mother believed he was: a heretic who had deserted the way of righteousness. He told how Lavina had left with his parents to obey their will, and certainly not her own.

Was that not the way of the cross?

Scott tapped a pen, pursed his lips, and listened closely.

"My truck, my clothes, my television, my phone—my whole life is a sin, according to my mother. I live in disobedience to my parents' wishes, so I am not honoring them as God commanded. I am a heretic to the Amish church."

"To their rules," Scott said quietly.

"Yes."

"So now, since you were reminded of this, you're brimming with guilt."

"Yes, I am."

"And you feel Lavina did the right thing."

"She did."

"So, what keeps you from going back?"

"You wouldn't understand."

"Try me."

Amos told him about the tangled web in which he was caught, the dysfunctional relationship of his parents, the constant stream of Cathy's power over her mother's mental state, his father's fear of them both, all a dark vortex hidden away behind the façade of being in the *ordnung*, obeying the rules except what could be hidden away.

He finished with, "But they're right, have God's approval, because of being Old Order Amish, and I am wrong. Everything I do is wrong, and all I wanted when I left was to be free of that hypocrisy, that suffocating knowledge of muddled truth."

Scott nodded. "Are you guilty in front of God?"

"You mean, for leaving, or for driving and dressing different?"

"Both."

For a long moment, Amos weighed his thoughts.

"Not when I'm alone. I have no personal convictions against material things."

"No guilt at all?"

"No. Only when I think of my Amish upbringing and the dishonor I am to my family."

"You know, I can't tell you what to do. Everyone's path is different. God may have led your sister for a reason, as He is leading you."

Amos shook his head.

"According to them, the devil is leading me."

"Do you have a plan for your future, Amos?" Scott asked, leaning back in his chair and propping his elbows on the arms.

"No. I mean, well, maybe."

"Can you tell me?"

"No. I'm embarrassed."

Scott waited.

"I mean, I'm not sure. I started this course. From a college. I'm not smart enough, though, so I probably shouldn't be doing it. I just started."

Scott encouraged him, and Amos released a torrent of hopes and dreams, the need to help others who lived with complexity beyond their own understanding, who filled the deep void with anger and violence, with drugs and alcohol, telling themselves this is who they were, blaming parents and relationships, hating.

"Sounds like you do have a vision."

"I guess. Well, not really." Amos shrugged his shoulders. "It's stupid. The whole notion of it. I mean, who do I think I am? I never struggled with drugs or alcohol. So how would I know? I just feel as if maybe I could learn to help confused young men, somehow. If God is with me anyway, which today, I'm not sure about. For all I know, I'm a lost soul."

Scott shook his head.

"You accepted Christ as your Savior, Amos. You were baptized in His Name. And now you are being called to serve Him. It's that simple."

"No, it's not simple. Not at all. I may have done it the wrong way."

"You're saying our Jesus is different than the one in the Amish church?"

"No. Well, kind of. I mean, our way requires obedience to the law."

Scott brought his chair down with a thump.

"Alright, Amos. I understand what is going on here. I see the picture pretty clearly. But you have to figure it out on your own. Search the Scripture and keep praying. Come to church and don't give up on your course."

"It's over my head. You have to realize, I barely made it through eight grades in a parochial school. I am actually dumb. Stupid."

"Okay then." Scott grinned. "Just keep working on it."

Amos sat, unable to finish what had been started.

"Do you think I'd have peace if I followed my sister?"

"That's up to you, of course. My own personal conviction is, you have taken your eyes off Jesus, and you're sinking, like Peter when he walked on water. You're forgetting who saved you."

When he arrived home, he had a call from Joseph at the big house. Could he come check a leak behind the washer in the laundry room? In his fashion, he explained in detail what he believed it was, but he wasn't sure. He did not want to call a plumber if he didn't have to, the way they charged exorbitant prices.

He looked up "exorbitant," smiled to himself. He'd thought so. Then he remembered the text from Anna Riehl. He wanted to return her inquiry but was afraid of what was sure to come. Quickly, he took up his phone, messaged her without thought, and left his phone in the house as he made his way up the drive to check on the washer.

Through the gloom, the yellow light through the tall windows gave the grand old house a welcoming glow. He thought of all the love within its walls, the blessed white-haired couple who had done so much for him. He owed them his life. Through them, he had learned there was a love that held no conditions—no high bar had to be cleared to win their approval. It was love in its purest form, and neither one of them knew how much he had longed for that.

He knocked, let himself in, and called, "Hello, it's me!"

Lila came from the kitchen, wiping her hands on a towel. She walked slowly, placing a hand on the doorframe, the top of the washer.

"You're always so good about coming quickly, Amos. Joseph is having a bit of a fit about this leak. I put a towel down."

Joseph came from the living room, his thick white hair standing up, his brow furrowed.

"Well, now, there you are. Always on time. You're a good man, Amos. I don't know how we managed to keep this old place afloat without you. Yes. Now here. Look here. Darling, would you get my headlamp for him? I left it on the table."

Lila nodded, made her way carefully.

Amos found the leak, went to the toolshed for a wrench and pliers, a tube of PVC caulking. In the fog and drizzle, he heard the shrill call of a kestrel, the small hawk that wreaked havoc on the songbirds' carefree existence.

The thought of spring filled him with a jolt of unexpected joy, the glad realization of better things to come.

Could he possibly apply the feeling to his future?

He tightened the pipes, applied the caulking, and sat on his heels, watching for the telltale drip, grinning up at Joseph who hovered anxiously.

"You think that will solve it?" Joseph asked.

"I would hope so."

Lila came back from the kitchen. "Now, Amos. Nancy made a wonderful beef stew, and we have fresh sourdough from Harper's. You must stay and we'll have an early dinner. You will, won't you?"

"Sure. I'm actually starved. I just came from the gym."

Lila clapped her hands like a child.

"Oh good. I'm so glad. It's quite a lot. The Dutch oven is over half-full, and I'll have to freeze it if you don't stay. I'll get the table set. Is it okay to eat in the kitchen? We must call Lavina. Joseph, dear, would you place a call to her?"

Amos felt the discomfort, the heat in his face.

"Uh, Lavina isn't here."

"Oh, I'm sorry. Will she be back later? I'll keep a portion for her!" Lila was concerned, her eyebrows raised, creating deep furrows in her lined forehead.

"She, uh, well . . . my parents came for a visit, and she packed her things and accompanied them. My mother hasn't been well and needs her help."

A white lie, but so it must be, Amos thought.

"Oh my. I'm so sorry. She will be terribly missed, but of course she needs to go back. A mother comes first, always. Bless her dear heart. What a lovely girl. Like a ray of sunshine."

Jospeh expressed an identical opinion, then worried about a girl to keep up with the cleaning, always planning ahead.

Lila brought plates to the able, asked Amos to bring silverware.

In the glow of the hanging lamp above the table, Amos considered the white-haired couple on either side of him. He felt so much love, an ardent devotion to serve them as long as they lived. If only he could summon this emotion for his own parents, and for Cathy. They were his flesh and blood, and he owed them some kind of love and obedience, didn't he?

In spite of their shortcomings, they were his mother and father—surely that should mean something.

Quietly, he spooned the beef stew into his mouth, chewed and swallowed, wiped his mouth with the provided napkin, his thoughts far away from the table.

"Amos, you haven't elaborated on the state of your mother's health," Lila remarked, as she picked delicately at a piece of beef.

"She has trouble with her nerves at times."

"Really? The poor woman. That is troubling and most certainly no fault of her own. Mental health is misunderstood so much of the time."

Joseph nodded. "We need to include her in our prayers, isn't that right, Lila?"

"Oh yes. Well, she'll have Lavina now. She will be a big help. Is she on medication?"

"I'm not aware that she is. It's hard to persuade her to see a doctor," Amos said, avoiding their clear, innocent gaze.

"At any rate, we wish her the best. Now, what are we going to do about a house maid? Nancy has enough," Joseph said, buttering another slice of sourdough bread.

Amos thought he could eat the whole loaf. Crusty, hard on the outside, thick and chewy on the inside, it was the best bread he had ever been fortunate enough to taste. He reached for another slice. Was it his third? He looked at the amount left, embarrassed.

"Well, Anna is coming back in May for spring cleaning. Could we persuade her to work on a regular basis?" Lila remarked.

"We need to inquire."

"Amos. I believe you would have her number."

"I do."

"Then you make the call for us."

They sat back, beaming, waiting expectantly.

"I . . . I can dial, and you ask her."

He patted his pockets, puzzled. "Oh, I left my phone at home. I'm sorry."

"No, no. It's fine. You just call her when you return, then give us an answer. Will you, please?"

"Of course."

And so the evening ended with effusive thanks from the old couple, waving away his offer to help with the dishes. Lila would wash and Joseph would dry, while they listened to their old-timey music on the radio, they said, all smiles and generosity.

Joseph grinned. "And it only depends on the song, whether I'll take my little lady around the kitchen for a dance."

Lila laughed, a sound like tinkling bells.

As Amos walked down the drive in the deepening gloom, his heart ached with a new longing to have what Joseph and Lila had. A rare and beautiful love, a love withstanding the test of time.

He stalled for time. He paced the kitchen, put a load of clothes in the washer, wiped the countertops and rearranged the refrigerator.

Finally, he sat down, found her number, and touched the screen. Did he even want her back working at the big house?

She answered on the third ring.

"Hello, Anna. This is Amos."

"I saw by your number. How are you?"

"Doing okay. Uh, the Smiths need someone to clean for them. Lavina went home."

"She went home? Why?"

"My parents came to take her home with them."

"She was okay with that?"

"Yes."

"Hm. Well, whatever, I guess."

"Can you work for them?"

"Like, now? Immediately?"

"I guess."

"I can do Thursday. Is it every week?"

"I think so."

"Someone will have to pick me up."

"Okay. Eight?"

"Sounds good."

"Bye."

"See you."

Amos swiped, sat staring at the floor, thoroughly ashamed of himself. What a pitiful, stilted exchange. He was a moron, a coward. Why couldn't he have thought of one single witty thing to say? He was the dullest, most unexciting human being on earth. No personality at all. He should never have called. Refused. And he had not even thanked her for the text.

Well, sooner or later she would have discovered his lack of courage, his slow-witted ways, so why not now? Besides, they'd taken time off, and things had not changed.

How could they? He was devoted to the old couple, loyal as long as they lived, but still confusion cast its moiling shadows over him.

Why?

Why could he never feel this way about his parents? Even his gentle, quiet, mostly happy father. He had never done him wrong.

He guessed maybe that was his own fault, the resentment welling at the thought of his father's inability to speak for himself, to take on the role of a leader. Cowed by his wife, he found it more comfortable to fade into a fog of denial, allowing his wife to be the driving force.

What strength it would require, though. He could not imagine what would happen if he raised a shield against her or presented a dagger of truth. The entire household would be turned on its face.

A weary acceptance overtook him, and he shivered.

Was he, then, better than his father, choosing to leave, to hide away from the upheaval? He needed guidance. He could not think of Anna, of a serious friendship, without learning what was required of him.

For a man needed to take on the responsibility of a wife and children. A family. And how did one choose a helpmeet, a partner . . .

How could he make sure he chose someone who was totally unlike his mother?

There it was. That was his fear.

He thought of how his mother turned into another person in church—friendly, talkative, the life of the party, exchanging jokes and bits of humor, often at his expense. Trouser patterns, sizes spoken loudly, eyes rolled, a hand to her mouth as she giggled.

He had slunk away, blamed himself for overhearing—he should have been out playing with the others. Someday, he dreamed, he would be thin, agile, fly around the baseball diamond amid cheers, receive wide grins and high fives and "Way to goes." His pants size would be the same as the others. Then the others would accept him.

But no. Instead, he had found acceptance elsewhere, away from his family and community. He had stepped slowly, with increasing confidence, but had slipped backward after his parents' last visit.

He had tons of debris in his mind, but suddenly he knew the first step was to resume visits to a counselor and stick with it.

Chapter 4

Lydia Beiler was having a complete meltdown. The ministers had paid them a visit. It was a kindly one, but a reminder to rid themselves of the electricity they were still using after five years. The allotted time to change to diesel-generated compressed air was a year or two, which they had stretched beyond the limit.

Raymond felt sorrow, and a certain helplessness, knowing the funds for this costly changeover were simply not available. He had thought perhaps a few solar panels would be cheaper, but after asking around, he'd found that option to be nearly as expensive.

He tried reasoning gently, then a bit firmly.

"Lydia, listen to reason. We are Amish, pledged to keep the *ordnung*, and we've already been given a few years of grace. I'll go to the bank, maybe open a line of credit, using this home as collateral."

"I'm not going back to a wringer washer."

"You don't have to. We can get a battery-operated automatic. They're allowed. I hear they work slick as a whistle."

Pouting now, she gave no reply.

"I think six or seven thousand should cover it. With the water pump."

"What? You're not thinking of changing the water pump, are you? No. That thing is twelve feet underground. Who is ever going to know?"

"Alright, Lydia. But we'll have to get rid of the freezer. A propane gas one is around two thousand, unless you want to put our electric one over in the Troutmans' shed."

Lydia crossed her arms, stuck out her lower lip, and said she was moving. They could make a hundred thousand on this place and purchase a new house where they could use electricity again.

"Only for a few years."

"Not if we go to another district. I'm not staying here."

"Lydia, let's not be rash. We're settled here. We knew we'd have to switch from electricity eventually. Should've done it a few years ago."

Lavina was reading in her room, had heard the crunch of buggy wheels on gravel, had heard what transpired. She braced herself for the storm.

Lydia slammed dishes and doors, refused to answer questions, went to her cleaning jobs in a fine state of wounded martyrdom. The supper table was a study in suppressed fury, until Cathy rose to her feet, slammed her chair into the table, rocking water glasses and scattering utensils.

"The only smart one around here is Amos. He got himself out of this dysfunctional mess of a family."

"Cathy, sit down," her father implored, very quietly.

"Why would I? So she can go right on with her psychological damage? You know what, Mom? You need to grow up."

Cathy stomped upstairs and her mother retreated to her bedroom where her weeping could be heard from the kitchen table. Lavina and her father picked half-heartedly at food gone cold. Lavina felt a strange and distant sense of calm, and her father glanced shamefacedly in her direction before shrugging his shoulders.

"Should I keep the electricity?"

Lavina shrugged in the same defeated manner.

"She'll find a new home, is my guess," she murmured, keeping her eyes on her plate.

"*Ach* my."

A thousand unanswered questions swam in Lavina's mind, a restless swarm of right versus wrong. How could her mother condemn the lifestyle Amos lived when at least he was honest before God? How could she maintain the claim to being a better Christian because of the Old Order, yet her thoughts and actions were so far from obeying God's Word?

"I don't know if there's much to be done, Lavina."

"Dat, must you always give in to her?"

"If there is another way, I haven't found it."

Wearily, Lavina rose to her feet, scraped dinner plates, and drew hot soapy water, her lips moving in prayer.

Lydia hired a local driver and set out on her quest for a new home, leaving when Raymond was at work turning spindles and whistling the melody to "In the Sweet By and By." One of his coworkers brought in a package of homemade deer jerky, which he enjoyed with an ice-cold Coke and considered his day blessed indeed.

For there truly were abundant blessings in his life. He had counted six male cardinals at the feeder this morning, their plumage breathtaking. That in itself was a gift. And his father stopped in soon after he got to work, having gotten over his bout of the flu. It was a pleasant visit. Plus, it looked as if his turkeys were getting ready to start laying eggs, and his incubator was ready. He really looked forward to watching the eggs hatch and then seeing the scrawny little turkey poults racing around. He smiled to himself.

Somewhere in the back of his mind, however, was the niggling episode of last night's supper table and the need to go to the bank. The whole thing was blown out of proportion, but he guessed maybe most women were good at that.

He chuckled to himself.

In a week's time, Lydia found a small Cape Cod, white with black shutters and a porch along the front. It was on two acres with a shed that could be renovated for a decent barn. One tree only. Plenty of wind on that hill, and no leaves to rake. They'd all blow away. Plus, the kitchen was stunning. "Renovated," the realtor said. It was all white. Oh, seriously, she loved that kitchen.

So, with Raymond in tow, blessed to be back in her good graces, they put in an offer of three hundred thousand and listed their current house for eighty-five thousand more.

Tense, anxious days followed. Phone calls were made two, three times a day, checking if there were any bids. Friends and family spied the real estate signs, asked what in the world was going on.

Lydia had a solid answer prepared. She said they couldn't expect the two girls to be there forever, and with Amos still unrepentant, well, they didn't need that extra bedroom. Yes, it was too bad they had to move to another district, but my, her knees had been aching of late, and it was too much, keeping up with that huge, wooded lawn and landscaping. She gave a gentle touch of her handkerchief to her eyes when she spoke of Amos not being there. Just so sad.

She soaked up her friends' sympathy like a sponge, became heavy and inflated with it. *Yes, it is a shame, Lord knows we did the best we could. He was just hard to reach, even as a small boy. But I must accept the lot God has given me.*

Anna Riehl breezed into the big house in her brown dress and matching bib apron with her small white covering set on her honey-colored hair. She chirped her greeting like a Carolina wren and was welcomed back with open arms and a gentle handshake from Joseph.

She smelled like wet soil, bright February clouds, and the residue of her lavender hand cream. She sat for a few minutes to catch up on the news, then set to work on the third floor. She had a bird's-eye view of the property, including the small gatehouse at the end of the winding drive.

His truck was there, so he must be around somewhere.

She scratched her eyelid, blinked to clear her vision, then turned away from the window. She decided if they met today, it was meant to be. If not, it might all fall into place later. Or never. Who was to know?

Anna had a very clear sense of who she was and what she was about, exuding confidence like the scent of a flowering tree. But she wasn't sure about Amos. He seemed to have underlying issues. He'd told her bits and pieces about his home life, but she was wary of giving that too much weight. People needed to get over that wearisome "bad childhood" excuse. It was in the past. Let it go.

Still, she considered, perhaps she wasn't aware of how painful some individuals' childhoods had actually been. Hers had been great. Really.

So when she went downstairs for the mophead and rounded the corner of the laundry room and came smack down face to face with him, she shrieked, "Amos! You scared the daylights out of me."

"I could say the same thing."

And then, they merely stood, openly taking stock of each other. She found him taller, his shoulders wider, his hair and beard trimmed better, his brown eyelids drooping more with a certain kind of sadness. She chalked it up to maturity, she supposed. He exuded strength, clearly no longer a boy. For the first time in her life, she felt at a loss.

He saw the same short, soft young woman he'd remembered, the blonde streaks in the caramel color of her hair, the round face with big green eyes alive with blue and brown specks, a face he would always remember as the cutest, most amazing beauty.

Last night, his counselor told him it was necessary to practice courage, to think highly of the act of being a man. This all came to mind now, and he knew this was the best chance to start.

He touched her shoulder, the plump roundness of it, and looked into her eyes, not allowing another moment's hesitation.

"I missed you, Anna. Very much."

She swallowed, coughed. "Yeah, me too."

"You're serious?"

"I am."

Amos took a deep breath.

"Well, you're here now. Isn't this great? You'll be here every Thursday."

"Looks like it. I love this old couple. I always look forward to being here."

"Because I'm here, right?"

"Amos! Whatever," she laughed, a bit shakily.

"So did you do all your thinking about us yet?" he asked, still holding those wonderful eyes with his own. She looked away, her face turned downward, just as attractive at a different angle, the dark lashes sweeping the tanned cheeks.

"I thought, yes, but it's an ongoing process. My parents are liberal, and kind, but they can't quite wrap their head around me leaving the Amish. You know it's a hard pill for most Amish parents to swallow. I can barely stand the thought of hurting them."

Amos nodded.

"Would you return to the Amish for my sake?" she asked bluntly.

He smoothly avoided the question. "Look, why don't we get our work done and then I'll take you somewhere for supper? You could call your parents to let them know."

"Seriously, Amos. You seem so . . . different. When did you get so confident?"

"Grew up a bit, I guess." He smiled. Then, more seriously, "And counseling. I'm back to seeing a counselor. I won't pretend it's easy, but it really has helped."

"Okay, that's good. Anyway, yes, I'll go. Let's get to work."

SHE WISHED SHE weren't in her work clothes, but there was nothing to be done about that. Meanwhile, he showered, shaved, combed his hair, and put on a brown shirt to match her.

He laughed when she noticed and commented on it.

They drove to town together in his truck. He slowed, asked if Bart's was okay.

"It's a bar. No, not with my covering on. I will not go to a bar."

"Sorry, didn't think about it."

"You're a man. Men don't think about such things."

He looked at her, but she was not laughing.

"Sorry, Anna. I'm sorry."

"Don't be."

But her voice was small. When he turned the wheel, looked in the rearview mirror, then twisted his upper body to watch for oncoming traffic, she realized how big, how solid and manly he was, and felt an unfamiliar sense of being shy. She wasn't sure how to handle this new, confident person.

They settled on a simple diner, which Amos said wasn't great, but she said she could eat a double order of everything.

"Where were the Smiths this afternoon?"

"He had a doctor's appointment in Harrisburg."

"They drove themselves?"

"I think."

They were seated, ordered drinks, pored over menus, but for both, it was hard to concentrate, the way their eyes kept going back to each other. Of their attraction, there was no doubt.

Amos recognized this as the real thing. It was only his lack of confidence that had pushed them apart before.

But there was the thorny issue of his going back to the Amish, to lay down his life for her. He knew he had to answer her question from earlier. He brought the topic up gently, asking how it had gone when she'd spoken to parents about their relationship.

She said they'd given a firm no. No, they could not give their blessing for her to be English, to abandon the head covering, which was so important to them. If this Amos Beiler was serious, then it was up to him to forsake the ways of the world and come back to the Amish, which was the right thing to do.

She shared this with him, halting between sentences, sometimes close to tears, but without holding anything back.

Amos took a deep breath, his eyes wandering across the restaurant's patrons, seeing nothing. Finally, he told her if that if that was her answer then he'd have to have time to consider his own convictions, his hopes and dreams.

"To return for you alone, without considering whether I could stay true to the Amish *ordnung*, wouldn't be fair to either of us. I just don't know."

"Oh Amos. I was so afraid of exactly that answer."

"Can you give me time?"

"And not see you in the meantime?"

"I'd like to keep seeing you. Will your parents allow it?"

"I haven't asked."

"Let's not sneak around. I'll go meet them soon."

The remainder of the evening had been ruined for her, and he was keenly aware of this, so he took her home early, helped her from the truck, and took her into his massive arms, folding her tenderly against his chest. Her head barely came to his shoulder, and she seemed incredibly small and soft. They were both crying when they parted, both full of unbearable sadness.

Amos drove home slowly, picturing himself driving a horse and buggy, giving up his truck, his phone and computer, his hopes and dreams of helping troubled and orphaned youth. Yes, that particular dream seemed completely out of his reach, but the Scriptures he read encouraged him constantly. God was the Giver of all, and if you set your hope on Him, He would make a way.

This he believed with his whole heart.

But now there was Anna, and she as precious as a rare jewel. It would take time. All he needed to do was seek His face, to stay close to God, to seek a life of service to Him, and everything would fall into place.

He sought her out on Thursday the following week and found her seated with Joseph and Lila, her hand on Lila's shoulder. He had to look carefully to see that Lila was softly weeping, her gnarled fingers clutching a soft white Kleenex, the backs of her hands crisscrossed with heavy blue veins. Her old hands were trembling.

Joseph sat facing them, his lips trembling as well, his large, knobby hands clutching the arms of his chair.

Amos sat down beside Anna, raised his eyebrows.

"Amos, I just received a diagnosis from Spirit Lutheran Hospital in Harrisburg. The prognosis is not good. Elevated white blood cells, deficiency in red cells . . . it explains my lack of strength and energy. We're going back tomorrow," he said.

"I'll take you. Please allow me."

Joseph nodded gravely but smiled his gentle smile afterward.

JOSEPH WAS DIAGNOSED with acute lymphatic leukemia, and at his advanced age, there was not much to be done. He accepted it with a calm demeanor, his watery blue eyes searching the face of the doctor before him and then wearily nodding his head. A man of faith, there was an assurance in Joseph's eyes, but he did not look forward to the days of pain and disease ahead.

Lila sat beside him, one hand gripped in his, her eyes brimming. Amos felt large, awkward, his mind unable to comprehend the verdict.

The doctor was small, with dark skin and glossy black hair. In an Indian accent, he gave Joseph the specifics. At most, a year, perhaps two remained for him, unless he considered treatment.

Joseph shook his head.

They admitted him that day for further testing, and Lila refused to leave his side. After he was comfortable in the narrow bed with rails on each side, the smell of antiseptic and Clorox heavy in the air, the pale walls and heavy doors surrounding them, they stood quiet. Lila was on one side and Amos on the other.

"Make a list for him, would you, Lila?" he asked.

In her shaky script, she wrote the things Joseph would need, as Amos watched attentively. Joseph pleaded with Lila to return with Amos where she'd be more comfortable.

"No. No, Joseph. I will stay right here."

"You won't be able to rest, dear."

"That's for me to say."

And so Amos drove through the city on a dull day in March, when low clouds obscured the sun, the bare black trees a mass of skeletal branches whipping in the wind, the road ahead of him filled with gray chemical-splashed vehicles from recent wet snow and rain.

So, this was what it came to, then. Joseph would soon die, and who was left for Lila? There were a few very distant relatives, a group of friends from church, neighbors.

The Larkins would want to know.

His job might be in jeopardy, but this he would face when the time came. If God closed one door, He would open another, and he would need to follow His leading. He was aware of his own fledgling faith, often unsure of anything, caught between his upbringing as an Amish person and his years as an outsider, an English man. He would never find all the answers, and that was OK with him. It was a journey and he'd take it one step at a time.

THE OLD HOUSE was silent as a tomb, the wooden shutters making small scraping sounds on the west side. He turned lights on, checked the thermostat, lowered it five degrees, then remembered the housekeeper.

She'd likely gone home for the day.

The following morning, lights were on all over as he made his way up the drive in the cold drizzle, low clouds scudding overhead like restless, heaving puffs of smoke. He let himself in the back door, called out for Nancy, and stopped in his tracks when she accosted him in a fine temper.

"Where is everyone? The house is cold. No one's home. Am I supposed to make breakfast or not? Was anyone planning to tell me anything?"

Amos shrugged off his coat, went to the coffeemaker, and got down a mug. As he poured, he told her to sit down and he'd tell her.

"Who turned the heat down?" She still stood, ignoring his invitation to sit.

"I did. Listen, it's not good. They're in Harrisburg at the Spirit Lutheran."

She stopped, wide-eyed.

"Joseph has leukemia. He's not accepting treatment. The doctor gave him a year, maybe two."

She inhaled sharply and found a seat at the kitchen island, both hands gripping the mug before her.

"Well," she said gruffly.

"I know. He's like a father to me. Or a grandfather. He's the best." Amos felt ashamed to hear the tremble in his voice.

"Yeah, well, that may be, but do you realize if they're gone, you and I are out of a job? I don't know how I'll survive. Tom doesn't care about finances, and that double-wide is not paid for. I ain't getting any younger, and my kids keep moving back in. They can't keep a job, either."

She put her head in her hands.

At first Amos was annoyed that Nancy was making this all about her, but then he felt a tender pity well up. This fifty-something woman carried the responsibility of survival in a world where it was each man for himself.

"Nancy, it'll be okay. Lila will be here."

"How long, Amos? They're in their nineties, and you know it."

Amos held his tongue. She never expressed an ounce of sympathy for her employer, only thought of herself. But he knew her life was lived from one paycheck to another, and nothing to fall back on. He had only himself to worry about and was in no position to judge Nancy.

"I'm going to try and bring Lila home with me today, although she gave me a long list of things she'll need. Do you mind packing a bag for them? I'll leave around lunchtime."

"Joseph staying?"

"I don't know. I'll find out today."

Amos worked on the new zero turn mower, changed the oil, sharpened blades, then realized he needed to get going if he wanted to make it by one o'clock. He thought of how spring work would soon begin, and for a while, life would go on—the times of mowing, pruning, mulching, building fences, and keeping the place in top condition.

He realized anew how much he loved his job, his home. The best days of his life had been spent here. *One day at a time. Appreciate it all as much as possible,* he told himself.

A text from Cathy. He stopped, read the words, cringed at the harsh expletives.

Moving. His parents were moving.

Again?

He gripped his phone. "Preachers came, Mom in an uproar," the text said. "Here's the address. You have to come help us out."

He sighed, walked on, his thoughts centered on his father. Likely, he didn't want to leave the house in the woods, but his life was smooth if he shrugged his shoulders and allowed her to lead. He wondered why the preachers had come, but decided not to ask.

"Whatever works, I suppose," he said out loud, lifting his face to the cold drizzle. He heard the chirping cry of a blue jay from branches overhead.

Chapter 5

Joseph came home after a couple of days and was settled in the living room with the tall windows that had the drapes pushed aside to let the sun stream in. A comfortable bed capable of being raised and lowered was dropped off and Amos had helped to set it up. He moved the birdfeeder to where Joseph could see it outside the window from the bed.

Hospice came twice a week. Lila like a wisp, an angelic white-haired figure who served his food, took him on short walks through the house, read to him, hovered, cared, and loved her dying husband with every fiber of her small being.

On the third Saturday in March, Amos left them in Nancy's care and went to help his parents. It was a sunlit day with fast moving clouds and a brisk wind. He could feel the gusts against the side of his truck and steered accordingly, hoping his mother was not in ill humor in this wind.

He looked at his phone, turned on State Route 186. Where was this place?

Barren fields, unkempt forest, and fence rows. A gray doublewide, a white mobile home with a sagging front porch, a rusted red Jeep. The road wound downhill, across a brown creek like butterscotch pudding. Up the next grade, and there it was.

He checked the address. Yes. Then he spied buggies, a moving van, black-clad men carrying furniture. Probably extended family and church friends.

He stopped the truck but was in no hurry to join the men. Apparently, they had plenty of folks to help. Maybe he should just go. He felt a rush of anxiety, a surge of old memories of being left out, of feeling huge and clumsy. He could see in his mind his mother's eyes filled with disgust, skimming over him with spiked bristles of pain.

He needed to be a man of courage, his counselor said. "You're your own person now. You're not defined by your mother's opinions," he'd said.

His teeth hurt from clenching his jaw, so he steadied himself with a deep breath, opened the door of his truck, and walked across the yard.

"Amos!" Cathy, in a red dress and black pullover, her hair piled on top of her head in huge rolls.

He broke into a wide grin. She hugged him, a sideways half-hug of polite greeting.

She looked up at him. "I hardly know you, Amos. What is up? If I didn't remember your fat days, I'd think you were handsome. Your face looks different."

"Thank you."

"Oh, you're so English," she shrieked. "Thank you?"

"A man can accept a compliment, can't he?"

"Not an Amish man, and you know it."

He waved her away. "Come on. Let's help."

She stopped, put her hands on her hips.

"Look at this junk hole. I can't believe they bought this. It's the ugliest house we ever lived in. You know why we moved?"

"You told me enough to put the pieces together."

"She absolutely can't give up. You should have heard her. I have zero respect for my parents. Dat's like a limp, wet dishrag."

Amos said nothing. She looked at him, balled her fist, and hit his stomach, hard. "Seriously, like iron. How in the world did you do it?"

"It's called working out," he said, grinning.

And then the rest of the family spied him. A general fuss was made, mostly about his appearance, the years since the uncles had seen him. The old grandfather had tears in his eyes, and Amos absorbed the warmth of his grandmother's soft hands on his.

His grandparents had always been accepting of him, no matter his size or the condition of his skin. He was their grandson, and they loved him as he was. For this, Amos would always be grateful.

There were plenty of questions, curiosity about his life, but there was kindness. Since he had never become a member of the Old Order, shunning was not necessary, which made acceptance easier.

Then he spotted his mother coming his way, a heavy woman with a wide backside, rounded shoulders, and a thick waist, her face flushed with exertion, her eyes taking in his appearance, puzzled.

"Amos." She extended a hand, wary of him.

"Hello, Mom."

For a few seconds their eyes met. Her eyes darkened with a certain pride, and he stood his ground, never wavered until her gaze fell away.

"You can help Dat," she said, moving away with her head held high.

He greeted his father who had stayed in the background as always. He appeared aged, his hair thinning, his back stooped more.

He needed a new hat. Amos spied the broken-down sneakers on his feet, the laces frayed, and a pang of tenderness took his breath. Doing without so she would have enough.

He turned away before rage would overtake him.

Then dear Lavina, who ran into his arms and allowed herself to shed a few tears before holding him at arm's length and smiling with gratitude. She caught him up quickly on her life. She was having fun on the weekends, and she'd been texting someone.

"You don't know him. He's from Lancaster."

He raised an eyebrow, gave her a playful shove, then went to make himself useful. He lifted the heaviest furniture and boxes with ease, bringing a flurry of jokes, hands pinching his solid arms.

Then it was time to break for a snack. He'd forgotten the amount and variety of high-calorie foods set in array on a day such as this. And this was only a morning break. Homemade doughnuts, three different kinds of cookies, pretzels and cheese and potato chips, yogurt and granola, coffee, tea, and hot chocolate. Someone carried in an immense foil pan of breakfast casserole with a pot of steaming sausage gravy.

This was the best part of home as he remembered it. Loved ones coming together to support each other, food a comfort to his aching soul. He was different now; this he knew without doubt. The painful ache of carrying shame and guilt was gone, somehow. He had no memory of having discarded it by himself, so perhaps God in his mercy had replaced it with courage and grace. He enjoyed his food in moderation, the way he'd learned to, talked and laughed with his uncles and cousins, accepted compliments and kindness like a gift.

He went upstairs to help the girls and found Cathy throwing a huge fit about the lack of space.

"I hate this stupid house," she stormed. She threw a candle at the wall where it dented the drywall, fell to the floor, and rolled under the dresser.

"My room is the size of a mouse nest."

Amos laughed. "A bit bigger than that."

"It's not funny. Mom is mentally ill. Look at this crappy place."

Lavina poked her pretty face around the door of her own room.

"Be happy we each have our own room, Cathy. It could be worse."

"Oh, la-de-dah, Lavina."

Amos lifted mirrors, screwed them to heavy oak furniture, set up the bed frames and carried box springs and mattresses. There was no attic, only storage under the eaves, through a small door, into a dark, dusty enclave Cathy pronounced "evil."

"A strong word, Cathy," he said quietly.

"What? Who are you to say anything? You make me sick, being English and driving that truck, then acting all smarmy with religion."

A sharp retort was on his tongue, but he caught himself and turned away, hurried down the stairs, and left Cathy to herself. He knew none of this was easy for her, the control she prized above all else corrupted by the whims of their mother.

But her words made their way into his conscience and he floundered, wondering if there was a certain truth to her cutting remarks.

Did he uphold a sense of self-righteousness, a bargaining with God, if he drove a truck and dressed in English clothes? Or did Cathy simply hold the same power over him she always had, making him second-guess himself?

Either way, he'd have to search his motive for correcting her on the word she'd used to describe the attic.

She was, unabashedly, herself. At the same time, she was well on the way of becoming the one person she vowed never to imitate. Her own mother.

He found his father trying to fit the essentials of a barn into the shed designated to contain his driving horse, the buggy, his turkeys, and all the tings he'd kept in a much bigger barn. Two of his brothers were building a door for the makeshift horse stall, keeping up a lively conversation about Amish life in general. Taxes, Amos Rueben's Crist's horse foundering, the method of treatment, Aunt Annie's MS diagnosis.

Amos listened as he lifted feed bags, carried bales of hay, and stacked them in the corner.

Uncle Dan pushed back his hat, observed.

"You're like an ox," he called.

"What?" Amos stopped, lifted an eyebrow.

"I said, you're like an ox."

Amos laughed.

"So tell me, Amos, when are you coming back to the Amish?"

"I don't know. Probably never."

Dan shook his head.

"I . . . think I'd like to start a home for troubled boys. Something along that line. I'm taking some courses online."

"Huh. They all say that. It's the guilt of the *ungehorsam* (disobedient), trying to get back into every one of God's graces by helping others, doing good. You're not going to wiggle back in like that. Only one thing's gonna help you, and that's to come back to the Amish."

Uncle Elam, the older brother, clucked his tongue.

"Be careful there, Dan. Some people can work out their salvation in other churches. Not always good to be so narrow-minded."

"I guess, Elam. It's the old conservative way, I know."

This remark left an impression on Amos. It showed temperance, a willingness to bow to one another, finding a medium, considering another's view.

He found himself telling them of the boy taking things from his curbside dumpster container, the need to help, but knowing he had no knowledge or the funds to start up a venture like that.

His father had listened to this exchange quietly, but he stepped up beside Amos and nodded, a hand on his shoulder.

"I believe in Amos here. He knows firsthand what it feels like to be made fun of, to never fit in, no matter what. Yes, it's hard to see your children make choices you don't approve of, but we have to let go, give it to God, who is the ultimate and only true judge."

"That's so."

"I guess you're right."

An awkward silence, then, till Amos confessed he had no idea how this dream would ever take shape. It was all in his mind, not even at the starting point. They all encouraged him, however, which was an unexpected gift, filling him with gratitude. He felt a part of something much bigger than himself, grounded and rooted in generations past, something he could not name, but knew was there.

The men were called in to dinner then, and Amos found a table groaning under the weight of soups, stews, salads, pulled pork sandwiches, ham and cheese wraps, cakes, doughnuts, cookies, and vanilla pudding. Another table held more coffee, tea, hot chocolate, apple pie, and chocolate shoofly.

He ate, enjoying every bite. He poured milk over his chocolate shoofly and was taken back to times when he hid in the barn with huge portions of dessert, away from prying eyes, mocking voices. Shoving food into his mouth, breathing in that snuffling way, inhaling great mouthfuls—it was the only way he'd known to fill the gaping emptiness inside.

He looked up, found his mother's eyes on him. Again, he faced her head on, did not look away as he chewed his dessert. Her eyes darkened, slid away. Loudly, she said, "What kind of magic potion are you taking, Amos? Eating all that food and keeping the weight off?"

He heard the counselor's words about courage.

"No magic, Mom. I eat healthy most of the time and work out four or five days a week."

"It's more than that and you know it. We aren't all dumb Amish. I know the pills you take."

She set her shoulders after a slug of hot chocolate.

"No pills, Mom. Seriously."

"I don't believe it."

He shrugged, turned away. "Believe what you want," he said, weary now.

She brought victorious eyes to his face, a slow smile spreading, a quick hand to wipe crumbs from her dress front, expecting smiles from the observing sisterhood. She was puzzled when none appeared.

Little did she know the reproach this exchange generated among the relatives. Behind palms held to faces, the women spoke of her unnatural animosity toward her son. They understood Amos much better than they ever had, but who would be brave enough to stick out their neck and put Lydia in her place? A general chorus of, "Not I, not I, said the little red hen," and so forth, followed by tittering behind her back.

They didn't believe Amos took forbidden drugs, not for a minute. Why would a mother try to embarrass her son like that? Perhaps she should get after that Cathy for once and leave Amos alone, *gel* (right)?

But no one said a word to Lydia, who didn't show her face in the coming months, painting and renovating as fast as she could. Yes, they had a little chunk left over, and after the barn was built, she planned on new shrubbery, cement urns for the front door, stamped concrete walkways, and lawn service.

They'd be the talk of the neighborhood. Not that the neighborhood was much, those fat women in pink hoodies driving old clunkers with dogs hanging out the windows and no muffler to speak of.

Well, she fully planned on keeping her electric, too. Nothing wrong with that. She loved electric lights, could see no sense in DeWalt batteries. She flipped switches, even went so far as to buy a lamp for the living room at the Goodwill in Rochester. She set an end table beside the couch, placed the lamp on top, and arranged a small copper plate and a framed verse beside it. She stood back and admired the result.

Now, that could be in a magazine. The colors, the textures.

If she wasn't Amish, she'd be a designer. Interior designer, she thought they were called. Now that lamp was perfect. No one would ever know if it was electric or battery operated, with the cord going behind the couch.

She was just so proud of that lamp.

The following Saturday night when Cathy came downstairs wearing so much eye shadow and mascara, she berated her roundly, saying it was all vanity. "All vanity! Did you hear me for once?"

And Cathy shrugged, pointed her made-up chin in the end table's direction, and said she'd like to know what that electric lamp and her little idols represented, which put her mother into a slow burn.

Raymond peered around the daily paper, looked at the lamp in question, then at Cathy's cosmetics and chuckled in a place deep inside. It seemed of late he didn't need to take anyone's side. The truth would be like a caterpillar working its way out of its own cocoon.

He was still happy. He liked this little house. He really did. It was bright and airy, with large windows and freshly painted walls. His barn would soon be completed and he would have plenty of room for his turkeys. Maybe a few goats eventually. Their mortgage payment was less, and Lydia was pleased to have a few thousand in her checkbook. As he always did, he thanked the Lord for his many blessings.

Joseph and Lila's old house withstood the March winds and the skies weeping in April, but it seemed to crumple under the weight of its beloved owner as the disease in his blood took its toll. The rooms were hushed now, the lamps shaded or turned low as Joseph lay on his reclining chair, or on days when his legs tormented him, in the hospital bed by the window.

He told Lila they should place a call to their attorney, but first he would like to speak to the Larkins. They'd been good neighbors for years and he need to share his plans with them, seeing how their land was joined.

In due time, Jim and Faye Larkin brought their daughter Skye to have tea and scones with the old couple. Joseph and Lila planned it for a time when they knew Amos would be busy elsewhere, wanting to keep their discussion private. The neighbors were shocked to find Joseph deteriorating so quickly, with Lila so thin she was almost translucent.

Joseph spoke of his last will and testament, hoping they could receive it generously, knowing they had always planned on acquiring this property for themselves. In his gentle way, Joseph explained his plans, the Larkins masking acute disappointment with well-appointed smiles and assurances, which greatly relieved Joseph of his burden. They made a great display of well-wishes, promised to return often, and then climbed into their Infinity where Jim proceeded to pound the steering wheel in frustration. Faye let out an expulsion of air, while Skye said she had always been afraid of exactly this scenario. But, she said, they had nothing to worry about— she had her ways.

That evening the three of them lounged in the family room in front of the fireplace, drinks in hand, Faye's sandal hanging from one foot as it bobbed continuously, Skye staring into the flames, brooding.

"Daddy, you know I always wanted that land for riding. I will have it, one way or another."

"It's pretty much gone, darling," he said, throwing back his drink and going to the mahogany bar for another.

"Not if I can help it. I have the perfect plan. He has no idea I'm divorced, and he doesn't have to know."

She pulled a ponytail holder from her hair and shook her head, ran her fingers through the luxuriant mane. She tucked her feet up beneath her, sipped her drink.

"You go, girl," her mother encouraged, raising her drink.

THE ATTORNEY, OLD Luther Barrows, crotchety in his faded wool suit, hat, and walking stick, shuffled his way up the porch steps to the gold knocker, lifted it once, twice, and waited till he heard footsteps.

Amos stepped back, took the man's hat, and showed the way to the living room, where Joseph sat in his chair, thin and weary, lost in his best twill suit, his bow tie perfectly straight, his feet in warm house slippers.

Lila was like a wisp of morning fog in a lavender dress, her hands restlessly smoothing the skirt, over and over. Amos was in a button-down shirt, oblivious to the evening's plans.

There was talk of the weather, the time for tax returns, inquiries about his health, and Lila's.

Joseph motioned with his hand.

"Now then, Amos. I want you to sit beside Mr. Barrows, so as not to miss a word. We are not reading my last will and testament as of yet, only allowing you a certain peek into what is to be. A bit unusual, but we want you to understand the stipulations of our undertaking."

Mr. Barrows cleared his throat and shuffled two heavy pieces of paper, held them to the light and began to read.

The words came slowly, in the attorney's soft burr, and Amos paid close attention as sentence after sentence rained on his understanding.

Like a son. Bequeath. Property. The care and responsibility of the occupants. The sole owner. Ownership included acreage and present structures. Living rights for Lila. Inheritance.

The room spun, righted itself. Courage. He must exercise courage. He set his lips in a thin line, sat up straight and clenched his hands. He looked at Joseph, the attorney, and Lila, shook his head in refusal.

"I don't think this is right. I haven't done anything," he choked.

"It is right and good," Joseph said, a tremble in his voice.

"What would we have done without you?" Lila asked. "We could not have stayed to enjoy this house in our golden years."

"Will you accept?" Mr. Barrows asked.

Amos put both hands on his knees, shook his head, steadied himself.

"What if I'm incapable? I don't know anything about property ownership."

"You will learn."

And still Amos struggled under a sense of failure pulling him down, his unworthiness for a gift far beyond his understanding.

Finally, Joseph said, "Amos, this is what Lila and I want. It would mean a great deal to me to know that you will be here to keep Lila company after I . . . after I go to be with our Lord. And there's nothing that would make us happier than to think of you enjoying our home and property for years to come. Please receive it as a gift."

So he signed with a shaking hand, sat back, and began to tremble, his teeth chattering. He knotted his fingers tightly, worked at breathing deeply to calm himself.

He hugged Lila tenderly, then Joseph, who wiped tears.

He thanked Mr. Barrows with a firm handshake, then turned to take the tea tray from Nancy, who appeared worn down, her hair frizzy, her uniform wrinkled and stained.

"That's all, Nancy. We'll take care of Joseph tonight. Thank you, dear, and have a nice evening," Lila said, reaching out to pat her arm.

Nancy nodded, left the room.

Amos poured tea, his fingers thick and clumsy, but managed. He passed tiny plates, scones, and sandwiches without crusts, cut into triangles. Mr. Barrows was jovial now, reminiscing. He remembered this house from decades ago in its golden years. The garden parties and elegant dinners. It was worth millions now, he said, thanks to how well it had been kept up.

Joseph's strength was failing, and the old man took his leave, Amos seeing him to his car.

He gave Amos a wink, and the car moved off into the night.

Amos turned to go back but was stopped by the vision of the house beneath budding trees, welcoming yellow light pouring from windows, the great height and dormered roof, the wide chimneys and perfectly trimmed hedges. He bowed his head, felt the crushing responsibility now upon him.

Did he want this? He felt the weight of his own lack of talent, his meager eighth-grade education. What was he, really? A fat child, slow, cumbersome, a face like burnt oatmeal, no backbone to speak of. Why him? Why had he taken it? Would he even be capable of caring for Joseph and Lila until the end of their lives? Inexperience, helplessness—it all threatened to squeeze the life out of him.

Courage. He would be a man. It was an incredible gift, almost beyond human comprehension. He loved this place dearly, and he loved Joseph and Lila even more. And with his future finances taken care of, he could use his own savings to help others. He thought of Nancy and realized he could probably pay off her double-wide to ease her burden. A slow joy spread through his veins. This was not all about him. This was about receiving and giving back. This unspeakable gift of grace was meant to be shared.

And he walked forward, his steps firm.

That first evening, he took his new responsibilities seriously. He helped Lila brush Joseph's teeth, learned how to administer medication, to put him to bed without causing pain or injury. He learned to set the fan a certain way, the proper heat setting, where to set the ice water and Vaseline, the soothing peppermint lozenges for his dry throat.

He drew up the clean white sheet—did Nancy iron them? —the soft velour blanket, touched the thin shoulder gently and bent to say good night.

"Thank you, Joseph. I am grateful," he finished.

The old man's mouth trembled, the blue eyes filled with tears.

"I have loved you as my own, Amos," he whispered, closing his eyes.

Lila assured him they would be fine, but already he knew he could no longer spend his evenings at home. He was needed at the big house.

But as he walked down the drive, he felt the unreality of it all, the future spread before him, his dream attainable.

What about Anna? He would need a willing partner, one who shared his vision, someone with strength, stamina, a woman of courage.

Oh Anna, you're the perfect fit, he thought, even while remembering the obstacles in their path.

In his own strength, he'd be pretty worthless, he figured, so he'd have to learn on God, like the Bible said and like Scott had told him.

His idea of God didn't always match Scott's. Amos had always thought of God as fierce, powerful, pointing an accusing finger, flipping people into a lake of fire if they did wrong. Scott said He loved us enough to give His own Son, which Amos couldn't argue with. Which version of God was the right one? Could they coexist? He had so much to learn.

Chapter 6

Anna swung her large brown backpack over one shoulder and ran up the steps to the front door. She let herself in quietly before hanging her bag on a hook in the foyer. She made her way to the kitchen where she met Nancy Farmer, her head in the refrigerator, thumping Tupperware containers of leftovers on the island behind her.

"Morning, Nancy," she trilled, a bundle of energy, bringing in the scent of the spring morning, lilacs and forsythia, dewdrops and night mist.

"Whatever. Get yourself some coffee."

"I plan on it. Hey, you know what happened last night? You know my dad is a real stickler for tradition? Anyhow, he won't let my mom use a gas-powered tiller, says they don't dig deep enough, hitches up his powerful Percheron, he only has one, puts him to the one-horse plow and away they go—Mom watching, of course. The horse wouldn't turn when he was supposed to and trampled all over the magnolia, the holly bushes, and two lilacs. You should have heard her. You actually may have, wherever you live." She laughed, a deep sound like bells.

Nancy faced her, hands on her hips, elbows in fight mode.

"I'll trade your mom's problems for mine. What are a few trampled bushes? Really?"

Anna poured creamer, stirred, tasted, added a bit more.

"Huh. You don't know my mom. She loves her landscaping."

"Yeah, well. My landscaping around my famous double-wide is junk cars and dog houses, weeds, and one half-dead maple. So tell her to chill."

Anna watched her yanking lids off Tupperware containers, sniffing and emptying them in the trash can. She was quiet now, a bit hurt.

"So, what's today?"

"The laundry. We have to move that washer and dryer."

"Closets?"

"Yep. All of it."

The back door opened, with Amos stepping through, rubbing his arms, wearing a dark T-shirt.

"Colder than I thought. Morning, both of you."

"Good morning, Amos."

He caught her eye, both smiled.

He was bursting to tell her everything, all the things that had occurred last evening, which still seemed like a distant dream. But it would not serve any purpose, other than elevating his status. He was a man with an inheritance now.

He looked at her and found her looking back, an incomprehensible expression in her eyes. He raised his eyebrows, lifted palms to the ceiling.

"What?" he mouthed.

She shook her head.

He let it go. "Okay, listen. Anyone who isn't busy can help rake leaves out of the hedge, out of lilacs and rugosa, not to mention beneath the white pine."

"Use a blower," Nancy growled.

"Nah, this is a job for rakes."

Amos went to check on Joseph and Lila, who were both seated on chairs, dressed and reading their daily devotionals. Joseph told him in a strong voice he'd had an outstanding night's sleep, so if he needed help outside, he'd volunteer.

Lila waved a hand, grimaced.

Joseph continued. "Amos, there are no words to describe the letting go of all the things you love here on earth. No matter the flowery verse or the assurance of Scripture, we have a real battle with flesh and blood. I would love to traipse around my beloved grounds, but it is no longer possible. I must give up and accept my illness. It ain't no fun," he finished, grinning his old grin. "Is Nancy in?"

"She is."

"Would you ask her for an earlier breakfast? Skye Larkin is paying us a visit, after nine sometime."

"Skye Larkin? Is she back home?" Amos asked, incredulous.

"Yes, I believe she's living with her parents again."

Amos left the old couple as quickly as possible, without giving away his shock about Skye Larkin. Why was she back now? Hadn't she gotten married? Maybe it hadn't worked out.

For a long moment, he contemplated the choice he had made, was making, by leaving the Amish and becoming a part of another culture, which included divorce. How easily a marriage could be dissolved, how easily another partner was chosen. He wasn't sure about any of that, unaccustomed to living with it, had never thought about it much.

Why though, did he lean toward a girl from a plain background? Because he was raised plain, with conservative values, that was why. His thoughts raced suddenly, thinking of his parents, how his father gave his life to appease his strong-willed mother. If they weren't Amish, would his father have stayed with her? And his grandparents, married for over fifty years—how had they fared?

He went to the door of the garage, looked toward the big house, could not fathom the fact he would be the owner, a recipient of so great a gift.

How would he spend the remainder of his days as a wealthy landowner?

The only clear plan was the dream he still harbored, that of helping others who had not been given the gift of a stable home, the ones who survived abuse, neglect, or worse. His own insignificance raised its visage, mocked him with doubt and his own *dummheit* (stupidity), that inability to complete his work at school or hold down a normal job.

He turned away.

With his bumbling efforts, he could very well lose this home and the land around it, the grounds he loved. Joseph had been his rock, his guiding star. The patience and encouragement from him had enabled him to learn slowly over the years.

Who would teach him the management skills he lacked entirely?

He needed a helpmeet, someone by his side, and he could only imagine Anna. He needed her confidence and energy, her rosy outlook.

He fell on his knees, bowed his head, and lifted his troubles to God, begging for guidance in these weighty matters.

WITHIN A WEEK, a low vehicle wound its way up the drive and turned in at the gatehouse, the purring engine coming to a stop. Skye Larkin swept back her hair, took a quick look in the mirror, and opened the door. She walked confidently to the small front porch and lifted the brass knocker.

Footsteps, and Amos appeared. She'd forgotten his formidable height, the size of him, older now and even more appealing.

"Amos, hello. Remember me?"

He took in the sight of her, the mane of hair, the perfect features in the unforgettable face.

"Why hello, Skye. Of course I remember."

He stepped back, "Come in."

"I will, certainly."

Amos experienced a sense of caution. She was stunning, as always, and he was only a man, appreciating beauty when it was presented.

She raised her arms, zoned in for the expected hug, which Amos could not avoid. The softness of her, the scent from the thick hair, her form familiar.

He stepped back, but her hands stayed on his arms.

"It's so good to see you again," she said, smiling, tilting her head to evaluate him. "You're looking good. Very good."

"Thank you."

"So, here we are again, huh? You got anything to drink?"

"Tea. Coffee. Soda." He lifted his hands, palms up.

"I'll take a cup of tea."

He turned to the kitchen, asked her to sit at the table.

She lowered herself gracefully, crossed her jean-clad legs, and praised his housekeeping, the charm of the cottage.

"It's just too cute," she finished.

She launched into a labyrinth of her dubious past, her relationship with Paul, how they'd split up but then gotten back together. Her parents had been thrilled. Paul had all the status and wealth they could ask for.

As he poured the tea, he listened closely, never heard the word "married." Things had fallen apart, bit by bit.

"He's married to that firm. He worked from eight to six at the office but was tied to his phone twenty-four-seven."

Her foot swung restlessly. She tried her tea, the heavy lashes lying on the freckled cheek.

He wanted to ask, but felt the time was not right. If he was honest, he was enjoying her company immensely, the way she mouthed her words, the smooth contralto of her honeyed voice. She was brilliant, observant, well-versed in the ways of the world, moving in moneyed circles.

"How's everything for you, Amos?"

"Much the same. Working, going to the gym."

He smiled at her, and she smiled back, exposing the perfect teeth. He thought of Anna's adorable little protrusion of her two front teeth.

"So, you're still the groundskeeper, the all-around handyman for the old people?"

"That's me."

"You haven't furthered your education?"

"No. Well, I acquired my GED."

"That's only high school."

Amos drank his tea, felt the prick of irritation. "Yeah."

She would never find out the tremendous effort the GED had required of him. His shirt had often been wet with perspiration as he hunched over his work, searching his phone for the meaning of words he had never heard, a vocabulary as foreign as another language.

He didn't want to tell her about the course he was taking now, the difficulty of deciphering the big words, the plodding determination it took to complete each assignment.

"So, you have no plans for the future, as far as education?" she asked, blinking the heavy lashes in a way that mesmerized him. She was like a beautiful cat.

"Well, no, I suppose I don't."

"You'll be happy with the wages Joseph pays you?"

"He pays me well."

"But what if you wanted to marry someone? Have children?"

"I suppose I don't consider it enough."

"You're not getting any younger."

"That's true."

"You know Joseph and Lila won't live forever."

"That's true, too."

She watched his face, her large eyes unflinching, but he gave away nothing. She had no idea if the fading old couple had spoken to him about the inheritance, and he had no idea she knew. The discomfort edged its way in, and Amos choked on a mouthful of tea, coughed, wiped his mouth with a napkin.

"Excuse me," he stammered.

"It's okay. So, tell me, have you been seeing anyone?"

For a long moment, he was silent. She waited, concealing her eagerness.

"I guess the proper answer would be yes and no. There's Anna, who you met once at Thanksgiving. We've gone out, but her parents don't want her dating me on account of my having left the Amish. Which is understandable. We're still trying to work it out."

"You're considering going back?"

There was an edge to her voice, razor thin.

"I can't answer that at this point."

Skye was smart, and she quickly recognized the need for restraint. He must not know she was aware of the fact of the inheritance, and she planned on keeping the secret well. She would move slowly, allow him time to tell her himself. For now, she would depend on her ability to win his affection, to keep him at arm's length. Oh, she knew exactly what accomplished her own long-range forecast of the heart.

ALLAN AND RACHEL Riehl sat with their daughter Anna on an afternoon when the lowered clouds wept a copious amount of rain mixed with bits of snow, so late in the year.

Their house was substantial, a new dwelling built in the fine workmanship of the modern Amish, the timber frame porch posts surrounding stone walls, complete with gray shaker siding and wide trim on the windows. A three-story house, an attached sunroom to the east, where Rachel's array of expensive houseplants would thrive in the light of the morning sun, the three bathrooms tiled in the latest style, hardwood floors in the latest design in doors and trim, fine molding along the ceiling. It was a beautiful house Allan had designed himself.

You knew there were Amish people living in this house by the matching horse stable in the back, sporting the same stone and timber frame posts, the garage doors wood-grained with small paned windows, the black-topped drive winding up the small grade, Japanese pines and various well-placed shrubbery at admirable spots.

Allan was a highly successful building contractor, enjoying the fruits of his labor. He was able to purchase a second home, which he quickly turned into an Airbnb, gathering his profits, which were significant, a fact he kept to himself, not given to boasting among his peers.

Twice a year he gave generously to the church, his conscience soothed for living well. He loved his fellow men, his wife and children, and now dabbled in the lucrative field of horses, which was a fast-growing enterprise among the Amish.

Life had always treated him well, and he considered himself blessed beyond measure. God was good, his days well-ordered.

Abraham of the Old Testament had been wealthy, his herds more than many others, and he had found favor in the eyes of the Lord, and so it must be for him as well, he always assumed. Each man is responsible for the gifts God gave him, and he had the gift of acquiring wealth, as had Abraham in the Bible.

But his sunny, well-ordered life had been rudely disrupted by his daughter Anna, who had never before given them reason for concern. His wife Rachel's view of *ordnung* had always been a looser version than some of her fellow churchgoers, dressing her little girls in the latest styles, even on into their teenaged years. She enjoyed a nice, well-decorated house, pleasing to the eye, as she enjoyed seeing her daughters dressed in comely style, their hair rolled in the latest fashion, small coverings worn on the back of their heads, and so forth.

But this new development was not good. Not good at all, and brows were furrowed. Anna wanted her parents' consent to date a young man who had left the Amish and lived a worldly life. The very thought struck fear in their hearts. One of their own forsaking the conservative Amish culture was truly unthinkable.

What would people think? Their own parents, old now, would die of heartache. There was so much at stake here. All their lives, they had known other families who experienced pain and heartache, losing children or relatives to the world, away from the safety of the Amish *ordnung*. They had never imagined anything like that would ever happen to them.

Cups of coffee stayed untouched, cookies dried out in open containers. A hand to her apron front, Rachel struggled to stay calm, while Allan listened in consternation.

"We want to see each other openly. He's a good man and doesn't want to sneak around. I know he's not Amish, but that has its reasons. Hear me out, is all I ask," Anna said, her voice courageous, well-modulated.

She told them his story, his dream for the future, his fine character and relationship with God, his faith in the blood of Jesus to save him, same as hers.

"Same as yours, Dad," she finished, her eyes pleading.

"But he's not Amish. He comes from a troubled home. There are two giant red flags, right there. No, Anna, I cannot give my consent. I don't care how nice this guy is."

Her father was firm, a man of quick, well-thought-out decisions.

Anna picked up her armor, prepared for the battle she had known would come.

"Have you thought of the fact he's made something of himself in spite of his upbringing?"

Allan eyed her with poorly veiled contempt.

"Made something of himself? How? He's a groundskeeper, for Pete's sake, Anna. He's what? In his late twenties? And he's still mowing grass?"

Rachel nodded in total agreement.

Anna was furious, but she took a few breaths.

"So that's how you measure a man? Really? By the amount of money he makes? You have got to be kidding me, Dat."

"Don't get smart with me, Anna."

"No, I'm serious. You have no idea what kind of man Amos really is. He's humble, truly humble from the heart. All he wants from life is to help other kids who don't have much of a chance, like himself."

Allan sat back, crossed his arms, the stance he assumed formidable, a display of authority.

"He's misleading you. Don't you know that's the first thing those who leave the Amish do? Good works, to ease their guilt."

"Not you, too," Anna whispered, in disbelief.

Rachel broke in. "Anna, we're only trying to spare you trials and temptations down the road. If we allow this union, we'll have to see many hurtful things later in life. English grandchildren driving cars, and each generation will be farther out. Who knows what the third and fourth generation will be like?"

Quickly, Anna reminded them of the Amish homes and clothes three generations back, which were very different from their own substantial home, the solar panels on the roof, the cell phones and trucks he owned in secret.

Stung, Allan quickly subdued her, and Rachel began to weep.

"I'm sorry, Mam, Dat. Forgive me. I can see this is going nowhere, okay? I'll abide by your wishes, for now. But I ask you to keep an open mind and let me have time to consider everything," Anna said, broken now by the sound of her mother's sobs.

"We're looking out for you, Anna. Wanting what is best for you in the future. There are so many available young men who are steadfast in the faith," her father pleaded.

"Steadfast to what, Dat? What are they steadfast to?" she asked, quietly.

"Well, to God. To the Amish way of life. We promise to obey, to stay with the Amish the day we are baptized. It's a pledge to God and the church same as my marriage to your mother. Right, Rachel?"

"So, God isn't anywhere else?" Anna sked quickly.

"Of course He is. Just not for us."

Rachel blew her nose, wiped her eyes, and nodded, her eyes red and swollen behind her glasses.

"One more thing," said Anna. "You were always so broad-minded about other churches, various people and denominations. Why are you being like this now?"

"Because you're one of our own. If you leave, it will never be the same," her father answered quickly.

A tense silence hung over the room, turbulent with unanswered questions.

Then Rachel spoke, asking Anna if she would feel comfortable driving a vehicle up the drive, knowing it went so hard against their wishes. How nice it would be, instead, to see her driving up with a horse and buggy, her little ones standing in the front the way they used to. To be Amish meant everything to them, and this much was clear: If this Amos loved her the way he should, he would make the sacrifice and join the Amish church.

Anna nodded, then rose from her chair, bidding them a good night before making her way up the oak staircase and into her bedroom where she switched on the lamp and sank on the side of her bed.

But they hadn't met Amos, could not pass judgment so quickly. Rebellion rose in her like a growing disease, choking out reasonable thoughts. Rain splatted on dark windows, ran down the panes and onto the roof, a dark, sullen night matching her mood entirely. The wind rattled the downspout on the corner, sending cold chills up her spine, but still she sat, unseeing. Questions assaulted her.

What even was Amish? A secluded lifestyle, one sheltered from the world. What was the world? She shuddered, knowing her view of the world was entirely different than her parents'. There were English Christians who were not of the world, their thoughts and attitudes changed by their own confession of faith in Jesus Christ. They had little or no convictions about dress, deeming it completely unnecessary, but lived a wholesome life dedicated to spreading the love they believed was God Himself.

How could this be wrong?

Did she even like being Amish?

For a long time, she considered this question, and eventually came to the conclusion that, yes, she did like being who she was. This was her identity. This was who she was. Every morning, she combed her hair in the fancy style of liberal Amish girls, donned her dress and bib apron, put on her covering, and went to work, comfortable in her appearance, in her way of life.

Why had God allowed Amos into her life? As a test of her faith? If only Jesus would appear at her door, in His robe and sandals, with his long hair and loving eyes. He could tell her what to do.

Did she truly love Amos Beiler, for himself, as he was? Or was this some sort of longing because she knew he was forbidden?

She thought of him as he went about his work at the Smith residence with dedication. She had never heard him say one bad word against them, or anyone else. He was even hesitant to talk poorly of his mother.

Plus, it was obvious the old couple's admiration bordered on worship of him. If only her own parents could see what they saw in him.

A weariness overtook her, and she reached up to remove the pins from her covering, held the piece of white fabric in her hand. Was it really a symbol of her conservative lifestyle, or was it a fashionable item of Amish style that complemented her fashionably rolled hair? She enjoyed the admiration of her peers when they asked where she got her coverings, noticing they fit so perfectly.

Who was the seamstress? Making coverings was a business, with thousands being produced by many different ones. You could pick and choose, which Anna understood very well. She always picked the latest style, in the way she was raised. Their home, their accumulation of wealth, the horse they drove, the clothes they wore—it was all Amish, but was it what the forefathers envisioned?

She sighed, laid aside the covering, and lifted the bib apron over her head, examining it as well. Who had designed this article of clothing? And what did it represent? Modesty, supposedly.

"Hey."

Her sister Barbie, clad in flannel pajama pants and a Disney T-shirt, her hair loose and shoulder-length, came into her room, sliding her feet on the rug in an exaggerated display of well-being. She flung both hands in the air, threw back her head, and trilled.

"Guess who just texted me?"

"Couldn't guess," Anna said, quickly hiding the heaviness of her thoughts.

"One guess."

"Okay. Sim's Levi?"

"No," Barbie shrieked. "I would never take him."

"I know. Jesse!"

"Yep. You got it. Absolutely. Read this."

Her phone slid under her gaze, the words plain on the screen.

"Hey, babe. What's up?"

Anna drew back, in mock surprise. "Babe? Really?"

Amid all Barbie's happiness, she wondered if they were really so separate from the world after all. She couldn't imagine Amos texting her "Babe." He was more respectful, more conservative than this young Amish man texting her sister. Didn't that count for anything?

Chapter 7

In the Raymond Beiler household, things were running fairly smoothly. Lydia had money in her checkbook, though it was being spent at an alarming rate between Lowe's, the greenhouse on Bells' Corner, and Sherwin-Williams's paint store. She'd have to save her housecleaning money if she wanted the stamped concrete walkways, but she could do that.

Thrilled with her sunny kitchen (how could she have thought her former home was worth the price?), her electricity, and the lower monthly payment, she whistled and sang her way through each room, wielding dripping rollers and narrow brushes, each room given the same almost white coat, the trim only a tad darker, to make it stand out. She was so pleased with the result, she told Raymond this was the best move they'd ever made, and he got all the credit, the way he'd encouraged her. This brought such a great rush of love for her he took her in his arms right then and there.

Lydia giggled and told him Lavina and Cathy would see.

It was all worth it, giving his life for his wife. It wasn't a sacrifice, but an honor to love someone the way he loved her, and he whistled his way through each bright day and thanked God from the depths of his heart and soul.

How glad he was he had married her. To come home to a steaming beef roast and mashed potatoes, with yet another room done to her liking and a smile on her face, was heavenly for him. Even Cathy showed a bit of common sense and stayed quiet about real or perceived grievances.

He built two flower boxes for the front windows, which she stained dark gray and filled with scarlet geraniums, purple salvia, and trailing vines. He helped her plant boxwoods and weeping cherry trees, a few hollies and azaleas, waving to old vehicles rattling past.

In due time, lawn service rolled up to the house, a green van with LEROY'S LAWN CARE in purple lettering and a wild display of multi-colored flowers all over it. Lydia was putting the finishing touches on the spindles of stair rails, so she dropped everything and went to the door to find a thin, wiry little man with a face like an old leather wallet.

"Yes, ma'am. You wanted an estimate?"

"Yes. I certainly do. But not the whole backyard. Our garden will be plowed there. Here. I'll get my shoes and show you."

They walked around the perimeter of the yard taking stock of the overrun lawn, completely golden with dandelions and red root. After much deliberating, he gave her the price of around a hundred dollars an application, four times a year. "Four hundred," he said deliberately, and she nodded happily. Not bad at all. She could manage that, my word.

But then that Sunday in church Sarah Fisher told her that she was crazy. What was she thinking, spreading all those chemicals on her lawn? Didn't she know that stuff was pure poison? It would give them all cancer. And Lydia sniffed and said that was a matter of opinion, that she wanted a really nice lawn for once in her life, which she figured was her own business, was it not?

She forked another slippery red beet onto her plate, tried to keep it speared securely to cut it with her knife, but it shot away across the table and came to rest in Barbie Lapp's apron. Lydia muttered something about these mothers no longer teaching their girls to cut their red beets smaller. These young women were getting downright sloppy.

Barbie poked Sarah's ribs with her elbow and they desperately tried to hide wide grins. They knew Lydia well. Too well.

Lydia remained a bit huffy as she relayed Sarah's opinion to Raymond, who replied that perhaps it was better not to discuss the lawn service with the other women. They then had a very silent ride the remainder of the way home.

She flounced out of the carriage, her skirt catching on the brake protruding from the floor, and down she went, hard, on the gravel, tearing the hem of her skirt, both legs revealed well above the knee, big and white, like two big fish.

"Oh. Uh. Ouch. Ow," she muttered, struggling to her feet as the hem of her skirt tore loose.

"Lydia. My goodness, are you okay?"

With red-faced attempts, she grunted and heaved, tugged at her skirt, and crawled across the gravel without answering. Finally, on her feet, she surveyed her lacerations and hobbled to the house, slamming the door as hard as possible.

Raymond's face twitched and his stomach jiggled as he unhitched the faithful standardbred and led him into the small barn. Then he broke into full-fledged guffaws until tears streamed from his eyes and he bent over, slapping his knees.

"Oh my," he chortled finally. Ah, his dear, funny wife. But a blessing in his life, absolutely.

Upon him entering the house, Lydia yelled hoarsely, "Raymond, did you use the B&W ointment?"

"Not that I can recall."

"See if it's in the girls' bathroom upstairs."

He followed instructions, squinted at small containers, and found a white one with a yellow label.

"Yup," he said under his breath, and took it downstairs to his injured spouse.

Out of the corner of his eye he caught sight of a black pickup and his heart soared. Amos. He was so glad. When the knock sounded, he was at the door immediately, welcoming him warmly, his brown eyes glistening with emotion.

"Amos, Amos."

"Hey, Dat."

"Come on in. Surely good to see you."

"Who's here?" Lydia called.

The plaintive voice from the living room produced the same stomach churn it always did for Amos. He gripped the back of a kitchen chair, his lips compressed.

"Mam."

"Oh, it's you."

"Something wrong? What happened to your knees?"

"I fell." Down went her skirt, a firm hand on each knee. "Nothing much."

Her eyes met his, a challenge. *Dare to ask one question, Amos. Just try it.*

"Come on out to the kitchen, Amos," Raymond interjected. You know how it is—you eat in church and you come home hungry. Coffee? You want popcorn? I think Mam made whoopie pies."

"I did not, Raymond. That's a lie."

Raymond winked at Amos and grinned. Amos shook his head.

"What happened?" he mouthed.

"Fell out of the buggy." Then he was overtaken with another paroxysm of giggles, hanging on to the back of a chair as he fought for control. Amos felt laughter begin in his stomach and then build until his shoulders were shaking. It took him by surprise, and it was beyond his control. The more his father laughed, the more he did.

It simply wasn't done. No one laughed at Lydia and got away with it.

He heard a sharp, "What's so funny?" from the doorway and instantly the mirth came to a halt.

"Nothing, Lydia. We were just saying how we eat at church and come home ready for a snack. Right, Amos?"

"Yeah, that's what he said."

"Amos, you probably don't even remember eating at church, it's been so long."

"Oh, I remember, alright."

Too clearly, the memory of quickly stuffing one delicious slice of bread with peanut butter spread—that lovely soft concoction of peanut butter and marshmallow cream, spread on homemade bread—into his mouth, stealthily reaching for another, hoping no one counted as he consumed rapidly.

Squeezing his too-large body into a tiny space between bench and table and wishing, wishing things were different.

"You probably go out to eat on Sunday, right? The way you English people do."

"Sometimes I do."

"You know better, Amos. You were taught not to spend money on Sunday. That is not keeping the Sabbath holy."

Amos had no reply, so he just sat in silence, waiting.

"Whatever. You were gone so long now I almost forget you were ever at home. Didn't you find yourself a wife yet?"

"No, I haven't married."

"Well, you sure don't look the way you used to."

This was said grudgingly, her back turned as she scooped coffee into the coffee maker.

"What's up with the electricity use?" he asked, looking around, catching sight of the working microwave, the lights. As soon as it came out of his mouth, he remembered what Cathy had said about the preachers visiting his parents at their old house. The pieces came together in his mind.

"You know how it is. You're allowed for a while. I figure the bishop in this church won't come see us right away."

They sat together that afternoon in a more civil manner than they had in the past. A certain acceptance had somehow occurred, like a laying down of swords, a tentative peace treaty. Amos began to relax, refilled his popcorn bowl twice, even had the nerve to tease his mother about the lack of whoopie pies.

"Oh," she said, "you should see how I've been working. Cathy has before and after pictures in her phone." She walked him through the whole house, which wasn't large at all, but he told her she'd done a great job. He said he loved the bright, airy feel of it, and she replied that she liked it more than any house they had ever owned.

He walked ahead of her up the stairs and she marveled at his well-built physique, the massive shoulders and sturdy legs encased in denim. An unexpected rush of pride washed over her, but she stuffed it away. He was an English man now, and she could not be pleased with him.

But my. She had never seen anyone change their appearance like that. He was still only Amos inside, though, and would always be a day laborer, likely never moving on very fast in the financial world, just like Raymond. Simple-minded fellows, both of them, like faithful mules, content to plod along to work each day.

Amos drove home that Sunday with no understanding of the storm of emotion engulfing him like a towering tidal wave. He wept so hard he had to stop the truck and clench the steering wheel as sobs tore through him with hoarse, feral sounds that frightened him.

His father had been glad, genuinely pleased. The warmth of it, the waves of hidden laughter together. The acceptance. He realized then, like the sun rising in the east, his father liked him. He was pleased to see Amos drive up and pay them a visit. His mother's cutting remarks seemed limp, somehow having lost their sting. Was there a chance she would come to the same acceptance?

No matter. All in God's time. The important thing was the way he turned to seek God's face, to walk with Jesus daily, as the minister had expounded in the lovely church he attended faithfully.

He had grown a lot at Scott's church, but after a while he'd found himself curious about other churches and stumbled onto this smaller one, a stone building in the middle of Rochester, set back from the street shaded by stately oaks, their immensity never ceasing to thrill him.

The church was good fit, like a comfortable wide shoe, and he had thanked God many times. He felt spiritually fed and his soul was satisfied as he listened to the wisdom of the white-haired minister, noticed the filled pews, the younger couple with children.

He drove on, feeling a certain healing. Who was to know of anything? A coin on its edge could fall either way. Who could deny the mystery of the future?

At home, he felt restless. He wanted Anna but knew contacting her was not a good idea at this point. He would walk a while, check up on Joseph and Lila.

He let himself out the door, into the aching beauty of a spring evening heavy with the scent of lilac and flowering quince. A piercing song from a pair of cardinals broke through his thoughts. The bushes beside him were alive with the twittering of frantic sparrows sparring for access to the old wooden birdhouse. The yellow house stood sentinel beneath the aging trees, beautiful in the early evening light. The wide black shutters were the perfect accent for the deep porches, the long windows glinting with sunlight.

He needed to repair that corner downspout, the way it washed the mulch away from the new globe arborvitae.

A nurse was hired for Sunday to give Nancy and him a break from their duties, so he let himself in the back. He found no one in the laundry room or the kitchen. There were a few dishes to be washed, so he turned on the overhead light and squirted Dawn dish soap, ran the tap, and began with the yellow sponge.

He became aware of a presence, then heard a mild "Hello." He turned to find a stranger, presumably the visiting nurse.

"Hello?"

"You must be Amos Beiler."

"I am. And you must be the nurse."

"That's me." She smiled, extended a hand. "Amy Forge."

"Amos Beiler."

"Good to meet you. Okay, I have him settled for the night. I'm sorry to report his condition today is not well. Has Lila considered hospice visits?"

Amos stared blankly.

"You mean . . . ?"

"Yes. It's time. He may not have long."

Amos lowered his eyes, needing a moment.

Amy was as tall as he was, her blue eyes almost level with his. She was not beautiful like Skye, but showed a certain attractiveness, a somber quality about her half-lowered eyelids.

"I really don't know. You'd have to ask her about that."

"Why don't you come with me and we'll try to approach Lila."

He put down his sponge, dried his hands on a dish towel, met her eyes and nodded. She nodded back.

Lila was like a wisp of fog in a white bathrobe, a green throw across her lap, the radio playing soft hymns beside her.

Joseph was asleep, so thin there was barely a mound beneath the blankets except for his feet. His breathing was shallow, labored.

"Lila," Amy said gently.

She reached over to turn off the radio, looked up and smiled weakly. "He's had a tough day today." The old mouth trembled slightly.

"He has. He's very weak," said Amy. "I wondered, shall I inquire about hospice for you?"

She shook her head. "No, no. Not yet. Not that. Let me have him a while, please."

Amy crossed her arms, stood quietly, saying nothing.

"Please don't think me impertinent. I know I'm a stubborn old lady, but having hospice come in is the beginning of the end."

Amos stepped up. "Whatever you wish, Lila. We'll honor your decision. Nancy and I will manage very well."

"You will?"

"Yes."

"Thank you."

They tiptoed out of the room and walked to the lighted kitchen without speaking. Then Amos turned. He was lonely, needed a friend to talk to.

"You have time for a cup of tea?" he said, then checked himself. "Oh, you might have a husband, children who need you."

"Oh no. Actually, I'm a long-distance runner. Marathons. Between that and work, doesn't leave much time for anything else."

"Wow! I'd love to hear about that. I mean, unless you were planning to go for a run or something now . . ."

She considered for a moment, then perched on a kitchen stool and began to talk. She lived among the Amish, always had, took the horse-drawn buggies in stride, the bonneted women at the grocery store. She heard his story with empathy, marveled at his weight loss. Naturally thin, her passion was running. There was a guy in her life, yes, but he was a rock climber and out of state half the time, so it was bit up and down. Not that she had time for much more than that from a relationship anyway.

The tea grew cold as they talked on. He found her fascinating. With her hair drawn back in a stringy ponytail, no makeup, she wasn't the kind of beautiful you'd see on the cover of a magazine at the grocery store. But her smile was wide and genuine and her laughter came easily, low and unhurried.

At ten thirty, she said she better get home to feed her cat. Amos thought of Fred. He missed him so much. He still felt a sickening wrench when he thought of his terrible death. He couldn't fathom getting another dog.

"Get a cat. They're easier."

"Look, I already drink tea. A cat would really tip the scales into old lady territory."

She laughed. "You want to run with me sometime?"

He shook his head. "I'm an ox. There's no way I'd keep up with your long legs."

"Just a jog. I'm not asking you to beat me in a marathon."

He looked at her. She looked back with her frank stare. There was nothing hidden in the depth of her eyes, that was sure. She was the most refreshingly forthright human being he'd ever had the chance to meet.

"OK, yeah. Give me a call."

They exchanged numbers. Both stood up, her face almost but not quite level with his.

"See you next Sunday."

"Sure. We can have tea."

And she was gone.

Amos went to check on Lila and found that she couldn't sleep, so he spent the night in the room at the top of the stairs, his phone beside him, for her benefit. He had fallen into a light sleep when the buzzing woke him. For a second, he couldn't get his bearings, then he remembered and grabbed his phone.

"Amos, would you come check up on Joseph? He's making sounds."

Quickly, he drew on his jeans and shirt, hurried barefoot down the steps, calmed himself before going to his bedside.

"Joseph," he said, very quietly.

The old eyelids flew open. "Amos."

"Yes. Lila wanted me to check up on you."

"I'm alive if that's what you mean. Go back to bed and leave me alone." He smiled, the old grin, and Amos tucked the covers over his chest and patted the liver-spotted hands, achingly misshapen with arthritis.

He heated milk in the microwave for Lila, brought her the mug, and sat with her in the dim glow of the shaded lamp until she drifted off to sleep, her head rolling to the side. Gently, he placed a pillow to one side, drew up the green throw, and took the empty cup to the kitchen.

The quiet house enveloped him, spun a cocoon of warmth around him, and he felt peace and gratitude. He was young and strong, he had the support of a fine lawyer and an accountant, and could manage the upkeep of this house he loved. He could only grasp the full extent of his inheritance in small pieces, bit by bit.

He had not told his parents at all.

In the morning, Nancy was a scary presence, her allergies on a rampage, nose leaking, throwing the most astonishing sneezes, wheezing and huffing into her medicated inhaler. She made waffles for Amos, and sausages, said if he wanted eggs he had to go buy them.

He told her about the visiting nurse, about her request for hospice. She nodded when he told her about Lila's refusal.

"It's about their dignity, Amos. It's going to be a tough road. Lila's not going to want a stranger taking over her role as Joseph's primary caregiver, but the reality is she's not going to be able to do it much longer. It's pretty much up to us two."

"I don't know if I'm going to be any good at this."

"You already are, Amos, so scrape up some moxie and be a man."

He ate his waffles and contemplated what she'd said. Was it a compliment or insult? It was hard to tell with Nancy sometimes.

After breakfast, he went to the living room, sat beside Lila, and asked if she'd slept in his quiet, humble way. She gazed at him with very blue eyes, the skin above them transparent with tiny blue veins threaded across. She must have been beautiful at one time in her life, a delicate beauty, and this greatly touched his heart. He took her hand.

"Amos, dear heart. You are the son we've longed for. I consider you ours. This morning, I want to let you know how glad I am to leave this world thinking of our blessed house occupied by someone we love, not sold to complete strangers. Will you promise me one thing?"

"Anything," Amos said softly.

"My gladiolus. The bulbs you dig and replant. Will you keep them going in our memory?"

"Of course."

"I know it's childish, a petty request. But how beautiful they are, and they will continue to multiply, a link from me to you from our home in Heaven."

She smiled, patted his arm.

"The day God sent you. He presented us with a rare gift, there is no doubt in my mind. I so wish I could have met your actual parents."

Amos stumbled over thoughts. The thought of his mother being in the same room as Lila made him immediately nervous. But if Lila really wanted to meet her . . .

"If it means so much to you, I could arrange it."

"Would you?" Her smile was tremulous.

"I'll try."

Joseph emitted a low moan from the bed. Lila tried getting to her feet, but Amos hurried over. Alarmed at his pallor, he took up the frail wrist, felt the weak pulse. He called his name, received only the fluttering of thin eyelids. Repeatedly, he said his name, placed a hand on his forehead, then turned to Lila.

"He's very low. Should we call for help?"

Lila was beside him, so small, reaching for her husband, calling him, becoming more distraught as the seconds ticked by.

Silently, Amos turned, tapped the three emergency numbers.

Joseph spent his last days in the Harrisburg hospital, the old heart laboring on, his eyes closed most of the time.

The doctors conferred, spoke in assuring tones, but Lila knew better, her eyes telling Amos all he needed to know.

She was accepting the truth and would gather the strength to face the coming departure. Twice, Joseph spoke, and always to Lila alone, words Amos could not hear, a confidential whisper meant only for her ears.

She stayed by his side, was there when he breathed his last, folded his hands and touched his face. She closed the old eyelids and wept in silence. Amos stood by her side, unexpectedly peaceful, the knowledge of a believer's soul gone to the mansions prepared for him.

He drove Lila home, his thoughts hidden away from her, but wondering many things. He was considered a gift from God for the old couple, but a disobedient heretic by his own mother.

Which one was he in the eyes of God?

He left Lila in Nancy's care, went to his own small house, showered and shaved, leaned the palms of his hands on the top of the bathroom vanity and stared at his reflection.

Who am I? Which one of these two descriptions is the truth? To deny one and accept the other would never be right. He had to face his past, find the courage to bring it to God.

Yes, he had disobeyed his parents, would continue to disobey them as long as he lived away from the Amish lifestyle. He was a disappointment to them, a shame to their pride.

And yes, he was a gift to Joseph and Lila, had been rewarded by far more than he would ever deserve. Their life had been a gift to him, too; they had taught him about love, pure and simple. He learned he could hardly do anything wrong in their sight, which was liberating, a freedom he had not thought possible.

Forgive me, Lord Jesus, for the disappointment I heaped on my parents. Help me to find the path you have prepared for me. If this dream is not blessed by you, then take it from me.

He began to weep, turned away from the mirror and folded to his knees. All he wanted was a deeper relationship with the One who understood him, who would always know the intentions of his heart.

Chapter 8

Amos stood at Lila's side through the visitation, greeted acquaintances and unknown relatives who flew in from different states, great-nephews or nieces, a distant cousin. They all spoke in loving tones, though Amos thought he detected a certain eagerness to know about Joseph's presumed wealth.

The service was beautiful—the great mound of flowers, the framed photograph of their only son alongside photos of Joseph, the memories of friends and the pastor who had spent many years with them both.

At the burial, Amos stood with Nancy and Lila. He felt a presence behind him and turned to find Anna, dressed in the traditional black garb of the Amish, her eyes lowered. Quickly, he turned away.

She had come. He steadied himself with a deep breath but could do nothing to stem the flow of joy like a bubbling spring.

He chose to stay in the moment, to hear the voice of the speaker at the graveside, to allow this profound event to saturate his heart.

He would always remember Joseph as a second father, a man of so much integrity, so much respect and knowledge.

He bowed his head, placed a hand on Lila's shoulder, and vowed to protect her as long as she lived.

The big house was surrounded by vehicles, every lighted window a beacon. The day was mild, a bit overcast, the lawn and surrounding trees and shrubbery glowing with a myriad of green.

Surrounded by her friends and acquaintances, Lila rallied to have conversations, to examine memories of bygone years, while Nancy and other hired help served tea and coffee, delicate pastries, and sandwiches.

He found Anna in the hallway, speaking to Nancy. He knew he could not back away, would have only this chance, so he stood, waiting.

Nancy looked up. "What?"

"Wanted to say hello to Anna."

"Feel free." And she headed to the kitchen.

"Anna."

"Yes, Amos."

"I was hoping you would be here."

He knew then, he would never feel differently about her. She filled him with a sense of direction, like a homecoming. She was not Skye or Amy or any of those girls at the gym, or the waiters at the Lodge, or any other attractive girl he had ever encountered.

"I would not have missed the service. Joseph and Lila have been good to me. Joseph is—was—such a kind man."

"Yes." Amos found himself tearing up, at a loss for words. Anna was one of the few people who had some idea how much Joseph had meant to him.

"Anna, I . . ."

A rush of color, an overwhelming scent of flowers, and Skye Larkin swung against Amos, slipping an arm through his, her great mane of hair hanging in loose waves, her face made up perfectly.

"There you are, you big handsome dude. I could hardly wait to get my hands on you."

She gazed up at him, a vision in floral hues and high heels.

"Hello, Skye," Amos said calmly.

"Is that all I get?"

He bit his lip, looked at Anna, who stood, resigned.

"Anna, you remember Skye Larkin? You met at that Thanksgiving dinner Joseph and Lila hosted."

"Yes." Anna offered her hand, and Skye took it. "Nice to see you again."

"You Amish do a great job of house cleaning, I hear."

"I love cleaning this gorgeous old place," Anna said, innocently enough.

"I'm sure you do. Well, hopefully you can keep your job now that Joseph is gone."

Puzzled, Anna looked at Amos, found his eyes. He raised one eyebrow, shook his head.

"Amos, come for a walk with me. These people give me the willies. Come on."

She tugged at his arm. Anna turned and walked away.

Firmly, Amos extracted the grasped arm and said he couldn't, Lila might need him. "Anna, stay for a moment," he called.

Skye flung her hair, gave him a sultry look, and said, "Later, then."

He caught up to Anna, followed her to the kitchen, and watched helplessly as she kept her back turned. She reached for two mugs and filled one with coffee. The refrigerator door was opened, creamer poured and stirred, all without facing him.

"Anna, I'm sorry that Skye interrupted."

She did not turn, said nothing. Quickly he walked to her, touched her elbow. "I couldn't help that."

Slowly she turned, her face upturned, her green eyes alight with a burning intensity. Without flinching, she looked deeply into his eyes, an honest appraisal.

"So, what is she to you?"

He told her their entire history, and she sipped her coffee, slid onto a barstool. She seemed to accept his story, believing him when he said he and Skye were not together and he had no interest in a relationship with her.

Taking a deep breath, she told him about the talk with her parents. Servers came into the kitchen to refill platters of sandwiches and crudites but paid them no attention. She told him of her struggle, how frustrated she was with her parents' stance. So liberal, yet when one of their own wanted to choose an alternative path, they were dead set against it.

His heart like an anvil in his chest cavity, Amos could not find the courage to accept the verdict, her parents' final disapproval. He felt the draw of desperation.

"Anna, don't say it yet. I'm not ready to hear that we are finished. Not yet. Not today . . ."

Her eyes rounded, grew liquid with emotion.

"Do you want this to work? I mean, you . . ."

"Yes. I do want this. I want to keep seeing you."

"But there's a dead end. I can't go against my parents. It's not right."

Amos sighed, suddenly exhausted. "Look, I have to go be with Lila. Stay. Stay this evening. Come to my house. I'll take you home."

She shook her head. "I told myself I wouldn't, Amos. I can't do it."

"Just to talk. Figure things out."

"They are figured out."

"Okay, but give me this one evening. Please, Anna. You can head to my place whenever you're ready and I'll meet you there when things wind down here."

She bit her lip, her eyelids lowered. She saw the pain in his eyes, his thinly veiled grief over losing Joseph, his deep weariness. Slowly, she nodded. "Okay."

He turned away, his arms aching to hold her, to tell her everything she meant to him, to feel the comfort of her soft body leaned against his own. The remainder of the afternoon was spent in a cloud of bewilderment, as if a dense fog had settled over him, and he saw only bits and pieces of his surroundings.

There were the Larkins, hovering over a very small and a very weary Lila, effusive, intimidating. He felt the need to protect, to turn them away, and so placed himself at her left, took her elbow, and bent to ask if she needed to be in her chair.

"Excuse me, please," he said, quite clearly.

Lila looked up, gratefully accepted, and he steered her away, seated her gently, placed the green throw across her lap, then left to bring her favorite tea.

Immediately, the Larkins took up positions on either side, a well-dressed couple intent on worming their way into her benevolence.

Amos brought the tea and a small folding table, which he lowered beside her chair, then straightened to meet the eyes he knew were watching every move. He was determined to take the pressure off of Lila, which meant being polite to the Larkins, though he wished they'd just leave.

"How have you been? Both of you. We haven't seen you for quite some time, have we?" he asked.

Mr. Larkin launched into an account of an extremely hectic schedule, which left no time to visit close neighbors, which was a shame, a complete shame, absolutely. Now that summer was on the horizon, perhaps life would slow down a bit and they'd have time for a visit.

"We'll certainly do better, now that Lila is all by herself. We can arrange to have James bring you over to our house as well. Would you enjoy that?" Mr. Larkin looked to Lila, leaning toward her eagerly.

"It would be interesting, of course," Lila replied softly.

"Amos, you will have to join us. We have a great pickleball court."

Amos nodded, smiled, said all the proper things, until finally they moved aside. He was greeted by other guests as they came to pay their respects and offer their condolences to Lila, and he shook their hands, listened to their kind words, told them to be sure to help themselves to sandwiches on the buffet table. The guests blurred together after a while and he felt almost as if he were in a strange dream. He knew Lila needed him by her side and yet he also began to feel like he had to escape. Eventually, he bent down and excused himself, telling Lila he was going to get some water. He was headed to the kitchen, avoiding eye contact with anyone, when he ran blindly into Amy, who backed off with her hands in the air, palms out.

"Whoa there," she laughed.

"Sorry, Amy. Wasn't thinking."

"Or looking where you were going."

She watched his retreating back, wondered if she'd ever seen a guy quite that nice-looking in a black suit and tie. It was very unusual of her to notice anyone like that. He wasn't like so many other men she knew. It was the way he spoke, the humility and genuine sweetness of him. She found herself wondering when he'd ask for that first time running with her.

Skye pouted, watched Anna leave, thought, *Good. What was she to Amos? Whatever. Short and decidedly not skinny. Well. It's not over yet.*

She went upstairs, thought of being the owner of this house. Good bones, sure, but she'd rip off this ancient molding and overdone trim work, get rid of these awful doors. The furniture was hideous.

She'd always had an eye for structure, placement, good design, and if Amos inherited the old guy's stash, well then, she'd finally be able to put her expertise to good use. He wouldn't know the first thing about it, coming from the Amish. They were all simple. Real hillbillies.

She caught sight of herself in the mirror of an old dresser, the intricate detailing of the frame appalling. Had she overdone it, wearing this dress? As usual, her mother had disapproved, but she was an adult now, capable of making her own choices.

The dress was stunning, with the large floral print, the bell sleeves and good neckline. Not appropriate for a funeral, perhaps, but appropriate for catching the eye of a certain groundskeeper.

But she knew the mission had gone awry.

Finally, Amos was released from his duties. Lila said there was no need for him to stay. Amy was spending the night, and Nancy didn't have a lot of cleanup to do. He double-checked with Nancy, who agreed that he should take off. He thanked her, then told her she looked nice in her navy-blue dress, which brought a wave of her hand, then a searching of his face, as if to assure herself he meant it. He slid an arm across her shoulders and squeezed. "You're the best, Nancy."

He felt so English, saying that. There had been a time in his life where that would have been unthinkable, handing out compliments, a display of affection.

He walked down the drive in the tranquil evening, the air as soft and mellow as the scent of a daffodil. He thought of Joseph, the emptiness his passing would bring. He missed Lavina. He should have told her about the funeral, but he knew it would only bring another battle from their mother.

His breath quickened as he approached the small cottage.

He told himself to accept the outcome of the evening, to find his courage, but none of this was going to be easy.

He found her seated on his sofa, a magazine on her lap, watching him silently as he entered. She'd removed her shoes, her cape and apron, her covering laid on the end table.

"Sorry. I sort of made myself at home."

"Good. I plan on doing the same."

He shrugged out of his suit coat, tugged at his tie, said if he was Amish he wouldn't have to mess with these things—not that he wore them very often.

He went to the hall mirror, lifted his chin as his large fingers worked at the knot.

"You need help with that?" she asked, getting to her feet.

"I can't seem to get it."

She stood in front of him, had to reach way up to undo the tie, then stepped away quickly, as if she had placed herself in a forbidden position.

Amos said nothing, but felt shaken.

"Tea?" he asked, hoping his voice was steady.

"Definitely your chai."

He smiled.

"That's one thing we agree on."

Small talk. What was it worth? It was necessary, as he poured boiling water, watched her face as she toyed with a napkin. Her hair was pulled back, but the honeyed streaks were natural, no hair color. She was not as conventionally beautiful as Skye, but she was so perfect—the round contours of her cheeks, the straight well-formed nose and slight protrusion of white teeth. He could not explain his feelings for her. It was as natural as the air he breathed, the clouds in the sky, and the earth at his feet.

They sat opposite each other at the small table in the soft light of the kitchen, found each other's eyes, and kept them locked.

"Amos, I . . ." She paused, afraid to go on.

"Anna, it's okay. I'm going to be okay. Seriously. Just tell me."

"I don't know what to say."

"Try."

So she did, in fits and starts, relating again the painful conversation with her parents, the unwilling, brick wall objection.

"I was not willing to accept their viewpoint then, but I'm slowly being broken down. I have to choose between two rights. It's right for me to stay Amish and be obedient to them, but it's also right to be with you, if that makes any sense at all."

"You feel right with me?" he asked, suddenly incredulous.

"Honestly, I do. I don't want to date anyone else. But there's just too much at stake. The price is too high."

Amos thought about this. Yes, leaving one culture for another brought a hefty price, no doubt. A way of life was deeply ingrained, especially the unique culture of the plain people. Was it possible to shake this identity, ever?

"If I could only find it in myself to return to the Amish, I would. I would do it for you, but I'm afraid. It's all the stuff from my past, but also, I just can't think of a future stuck in a way of life I don't believe in."

"You actually don't believe the *ordnung* is important?"

"Not for me. If someone believes otherwise, then they should never leave. I believe God gives us each different convictions. But as much as I want to, I think I'd be wrong if I tried to talk you out of your own convictions. Do you believe the *ordnung* is important, for you?"

Anna brought her spoon out of the mug of tea, laid it carefully on a napkin, kept moving it in one direction then another, a pucker on her forehead as she squared it up. After a long moment, she said, "What is *ordnung*? Who even wrote all the rules?"

"I don't really know. I guess way back in the day the forefathers wrote the rules to prevent their families from going along with the fashions and advances of the times."

"To stay separate from 'the world,' I guess. Whatever that really means."

"To stay simple, not being a part of the sinners who didn't care about stuff. I don't know."

"My parents don't honor all of the *ordnung*."

"Mine never did. Still don't."

Anna sighed. "But it's very important for the children to follow the parents."

They tried to find their way through a maze of indecision, of respect and honor to the old way, or breaking loose and following a dream you felt was God's will for your life. Anna's voice became smaller, with long halts as she obviously struggled for control. When she reached for a napkin and began an achingly quiet weeping, Amos felt absolutely awful. The self-blame was a crushing weight.

He rose, went to her, and hunkered down. Her hands went to her face, to hide the shame of her tears.

"Don't, please don't cry. Look, I'm not worth it."

She shook her head, took a deep breath, and swabbed at her eyes. Her hands fell away from her face, and he took both of them in his hands.

"Anna, I hate that I'm causing you pain. I've put you in an unfair position and I'm so sorry for that."

She shook her head.

"We keep trying to stay apart, then we are together again, yet we can never find answers. My parents say the day we're born our decisions are made for us. We're Amish, flat out. There's no choice to be made."

"Wow." Amos gave a long low whistle.

"I know."

Were there differences? Was one allowed to make his own choice because of mistreatment? Should he have forgiven long before he did? Was the devil leading him now, as some would say?

He felt the darkness, a sinister being, and an unnameable fear mounted. He consciously switched his focus to the face of God, and all of his confusion left. He was filled with the need to be patient, to walk slowly, one stone at a time, even if the waters around him churned and roiled.

He let go of her hands, straightened up, and went to the couch, where he fell back and let out a long breath, the exhaustion of the day released.

"Come sit. We can't figure it all out in one evening. Let's give it a rest, okay?"

She came to sit beside him—not too close, but aware of him.

Oh, she had felt his presence before seeing him at the funeral. He was so tall, so well-dressed and handsome, kind and humble, taking care of Lila like a son. Supposedly, he was "worldly," cast out. How could he be? He was genuine, she could see him giving his whole life to the service of God, whatever he was led to do. No, he was not "worldly" in the way people thought.

But why couldn't he make this same sacrifice for her?

"Anna, may I speak to you from the heart?" he asked, unexpectedly.

She nodded.

"Here goes. Okay, you are the one I think of. I dream about. I don't know why this is. I have other options."

"I saw that."

Amos laughed.

"But it's you I want. Your way of talking, your ambition and energy—all of it attracts me. Not to mention your face. I would never tire of looking at your face, your little teeth—everything about you. And I believe these feelings are from God because He is the author and creator of love. But I can't come out and say I love you until we make a decision one way or another. But I believe we are meant to be together."

"How, Amos? If you won't come back to the Amish? Why is that I have to be the one to give up my family, my life?" she wailed, her voice catching on a sob.

"Anna, you don't understand. There is nothing there for me. All the good I have found in this world is up there in that yellow house. I'm sorry, but you don't realize the impact my rotten childhood had—has—on me."

"You're not a child anymore. Maybe it's time you get over it."

He sat up and stared at her. "Anna, you weren't there. You don't know what it was like. You can't begin to fathom the pain and hurt and blazing rebellion against plain people who are supposed to be the salt of the earth, a light to the world and all it is . . ."

"Stop it. You can't lump them all together like that. You know as well as I do, there are plenty of good Amish people. Most of them would never hurt a flea, and I bet your mother did the best she could."

"No, she did not, in fact."

It was like a dam being broken, a torrent of freed water carrying every moment of self-hatred, bitterness, injustice, and shame.

To be so enormous, so out of proportion to his peers, with two pretty sisters and a mother's ill-concealed pride in them, the disgust on her face when he waddled home from school like the monster he was, a father who lived in the dark, cowardly shadows of his manipulative wife—it was a childhood injury that would never be forgotten. Never.

He sat still, waited, the color slowly draining from his face, his arms crossed in front of his chest, stubborn.

"So then, the mistreatment of your parents is the handle you use to justify yourself for being English?"

"I am English. I don't need to justify that."

"Then why did you go into all that detail?"

"I'm trying to get you to understand."

"Why you won't return to the Amish for me."

"Exactly."

She stared for a moment, then shifted as if to stand up.

"It's getting late. My parents don't know where I am."

"Come here, Anna." His voice had softened.

"No. I don't trust myself, or you."

"A very good thing for you to say. You're the most level-headed person, so sweet and *chide* (pure). Why do you waste your time with me?"

"Oh, believe me, it isn't wasted. I happen to like it here. At least when we're not arguing in circles."

"Fair enough. So, what's the game plan from here on out?" he asked. "Do you have one?"

"Not really. I mean, do you want to try going out with other people? See if you find an amazing Amish guy?"

Anna was silent, contemplating the opposite wall. She picked at a spot on her face, coughed lightly, drew up her stockinged feet, tugged at her hemline. Suddenly she snorted, then laughed out loud.

"That gives me the worst case of the blues. Can *you* imagine going out with someone else?"

"I'd rather not. But I also don't want to push you into something you'll regret later. I want you for myself, Anna. But maybe loving you means giving you the chance to see I'm not your only option. Maybe you don't have to leave the Amish for true love."

Anna stood. "I have a headache. Take me home."

In the starlit night, as the truck bounced over country roads, there were no more words, only the beginning of acceptance that they could not sort out their future. God would have to show them the way.

"Goodnight, Amos," she said, before the truck came to a full stop.

"Goodnight, Anna. And thank you for staying. Listening to my stuff."

She nodded, slipped away hurriedly, disappearing in the night like a vapor.

Clearly, she was avoiding any contact, any physical touch.

He waited till she let herself into the house, then turned the wheel and drove away.

He sighed. With Anna gone, his thoughts returned to Joseph. With Joseph's death, a chapter of his own life was closed. Joseph was gone. He was no longer in the big house, or roaming the grounds in his golf cart, driving the old Cadillac down the drive, his back ramrod straight, his narrow-brimmed hat square on his head. Dunking his morning toast in his coffee, saying there was weather coming, which meant snow or rain or wind, or all three of them. So this was grief. He allowed waves of it to roll over him, the sorrow and loneliness of life without Joseph.

Anna filled up the rest of his thoughts. She certainly knew her mind. She almost irked him, saying that stuff about his years at home. She wasn't there, hadn't experienced it, living in a loving, stable family with all that money floating around. How could she know?

He rolled down the window, breathed the night air deep into his lungs, and was filled with a sense of well-being. Actually, he decided, he liked that Anna spoke her mind, didn't hold back. It had been a tough conversation, but in the end, they had both confessed they did not want to see other people, that they wanted only each other.

Now wasn't that something?

He wanted to hang out the window, the wind in his face, whooping and hollering like a schoolboy. He marveled at the range of human emotion. How could he grieve Joseph while his heart soared with joy over Anna?

Chapter 9

He threw himself into the work at home, spent hours at the gym, a way of life for him now. It wasn't really an addiction, not fuel for vanity, but for his health and mental well-being.

He worked on his courses, received As and Bs, and was proud of his accomplishments. He spent time with Lila, picked the first strawberries and brought them to Nancy, who began to whip up a shortcake.

They were not allowed to touch any of Joseph's belongings. His shoes stayed in the laundry room, side-by-side, his old hat on its peg, the corduroy coat and plaid flannel shirts hung neatly. His Bible and Daily Bread pamphlets lay on the table between the two chairs, his eyeglasses on top.

Lila insisted, said she could feel his presence beside her.

The warm spring days turned warmer. Raspberries began to ripen. Amos believed there were good things waiting just around the bend, that all he needed to do was have faith that God would work it all out in His time.

He received the text message two weeks later.

She said she had decided to break up, this time for good. There was no sense in pursuing a courtship that could only bring heartache to her parents. He had no right to refuse the ultimate sacrifice, which was to return to the Amish way of life for her.

She finished with a firm reminder of it being the only way.

Amos entered a season of sleepless nights and dark days. He hardly knew when day ended and night began. He was lost in a stark, lonely world without joy or love. He'd been so sure. So positive things would work out.

He resented her parents, resented her, wallowed in self-pity, ate cherry ice cream and half a pan of cold lasagna, swallowed sleeping pills and Advil, tried melatonin, and still he lay awake night after night. There was no fairness in life. Lifted to the top of mountains, only to be dashed into the darkest cave, your neck broken with sorrow and loss.

Nancy watched him, thought the Amish girl took him for a loop. Lila was awash in her own grief, but she noticed that he was distracted, distant, and asked God to send him peace.

He talked to his counselor, who listened and gave a gentle prodding in the direction out of self-pity. They examined why he did not want to return to the Amish.

Amos wrote him a check for his session, decided it was all money thrown away, and did not reschedule.

Nobody could take the sting out of a breakup. Nobody.

He was done with girls. Done. That Skye better stay away, and when he thought of lumbering beside the agile Amy, skimming along like a gazelle, his face turned purple with embarrassment and his eyes burned with shame.

He mixed a solution to spray the fruit trees and set to work digging weeds around the base, applying a layer of fertilizer. He'd follow Joseph's advice and do without Round-up. "Poison," he'd said.

He found a few moments of happiness, alone in the orchard, and remembered his first meeting with Skye. She'd been so different then, so young and fresh-faced with her dog on a leash.

All morning, the sun grew steadily warmer until he went to the house for a thermos of ice water. He hopped off the golf cart and into the house, finding Nancy in the kitchen and Lila asleep in her chair.

Every Thursday he avoided the house, but this was Friday, so the coast was clear.

Nancy looked up. "What's up?"

"I'm so thirsty I'm starting to see things."

"Oh, come on. You're as dramatic as a girl."

"Huh."

"You've been a grouch lately."

"It happens."

"Yeah well, whatever's bugging you, I can beat."

"Try me."

"My Tom has pancreatic cancer. Diagnosed on Monday."

Amos was shocked. This was not good for Nancy or her family. The old double-wide housed many children, grandchildren, runaway cousins or down-on-their-luck relatives of some order.

"I'm sorry to hear it."

"You and me both. I don't know what I'm gonna do. Our insurance is crap, and them chemo treatments are through the roof. Did I mention it's stage four? Tom says he's not goin' through with no chemotherapy, but I don't know."

"Does Lila know?"

"No use loading her down with it. She's got enough. It's like her right arm's missing since he's gone."

"If there's anything I can do, let me know, okay?"

"How about a million bucks?"

She walked by, slapped his back, grinned a bit. He was amazed at her courage, the bravado it took to face the world with so much struggle and heartache at home.

Everyone had their own battle to fight, he thought as he hopped back on the golf cart and bumped back to the orchard. There was no way to avoid pain and suffering. You literally had to live a day at a time, do the best you could with whatever God chose to hand over.

He ached to confide in Anna but knew this was not possible. He'd go visit his parents tonight, see his mother's garden. Perhaps he'd find some companionship with his father.

His plans were changed when Mr. and Mrs. Larkin came to visit with Lila. Nancy hissed behind the closed kitchen door that he could not leave Lila alone with those vultures—she was too old and frail.

He quickly showered, threw on clean clothes, and sat beside Lila. He was cordial, but no friendlier than necessary. Amos had no idea they knew of Joseph's will, and the Larkins knew nothing of Joseph having told Amos, so the game of cat and mouse began.

"So, you're staying on?" she asked Amos, with only a hint of acid.

"I plan to stay for as long as Lila needs me, yes," he said.

"As the groundskeeper?" Mr. Larkin broke in.

"Oh, he's much more than that. Much more," Lila said quickly. "He's like the son we once had. Amos enabled us to stay here longer than we could have otherwise. He's part of the family."

Eyebrows were elevated, looks exchanged between the Larkins, and both began to speak at once, spinning a tale of properties bequeathed to lesser individuals who brought it to wrack and ruin in a few short years. You had to be very careful, sharp, in this day and age, and if she needed a good attorney, Mr. Larkin would leave his card, to be sure.

Oh, and when would be a good time to have Skye come over? She'd bought a jigsaw puzzle and was hoping to work on it with Lila soon.

Lila lifted a hand, laughed quietly, her good manners always first, and said, "My dear, I'm afraid she'll have to find someone else for that. My old eyes could never find the pieces. Although, that is a very sweet gesture. Indeed it is."

After they took their leave, Lila sat with Amos, both of them silent.

Lila would never intentionally talk down on another person, so she told Amos she supposed this old place was quite popular indeed.

She smiled to herself, giving a pat to her white hair. Lost in thought, her blue eyes dreamy, Amos knew she was telling Joseph about the Larkins' visit.

He left the house, walked aimlessly. A sense of despair weighed on his shoulders. The thought of being an impostor, a person assuming he had the right to inherit this place, rose like a sour bile in his throat. Perhaps this was meant for the Larkins, as good neighbors who would value the property, and if he went home and found his rightful spot in the world, everything would fall into place.

He was high-minded, thinking he could help anyone when he couldn't get his own life together. He needed to forget about Anna, but that was like rowing upriver. He tried, but the current of his feelings for her was too strong.

He became aware of movement through the brush and slid behind a tree, an act of self-preservation, instinctive. A dog, his nose on the ground, lifting his head, then sniffing the clover and brome grass.

Amos could see the animal had been beautiful, the sleek coat of a white Labrador retriever. He was filthy, covered in burrs, his eyes wild as he ran a zigzag course, searching for food, or perhaps for the scent of humans.

Slowly, Amos peered around the tree at the same moment the dog lifted his head, wheeled, and ran, his haunches tucked low as he scrabbled to get away.

Amos stepped out. "Hey, dog. Come here. Here, boy."

The dog slowed, stopped, his ears lifted.

Amos took a few steps in his direction, extended a hand.

"Come on, buddy. Come here."

The dog wheeled again and ran a short length, then stopped.

Amos advanced, a hand held out, talking in a low voice. The dog lowered his body to the ground. A low whine. Quickly, Amos made his way toward him, but when the dog grew uncomfortable with the close proximity, he turned and moved off, but more slowly this time.

Amos worked patiently, closing the distance between them. He tried to make eye contact, but the dog was low to the ground, his head to one side.

As he had thought, the dog was well-bred, a good bloodline creating the sturdy strength of the breed. When he was close enough, he began to talk again in a coaxing tone, his hand extended.

"Hey there, buddy. Good dog. Come on. Let me touch you."

He wished for dog treats, a slice of cheese, anything. The dog was thin, gaunt. A few feet, a foot, then inches away. He touched the top of his head, his hand slid to his ears. Slowly, the tail moved from left to right.

"Okay, buddy. You're good."

Amos hunkered down, stroked his ears, his neck. No collar. He hadn't realized how much he had actually missed Duke. For a long time, Amos and the dog stayed together in the hayfield, the verdant plants around them, the blue sky above, wisps of clouds like cotton.

Amos got to his feet, clicked his fingers, asked him to come on home with him. Would he? His heart hammering now, he walked a few paces, waited.

The dog rose to his feet, whined, looked over his shoulder. Then, as if he'd come to a decision, he wagged his tail and followed. Amos walked slowly, kept talking, looked over his shoulder, and still the dog followed.

All the way past the fruit trees, up to the driveway, past the azalea bushes, past the big house and on down the sloping drive.

He realized he didn't need to coax, or speak at all as the dog was close on his heels now. When Amos stopped, the dog stopped; when he started off, so did the dog.

When they reached the gatehouse, Amos told him to stay. He hurried into the kitchen and grabbed leftover meatballs, slices of ham, a bowl for water.

He was elated to find the dog sitting on his haunches, waiting expectantly. Amos offered a slice of ham, which was sniffed, then wolfed down, nosing his hand for more.

And a friendship was born that afternoon. He named the dog Champ, short for Champion. He bathed him, scrubbed the skin, combed and picked at burrs, delighted to find the soft white beauty of his coat. He dried him with a towel, stood and admired this gift arriving from nowhere. Would he ride in the truck to buy dog food, a bed?

Champ would not set foot in the vehicle, in spite of his best efforts.

Amos coaxed him into the house, shut the door quickly and went to town, purchased the necessary items, and returned to find the dog whining anxiously behind the closed door. When he opened it, the tail began wagging furiously, his face uplifted, tongue lolling. Amos realized he had a new friend, a welcoming presence when he came home.

Cathy was pacing the kitchen, hands outspread as she told her anxious mother about the latest drama in her life, how unkind Grace had been over the weekend, and what was she supposed to do about it? Grace was jealous because of Sam, and could she help that?

Lydia was washing dishes, half-listening as Cathy wailed about her state of affairs. She was actually thinking about the price of Roman shades at Lowe's, and how she could afford them if she used her Discover card and paid it off in six months.

"Mom, you aren't listening to me," Cathy yelled, stamping a foot for emphasis.

"Yes, I am."

She remembered the dark green blinds in her own mother's kitchen, the blinds recommended for all plain houses, but only the most conservative used them these days. They were depressing, in the *ordnung* or not. She couldn't imagine them in her own house but felt a stab of guilt, wondering if Amos would have stayed Amish if she had green blinds in her house. Sometimes the thought of Amos living like an English person made her so sad she could barely endure it. Would she always have to go through life, all her days here on earth, with that sadness hanging over her head?

Perhaps it had nothing to do with green blinds at all, but what was in her heart. She didn't know, really. She just knew she would likely never get to enjoy Amos and his Amish wife driving home in their horse and buggy, coming home for a nice visit.

Who was to blame? A lot of it was Raymond's fault, spoiling him the way he did.

"Mom, you are not hearing a word I'm saying."

Lydia took her hands out of the dishwater, grabbed a towel, and dried them, turning to face her.

"Cathy, I want to get the peas staked up this evening."

"See? Your work always comes first. You don't care about me. I should just stop talking to you."

Quickly, Lydia assured her she was listening, poured a glass of meadow tea, and sat at the table. This tea just didn't quite have the full flavor it should have. Seemed as if Rachel was right, it needed full, hot sunlight to bring out the real mint flavor of *vissa tay.* She should not have cut it so soon. She drank, watched her daughter leave the kitchen, noticed her bib apron was a bit snug. Should she say something? She'd noticed for a while already, watched the expansion of her waistline, the fullness in her face. She drank too much soda. She'd have to stop buying Coke.

Cathy was well beyond the proper marriage age, and that Sam she went out with wasn't close to settling down anytime soon.

And now she was getting fat. She bet twenty pounds had been packed on. Sam would never ask her to be his steady girlfriend if she became sloppy with her figure.

She sighed, finished the tea, and went to look for her wooden stakes and chicken wire. She stood by the edge of her new garden, plump arms propped on wide hips, and shook her head, then went in search of Raymond, who was nowhere to be found. Annoyed, she started rummaging through the pile of junk he deemed valuable, searching for the pea fence.

Suddenly, she picked up an item, held it in her hand, turned it over, and swiped at flakes of rust. The old meat grinder. Cast iron, with an oversized handle, a wooden spool at the end. How had it managed to come along with them through all their moves?

Butchering. They used to butcher their own hogs and beef, when she was a girl, and how she hated the thought of all that blood and gore. It wasn't right, the way her parents made her help with the grisly work of cleaning the hog entrails, using them to stuff sausages.

She never quite managed to perfect the technique but tore one hole after another as her father scolded, corrected, his stern visage above her, telling her she needed to hold the knife differently. She'd done her best, but it was never good enough.

Her parents were strict, aloof. She never told them of fears, real or imagined, never confided in them of her feelings. It simply wasn't done. They would have thought it silly. Unnecessary.

As she held the meat grinder, she could smell the disgusting scent of pig intestines, the desperation to scrape the white bile without tearing the thin membrane, the need to please her father if just this once.

She was taken away from the scraping table, set to work stirring lard, the fire beneath scorching her stockinged shins, her arms aching.

She was ashamed to feel the sting of tears.

Had she been too hard on Amos? For the first time in her life, she wondered if she had been like her father, quick to criticize, quick to correct. She quickly justified herself, thinking of his laziness, so clumsy and so terribly overweight. She would never know where he inherited his looks. His face resembled neither of them, certainly not Raymond.

She had been nice to him, though. Hadn't she?

She turned the meat grinder over, laid it on top of a fifty-gallon drum, then resumed her search, coming upon a bundle of old green blinds tied with baler twine. Now why had Raymond kept them? She was never going back to that hideous color. No one did. Well, maybe a few of the ministers, but none of her friends had green blinds.

But when she hired a driver and went to Lowe's, a small paper with measurements in her pocket, she still hadn't put that bundle of green blinds out of her mind. She found a helpful young man wearing the red Lowe's vest and asked which aisle to look in. She chose shades she truly loved, brown basket woven ones. You simply pulled down on them or pushed up and they folded like an accordion. So cool. Oh, she was on top of the world, her heart beating happily in her chest.

At the register, she whipped out her Discover card and a mountain of guilt fell on her back. She looked around, hoping there were no other Amish in the store to see the numbers she was putting on a credit card.

Over eight hundred dollars. It felt like a sin. It was a sin. Yes, she had sinned, was sinning as she hastily pushed her shopping cart through the automatic doors. Her eyelids fluttered as she rolled her eyes from left to right, watching for Amish people, hoping she'd make it to the van before anyone would see.

Her heart sank in defeat as Elmer and Sarah Stoltzfus stepped away from a black minivan and made their way carefully across the parking lot, straight in her direction. She turned her head, hoping to avoid them, but heard her name clearly.

Resigned, she stopped, turned to face them.

"Oh, why hello."

"Hiya, Lydia. *Schayna dauk.*"

"Yes, a very nice day."

Hoping to move on quickly without their speculation as to what was in her cart, she began walking away.

"Hold on, Lydia. Did you hear of Eli Yoder's house fire this morning? They lost most of their kitchen and *kessle haus* (kettle house). Something with the gas refrigerator. We're here to open an account for them."

"No. I hadn't heard. My goodness. I'll have to go over."

"You do that, Lydia. They'll need all the help they can get."

"I will."

She almost put the shopping cart on its back wheels in her urgency to propel the Roman shades away from them, the guilt as heavy and miserable as before. That was the thing about being Amish. Everything was a sin. She pushed at the guilt. She deserved these shades, if ever anyone did. She worked hard, earned her own money, so it was okay with God—she hoped, anyway. She'd go over to Eli's, help all day, make casseroles and bake a cake. She had stuff on hand.

And so she kept up a lively chatter with her driver the whole way home, and to prove she was charitable, she did not stop for a quarter pounder and a chocolate milkshake at McDonalds because Eli's had a fire.

She did go over the very next day, bearing two pans of lasagna and an apple cake with brown sugar icing. Her heart warmed to see the row of black and gray buggies parked along the barn, skid loaders scuttling like giant beetles, cleaning blackened debris, new lumber already being nailed into walls by straw-hatted men with colorful shirts wielding hammers and nail guns.

This was something, now wasn't it? The whole community pulling together as in the days of old. This was brotherly love, and this she wanted for her children. Amos would live to regret his choice, but she did not want to dwell on that now. Filled with the truth of a charitable spirit, she greeted acquaintances as she carried her heavy containers to the basement where the women had set up a makeshift kitchen.

She hated walking past all these men. She was not a small person, and felt every pound jiggling on her lips. Well, if these men had their minds in the right place, they wouldn't notice her size at all, now would they? She always felt so immodest in a belt apron, but that was the *ordnung* for going out. You had to leave that bib apron at home, and she felt the bib of the apron was part of being modest. But she guessed the ministers didn't think that, huh? You were actually supposed to wear a cape, but she wasn't about to work with a cape on, those pins at your shoulders a real threat.

She hugged Malinda, turned her mouth down in a display of sympathy, but thought it was no wonder her gas refrigerator exploded, as sloppy as they were. Eli's Sunday shirt was absolutely yellow.

Malinda took the catastrophe in stride, in her laconic style, laughing easily, saying, "*Hesslich, dess iss an mess,*" ("It's awful, such a mess,") but never once showing dismay or irritation. She sat on a folding chair, comfortably dunking chocolate chip cookies in her heavily creamed and sugared coffee, greeting the men and boys as they filed in for their morning break.

Lydia believed she might actually be a saint, the way the Bible said there were saints. She wondered if there were any, in this day and age. Maybe Raymond's parents, too sweet and kind for their own good.

She was happy here with the women of the community, though, felt a part of something much larger than herself. It was the sacrifice they made, the generous giving of themselves, lifting the burden of the unfortunate.

At three in the afternoon, she gathered her pans, prepared to leave, and was amazed to find the structure of a new kitchen and laundry room attached, with windows and doors put in place, a new roof across the entire house. She was so glad for Malinda, and she felt this gladness on her way home and into the evening. Yes, there was so much good among the plain people, and the next time Amos came home, she was going to sharpen her blades of truth. What was that Scripture? Like a two-edged sword, the word of God exposed the truth, and he was going to hear it from her if Raymond didn't take up his fatherly duty and expound it the way he should.

As she brushed her teeth that night, it came to her again. Had she been the one who was the cause of Amos's leaving? For a long time, she kept rinsing her toothbrush, thinking of Amos as a small boy, his teeth yellow with plaque, the aversion he had to a toothbrush.

Repeatedly, he'd been scolded, spanked even, told he looked awful with those yellow teeth. She cringed inwardly as she dried her mouth with a hand towel. Once, in anger, she'd swatted him across his head. Hit him hard, his face spinning away, his small dark eyes lifted to her face with what? Shame? Humility? No, it was neither, she knew now. It was surprise. He could not believe she'd done that, hit him quite so hard.

Justification came swiftly. He didn't listen to her. The Scriptures told you not to spare the rod and spoil the child. She wasn't sure where that was in the Bible, but she'd heard it enough times that it must be in there. Well, she hadn't spared the rod, and he still went English. And here was Cathy, still Amish, if a bit on the wild side, she supposed, although she'd get over it. She'd certainly proved herself a fit mother, going out to that big Smith place and nabbing Lavina straight out of Amos's clutches. She felt a sense of victory, which soothed her pride.

Lavina was at home, safe.

Chapter 10

Raymond was having a real time of it with those shades, grunting as he maneuvered the screw gun with one hand, the bracket with another. The evening was humid, and still over eighty degrees. Sweat ran down the side of his face and he felt the exhaustion in his arms. On the floor below, the opened cardboard box, bits of plastic, the directions and packets of screws waited.

Lydia stood beside the stepladder, increasingly anxious, knowing Raymond had trouble with that one shoulder anyway. Perhaps it was not a good idea, getting him to do this after work, but she was so eager to see how they would dress up the house.

Raymond stopped, lowered the screw gun, and climbed down, rubbed his shoulder and winced. "Sorry, Lydia, but it might have to wait. I think there's a storm brewing somewhere, the way this thing is aching."

"*Ach* my," Lydia said, the bitter taste of defeat on her tongue. Raymond felt genuinely bad for her, knowing how long she'd waited for these precious shades.

"I'll call Amos," he said, eager to please her, as always. "Perhaps he can come for a visit."

"Why? If you can't do it, he won't be able to. You know how he is."

He made his way to the kitchen, picked up the phone and dialed, then Lydia heard him speak. Torn between wanting her shades up and disliking the fact they would call on Amos for help, she stayed silent, hoping he wouldn't drive in here with that big truck thinking he was rescuing them from their own stupidity.

In half an hour's time, they heard his truck, and he was at the door, his eyebrows raised in question.

"What's up, Dat?"

He looked so different, he barely seemed like their son at all. He was so tall, so well built, and although he could not be called handsome, his face was ruggedly attractive. Grudgingly, Lydia admired his haircut, his small beard, wondered at the tanned skin. T-shirt and jeans, white sneakers. He looked like a very presentable English man. So clean, so—oh, she had to admit—so classy and soft-spoken.

She felt almost shy, as if this man was a stranger in her home.

"Hey there, Amos," Raymond said with his usual chuckle. "Thanks for coming over. Mom has been waiting quite some time for these shades, and now my shoulder is giving me a hard time. You think you can help out?"

"Sure. I can try. Hi, Mom."

"Hello, Amos."

The girls clattered down the open stairway and went straight to their brother for a hug, fussing about his looks and how was he doing, and how great it was to see him again. Amos enjoyed the general hubbub of them welcoming him home.

The three of them were on the floor then, reading directions out loud, grabbing at the paper, sorting through brackets and screws, with Amos in the middle, laughing, saying, "Give it here, Cathy."

Lydia caught sight of Raymond, his eyes large and soft, liquid with tears as he watched his three grown children, like days before, when they were small. His forehead creased then, and Lydia knew he was remembering the times when he'd felt so bad for Amos. Clearly, now the sisters adored their older brother, and Amos was soaking it up like a dry cast away sponge.

"Okay," Amos said, and got to his feet. In a moment, he was on the ladder with the screw gun, the work beginning with concentration.

The first shade was as gorgeous as Lydia knew it would be, and she clasped her hands in silent glee. But she was unwilling to show gratitude to a disobedient son, her pride intact, her sense of truth held firm.

Around the house they went, the girls helping, teasing, shaking the ladder, causing a shower of screws, and Amos hanging on, threatening them with the screw gun, Raymond shaking with genuine laughter.

Oh, but the shades went above and beyond what she had expected. She walked around, gently drew them down then pushed them up, over and over, setting plants on a windowsill, then another, stepping back to eye the effect.

When Amos finished, he stuffed all the boxes and plastic in a garbage bag and carried it out into the warm twilight of evening, the low blush of the sun's last light on the approaching night. He lifted the lid of the curbside dumpster, then turned to go back to the house. He stopped, took in the sight of the small white cape Cod with the steep roof, the rectangles of light from the windows, and thought it was like a photograph of a warm and welcoming home. He fought the rising bile of bitterness. Growing up, his home had been many things, but never that.

No, never.

In the kitchen, his mother was preparing a snack for him, asking him to sit down, which he found amazing. She didn't say much, her shoulders held stiffly in the way she had when she was nervous or upset, but there was his father, and the girls, chattering on. He heard gossip, the news of the youth, who was dating who, engagements, break-ups.

There was meadow tea, sourdough pretzels and cheese, a dessert with raspberries and cream, fruit. He ate an apple.

His mother raised her eyebrows. "Are you still on a diet?"

"I never was, Mom."

"Sure you were, Amos. Nobody loses so much weight without dieting."

He shrugged. "I just eat differently now. And go to the gym."

His mother's lips compressed, which meant the subject was closed and she didn't believe a word.

He turned to Cathy. "How's the latest guy you're seeing?"

"I don't know. Not great. I don't know how serious he is. I can't keep a guy. They never give up their cars and settle down."

She pouted, looked worn, no longer the vivacious, sparkling beauty of the past. "I don't know what I'm doing wrong."

"It's fine, Cathy. You just haven't found the right one," her mother trilled instantly, scrabbling to salvage her pride where Cathy was concerned, here in front of Amos.

Her disrespect raised, Cathy slanted her a look, said her mother didn't know a thing about her.

Lavina quickly changed the subject, an experienced diplomat, as Cathy cut an oversized square of the dessert, ladled it carefully on her plate, dug in with a spoon.

"What about you?" she asked, pointing the spoon.

"It's pretty complicated. Not sure you want to hear about it," he answered, twirling the core of his apple.

Fear shot through Lydia like a knife, causing her breath to quicken, her mouth like dry sand. Was he dating an English girl? That meant he would marry her and never come back to the Amish. Ever.

But the girls clamored, urging him on, and he told them only bits and pieces of Anna Riehl, the on again, off again details, her parents' objection.

Raymond lowered his face, became very still. Lydia took a deep breath, put on her armor and prepared herself for battle, detecting a hope of victory after all. When she finished, Amos was tight-lipped, his eyes hooded, with no answer forthcoming.

"Say something," she said finally, the color of her face heightened.

"You won't want to hear what I have to say."

And she didn't. There was only one truth, and that was for him to relinquish his hold on the world and come back where he belonged. This was God's will for him, cut and dried.

"You know I'm right."

How to explain? How to express what was lodged in his chest like an inoperable bullet? He didn't know where to begin, or where to stop, his feelings stuffed away, the cap shut tightly.

"Mom, Dat, you know things weren't always good here at home. I had a rough time, the way I was—big, dumb in school."

He paused.

"Oh, but we never noticed. We loved you just the same," Lydia spoke up.

Cathy's mouth literally hung open, and Lavina lowered her eyes, picked at the edge of the table. Raymond looked squarely at Amos, conveying something.

"What?" she asked, her voice higher than she expected.

"Mom, I'm sorry, but that's not the truth."

"Are you calling me a liar?"

He said nothing.

"My own son, calling me a *ligna*."

She began a sort of sniffing, an artificial weeping that left her dry-eyed.

"I'm only saying this, then I'm leaving. If you want to sort it out with me later, I'll be glad to return. I have no fond thoughts of anything related to plain life. Our home was often a disaster, as was my own life as a child. I was a disappointment to you, and you let me know in hundreds of ways. Sorry, but Dat never had the strength to stand up to you, and so I bumbled alone through my early formative years while you admired Cathy and Lavina. I had to leave if I wanted a better life, and I found it in that big yellow house with English people who are Christians in every sense of the word."

He got up and walked out, closing the door gently after himself.

Chaos erupted in the small white house after he left. Cathy carried on about how Amos had nailed the truth on the head, and he had every right to leave. Lydia was white-faced and furious, and Raymond shook his head forlornly.

Lavina spoke, then, in a normal tone of voice, saying they would all do well to search their own hearts. But she too had to agree Amos had spoken his truth, and no one could deny the validity of it. "Mam, you were a good mother in many ways, and likely you did your best, but no one liked Amos very much. Maybe Dat did, but he didn't show it much."

"When did it become commonplace for children to speak like this to their parents?" Lydia broke out, her nostrils flared.

"And when did it become commonplace to edge out one of their own?" Lavina answered quietly. "Animals do it—runts of litters, misshapen offspring pushed back—but not, I believe, in a household where Christ and His love is the Master. I'm sorry, Mam, I don't mean to be unkind, but our family needs healing, and it's probably going to hurt in the beginning."

A reasonable ending, then, with Lydia washing up the snack dishes, Raymond drying, soothing his defiant wife, saying yes, yes, the children had acted up, and no, no, it isn't your fault. He was rewarded for his loyalty many times, as he knew he would be this time.

For Lydia needed support, and he could easily supply it, knowing the rewards were to his gain. But a spark had ignited that night, setting Lydia down the confusing trail of introspection, wondering afresh if she had actually caused one of her own to desert them. From that night on, she felt the uncomfortable firing of her own memory, but only from time to time, and often at the weirdest moments.

Distant regrets, like a vapor, would pass through her, but she could always remedy the confusion by saying she'd done her best.

Just across the valley, not far as the crow flies, but a distance of fifteen miles or so, Anna Riehl sat with her sister Barbie in the humid evening, their bare feet sliding across the brown composite decking as they swung from the egg chairs suspended from sturdy metal hooks in the ceiling. There was no breeze, and it was still very warm, so the bit of swaying through the air brought relief.

Behind the house, they heard the creak of the garden shed door and knew their mother was putting her hoe away. She was always working, keeping their home and surrounding area a showplace, with energy left over. She came up onto the deck, a youthful-looking woman in her forties, still stepping much livelier than she probably should have, asking why they weren't in the shower yet.

"Talking, Mom. Talking. What sisters do," Barbie said.

Anna kept her eyes on the floor of the deck, said nothing.

"Good. So, fill me in. What did I miss?"

"A lot, Mom. Anna broke up with Amos. And she quit working there so she won't keep seeing him."

"I know that. And I'm sorry."

The space fell silent, the only sound from a few whining insects, the distant lowing of a cow. On the wide highway, a horn blared, an engine was accelerated.

"I wish it didn't have to be this way," she said softly.

Anna shrugged, too close to tears to speak.

"It's hard now, but someday you'll see the value of your parents making your choices for you. We can see nothing good coming from a young man who openly disobeys his parents. He is out in the world, and we are a people set apart from it."

Anna raised her face. "Are we, Mom? Are we?"

"Of course, Anna. There is no doubt."

Anna bit her lip. "It's hard to fathom sometimes. With all the changes we are experiencing in the years since I've been born. Our house, our way of life—it's not much different from English life. Thousands of homes aren't nearly as nice as ours."

"But there's no *ordnung* against a nice home. We are a hardworking people who were taught by their German ancestors."

"I get that. I do."

She sighed. Yes, she saw her mother's point, and it was a valid one. Amish people made the choice for their children, born Amish. You were expected to follow in their wake, and anything aside from that was a tremendous let-down. No matter if anyone felt they had a calling, or God led them to divert from the beaten path, it was all viewed as heresy, absolute abandonment of the right way.

Anna was mature beyond her years—a gift, her mother said—so she knew the answer was not black and white. She would bide her time, learn to pray in spirit and in truth, and wait on the Lord, as the verse on the plaque in their living room said. She believed she'd done the right thing by definitively breaking up with Amos, but her heart hadn't been in it. She couldn't help but hope that God would still make a way.

She would wait, and she would rise up as the eagle.

In the meantime, she would be fair, never judge the Amish way of life, but remain in God's love for those around her. She believed it was wrong to turn against a plain way to justify leaving for another culture, but could it be done a better way? The question was burdensome.

And so, she gave in to the wishes of her parents, who led her in the way of truth. Yet as late spring turned into the heat of summer, she missed Amos desperately. At a particularly low moment, she texted him. One short message.

Where was the harm?

"Thinking of you."

That was it, but it was a cry from the heart.

AMOS STOOD IN the doorway of the garage, down by the orchard, with Champ pressed up against his leg shaking visibly, a low rumble of thunder in the distance. He reached down to pet his dog, running a hand along his back, comforting him, as frightened as he appeared to be.

Amos loved a good summer storm, and by all appearances, this would be a humdinger. All day, the sweat rolled off in the high humidity, the leaves like limp pieces of cloth, dust devils whirling off as the atmosphere grew tense, the air brassy and yellow before he heard the rumbles in the distance.

His phone dinged. He was watching the Carolina wren, his little friend, prance around the top of the mower, chirping and tweeting to the hatchlings, who peered over the edge of the well-constructed nest.

Absentmindedly, he lifted his phone, saw her name, read the text. He took a deep breath. He did not feel joy, only a vague sense of acceptance. *Yes, Anna, I know. I think of you, too.*

But there's no use.

He spoke to God, asking him to show him the right way, as he'd done many times before. He did not text her back, reasoning in his mind that if he did, he would be starting up a relationship that could only end in pain.

It was up to her and her parents.

The rain came in a wall of wind, gusting across the orchard and up to the big house, bending the trees, whipping green leaves into a frenzy, their pale undersides mingling with the darker tops. Fir trees thrashed as the rain pummeled the roof. Lightning crackled, followed by a deafening roll of thunder, then another.

He knew Lila was standing at the French doors, thrilled to see the rain watering her delphiniums and nasturtiums in the window boxes.

His resolve remained in place till later that evening, as he lifted the mat by his door to sweep the porch, the rain having driven torn leaves and twigs across it. Champ lay on it the minute he replaced it, and he lifted his ears and looked over his shoulder when Amos ran the broom along his back.

"What should I do, Champ?"

No answer, of course, but it did not feel right to ignore the text message either. Was it? He decided there was no harm in a lighthearted answer, and sent, "Thanks. Same here." Then turned on the grill and made burgers, two for him and one for Champ. He was pleasantly tired out after working in the heat all day, took a shower and dressed in clean shorts and a T-shirt, then walked to the big house to check on Lila. He always sat with her a while in the evening.

Amy Forge had been there, she told him, and discovered her blood pressure was up. She laughed.

"It's those homemade potato chips Skye bought at the market. Sour cream and onion."

"She took you?" Amos asked, raising his eyebrows.

"She surely did. She's a very pretty girl."

"She is that."

"But I don't believe she's your type," Lila said, looking at him pointedly.

Amos didn't respond. Sometimes, he admitted to himself, he longed to have someone like her as his girlfriend. It would all be so uncomplicated, so easy and free, where nothing was looked down on, where folks made their own choices and lived by their own conscience and not someone else's.

"You want me to stay, Lila?" he asked, changing the subject.

"Not tonight. I feel fine, and Amy was here. Be sure to check the burglar alarm system and I'll sleep like a newborn baby."

She waved him off, and he did what she asked, then let himself out. The night was sparkling with rain drops everywhere, the macadam drive slick and wet. Frogs croaked from the swamp down by the road and a slithering in the hedge reminded him of snakes or skunks, maybe a wide-eyed marten. He loved nighttime, especially after a rain, like tonight, when everything was newly rinsed with rainwater, the air scented with moist earth and glistening drops.

He felt peaceful. He lifted up a silent prayer for Anna, that she would be able to accept God's plan, whatever it was. *Let it be, Lord, let it be,* he thought, allowing himself to rest in the peace that passeth all understanding.

THE FOLLOWING EVENING, Cathy called.

"Hey, dude?"

"How's it going?"

"Could you lend me a couple hundred dollars till next week?" she asked, in that whining tone setting his teeth on edge.

"Why?"

"Well, Sam and I have to pay our share of an Airbnb this weekend, and he's short. I just had to replace my phone, so we're both broke."

"Then stay home."

"Amos. Come on, you're always loaded."

He smiled to himself. If she only knew.

"Alright. I'll write you a check, but you have to come get it."

"Sam'll bring me over. You haven't met him."

"Tonight? It's late."

"Tomorrow night. Eightish."

She hung up. No "thanks," no "please," no asking about himself.

But she was his sister, and he loved her.

Champ barked the following evening, but not till he was ready for bed at nine-thirty. The crunch of tires, a car door slamming, Cathy's loud voice and a rapping, insistent.

Wearily, he went to the door. He wasn't in the mood for his sister and her flavor of the month, but he opened the door and welcomed them inside.

"Hey! This is Sam. Sam, Amos."

"Hey."

"How's it going?"

Sam was of medium height, longish hair, beard, jeans and a T-shirt, presentable enough, though shifty-eyed. It was Cathy that shocked him. Dressed in jeans and a too-tight shirt, her eyes were caked with black eyeliner and mascara and her hair was pulled back in a pony tail.

This was not obedience. This was not a plain lifestyle at all. Why did it sadden him to see Cathy dressed like this? Was it OK for him but not for her?

He went to his desk, sat down, and wrote a check for two hundred, handed it to her.

"Mom know you go out like that?" He couldn't help himself.

"She acts as if she doesn't, but she knows. Why? You got a problem with it?"

Her eyes, so like their mother's, challenged him.

"No. Your business."

He made small talk with Sam, was surprised to see his discomfort on the subject of where he worked, but let it go. Again, it was none of his business, although it seemed as if a twenty-something unmarried man should be capable of producing a few hundred dollars.

Cathy grabbed the check. "Thanks."

"Yeah, what she said," Sam said, grinning his voice slightly mocking. Amos lifted a hand, closed the door behind them.

So that was Sam.

Likely the name came from a long list of Samuels, from the devout followers of Bible names in times past. Among the Amish, names from the Bible had been chosen for centuries, and only in the last ten years had this made a drastic change, but again, only among the liberals. A large portion remained conservative, steadfast to the old way.

The modern ways seeped into plain churches in all kinds of ways. Everyone was only human, no matter how righteous they aspired to be. Times changed. Parents allowed rules to become loose and easy, resulting in youth who did not resemble the plain church at all, but ran wild, put on a display of settling down, but only settled into an unhappy marriage where real problems were never resolved.

But then, there were many who were sincere in their faith, living a just and honest life, one generation after another.

Champ whined to be let out.

"Alright, buddy."

He got to his feet but felt heavy, aged with sodden thoughts. He worried about Cathy, worried about the outcome of her life. She had always ruled the roost at home. How would that dynamic play out in her other relationships?

Oh, Cathy. You need to find Jesus and learn His way for your life. She'd find that humorous, her English brother praying for her, but that was what he did, kneeling by the couch with Champ whining to be let in.

At home, Lydia was still happy with her Roman shades and telling Raymond she couldn't believe how fast Amos had put them up. He really was not one bit the way he used to be, was he? And Raymond shook his head, no he wasn't.

If only he would drive in here with a horse and buggy, wear a straw hat and suspenders, his Amish wife beside him, then she would actually be proud of him.

"Right, Raymond?"

CHAPTER 11

AMOS WOKE, PEERED AT HIS PHONE, FELT DISORIENTED AND weighed down with an unnamable dread, a dark place rife with hidden danger. He rolled onto his back, plucked at the sheet, put his hands beneath his head, and stared wide-eyed at the darkened ceiling. His heart pounded. He realized the dryness of his mouth.

Taking a deep, calming breath, his mind stabbed in hundreds of directions at once, eliminating any rational thoughts. He wanted peace, reached for the God who never failed him, but like a rumbling train driven at maximum speed, his thoughts took over completely.

Fear lurked in every corner of the room, hyenas growling, their wild laugh waiting to erupt. He was icy with dread, then broke out in a cold sweat. The hyenas circled, waiting. He tried to get out of bed, but the expanse between his bedroom and the kitchen was too large, too exposed. There was nothing between him and the choking, clinging night.

He rolled on his side, put the pillow over his head to shut out the horror, but it persisted. He had to get away, somehow, so he threw back the sheet and leaped out of bed, walked quickly, stumbling through the dark to the kitchen where he gripped the countertop till the ends of his fingers turned numb. His breath came in ragged, congested heaves as sweat rolled off his face.

From his bed in the corner, Champ whined, then rose to his feet and padded over, looked up expectedly. Amos reached for the light switch, blinked against the illumination, reached to ruffle the dog's ears.

What was this? Had God forsaken him?

His past rose up—the decision to leave his family, the decision to drive his truck, to dress in English clothes and live away from his community. Suddenly, with astounding clarity, he knew he could not accept the inheritance from Josepha and Lila Smith. He was simply unworthy, would make poor decisions based on inexperience, squander the money. Wealth was never good.

This thought kept him rooted to the floor as more accusations were flung at him with terrible force.

He had never been worthy of any gift, never would be.

He sagged down on the living room couch, shivered now in the chill of the air-conditioned room. His mind traveled back to a Sunday night gathering with the youth in his teen years. It had been at Christmas, and the youth in his group had exchanged names, bought gifts for the person whose name you had drawn from the basket. He'd drawn a slip with Sarah Yoder in plain black writing.

Sarah Yoder was heavy and given to a sloppy appearance and a self-conscious laugh much resembling the braying of a donkey. She was often made fun of, like himself, although he never allowed himself to talk to her, so deeply ashamed of the likeness they bore for one another. Her family was troubled, his mother said, having no foundation financially, with that shiftless father and a mother given to nervous breakdowns, so no wonder Sarah was like that. They were poor souls, she said.

He hid the slip of paper for weeks, contemplated the embarrassment of telling his mother, who would tell him they were the perfect couple. Which, inevitably, was what she said, hooting with laughter that swarmed like an angry group of wasps, stinging as he fought them off.

She bought a gift, the one he remembered so well. A vase with silk flowers, a bottle of perfume. He'd suffered so much, but she assured him Sarah would be more than pleased, that her family had nothing.

He lived in dread till the Christmas gathering of the youth, where names would be revealed, gifts exchanged. He drove his horse and buggy through the cold that night, trembling with fear and anxiety of what was to come, and stood on the outskirts of noisy groups and wished himself dead.

To watch Sarah Yoder stand at the plastic Lifetime folding table, her hair in the usual disarray, her covering too large and pushed back too far, wrinkled and yellowish, her dress much too tight and too short, was painful for him. He recognized himself in her. She lifted the vase, blinked rapidly, and said too loudly, "From Amos Stoltzfus. Thank you!"

A swell of laughter from onlookers turned into a roar of approval when he stood, opened the oversized gift from her, and held it aloft for all to see. A backpack, and a heart-shaped box filled with chocolates. His face aflame, he mumbled her name, pronounced his thanks, and moved his bulk away, swiftly and soundlessly, seeing nothing. He was aware of the calls about them being the next couple amid wide grins and raised eyebrows.

That was the last Christmas he had ever spent with the youth, vowing never to put himself in that position again. He was unworthy of anything pertaining to a normal social life. He wasn't worthy even of Sarah Yoder. He simply did not fit the mold of other popular, good looking young men with a pleasing personality.

He was a failure, an oddity, like her.

Why then, had he been awakened by this strange sense of fear, the panic so real he could touch it? And why had this memory followed? He shivered, got to his feet, and went to the door, opened it for Champ, and sat on a porch chair in the humid midsummer night as he slowly regained his calm. He longed to talk to someone, anyone. He had to understand this deep conviction of being unworthy to receive this home, this wealth that must be suffocating his spirit, somehow revealing the lack of competence he possessed.

He put his face in his hands, tried to talk to God, who was always available, his only Friend. The presence of Jesus, the figure of kindness and love, the bedrock of his faith, his life. His spirit often sought desperately for communion with Him, and now he knew for sure He was nowhere to be found.

The hyenas waited on the perimeters of his mind, and agitation followed immediately. He got to his feet, paced the porch, afraid to look into the darkness around him. His hands began to shake as his knees weakened.

Champ whined, so he opened the door, but he stood, resolute, looked up at Amos, and continued whining.

"Come on, buddy," he said, his voice shaking, the words like sandpaper dragging across splintered wood.

He drank a glass of milk and went back to bed, and lay rigid and terrified as painful thoughts of the past motored through his head like a fast-moving car, swerving around corners and into dark roads crosshatched with fissures and steep ravines on either side. He wondered wildly if he was having a mental breakdown, if this was what it meant when people talked about someone losing their mind.

In the morning, after the night of being adrift with images of his past, he was bleary and pale, a certain element of normal well-being completely gone. He let Champ out, got dressed, brushed his teeth, and clung to the vanity top as he gazed at his bloodshot eyes. He was hideous, the red bulbous nose, the tiny slash of a mouth, brown eyes hidden in folds of flesh. How could he ever had imagined himself improved?

He couldn't eat, his stomach roiling with pain. The coffee was like charcoal water, that awful black stuff they had to drink when the stomach flu hit. Or black walnut extract water when his mother decided it was time for a parasite cleanse.

With sudden clarity, he realized he was a parasite. Amos Stotlzfus, a leech who siphoned away the wealth someone else had been deserving of. Joseph Smith, a saint, had amassed a fortune, by his own hard work and God-given ability, and he was like a choking vine, a parasitic undergrowth crawling up the trunk of a verdant tree, destroying it.

Yes. He had never been good enough, so what made him imagine he would be now? He had destroyed Cathy by going away and living the life of an English person. The fault was his alone.

So where would he start to make things right?

He longed to talk to Anna Riehl, to his sister Lavina, to Scott or his counselor. He had to talk to someone, anyone.

Not Lila, not yet. She was too old, too frail, and would not be able to carry the burden of his thoughts. He picked up his phone, considered who to call, but couldn't bring himself to try anyone.

Despair descended like the flapping wings of a vulture, obscuring his usual delight in a summer morning.

For weeks on end, he fought his demons at night, felt his prayers hit the ceiling and bounce back to mock him. God had never seemed farther away, and he could not conjure the white robes and dusty sandals of Jesus without fear of being cast away.

Nancy Farmer watched him as she stirred the vegetable soup on the stove, then came right out and told him he looked awful. Had he checked himself lately for ticks? He might have Lyme disease, the way he appeared washed out and anxious. Lila told him he was working too hard in this heat, and why didn't he take a break for a few days, she and Nancy would be fine.

He shook his head no, but Lila pleaded, saying his work would be here after he returned. But where would he go? What would he do?

He had no one to accompany him. He thanked Lila, promised to think about it, then returned to his own house and tried to schedule an appointment with a local physician, thinking perhaps Nancy was right.

Most offices closed at five, so he was unsuccessful, laid down his phone, and dreaded the night's arrival. He wanted someone. He needed another human being to help him regain his footing, but who exactly?

His latest fear had been debilitating, the fear of having lost his salvation, having committed the unpardonable sin. The angst had been so real, and now he felt he might have a brain tumor growing steadily, cells multiplying wildly until a large mass would snuff out his life.

At his lunch hour the following day, he finally scheduled an appointment, had a full physical, a comprehensive blood panel done, and asked for an MRI of his brain, which the doctor questioned with raised eyebrows. He insisted, however, citing painful headaches, and was given an appointment, only to find a clear brain scan.

Finally, he talked to his pastor about the act of the unpardonable sin. His pastor was a man in his sixties, white hair in thick profusion, which was a landing field for a restless hand.

He helped Amos tremendously, sitting in the quiet, pale-hued office with a print of Jesus on the wall, a framed photo of his family beside it. He explained in detail how the only unpardonable sin was the refusal to believe in God's grace, or the power of the blood of Jesus. Amos opened his heart to him, this man of God, which was surely what he was, and felt received, loved, even cherished.

With his chair reclining, his elbows propped on the arms, fingertips forming a steeple, the pastor explained how many folks who leave a plain lifestyle lose their identity and often at some point in their life reach this place of fear and displacement.

"Religion and its order, the outward appearance, can be a substitute for a spiritual relationship with God. I'm only saying it can be, it is not the same for one individual to the next. We all have to come to God completely naked, which is only a figure of speech, but it means we have to shed every trace of our own righteousness and recognize the only good is from the Father. Every good and perfect gift is from the Father of Lights, everything we may presume we have of our own, is a gift, given to us, not from ourselves."

Amos felt a great weariness of the mind. He was so tired, his mental capacity stretched to the limit as he fought the remembered taunts and insults, the fear and crippling despair. He had a hard time following the words the pastor spoke, not quite able to grasp the significance. He asked him to repeat his advice, then felt he was only being a huge burden and took his leave, but not without a promise to return.

At the end of August, when the relentless heat had lost its strength, he called Anna Riehl. He dialed her number and waited, hardly able to breathe, his heart pounding in his ears.

He waited, and after four rings, her voicemail.

"Hi, it's Anna. Try again."

Oh, my Anna. Her voice brought a wave of emotion so raw he could barely tolerate it. He needed her so badly. He tried again later in the day, after he'd eaten and was seated on the back porch, the grass having been cut recently, the trees surrounding it creating patterns of shadow and light.

She answered on the first ring, and he lost his voice for a few seconds, before regaining it, beginning with "Uh, yeah."

"How are you, Amos?"

"Um, okay."

"Why are you calling me?"

"I don't know. Missed hearing your voice, I guess."

"Oh. Well, that's nice to know."

There was a troublesome space of silence, before Amos stumbled on, hating every word.

"I just thought you might, you know, want to go away with me for a few days. Lila thinks I need to take a break. She thinks I'm working too hard, as hot as it is."

The same silence again.

"I don't know if my parents would approve. You likely haven't come to a decision, have you?"

"No."

"So probably not. I'm sorry, Amos."

"Okay, it's fine."

The silence was crippling now, hurtful and painful and raw, so he simply told her goodbye and cut off the communication between them.

He berated himself for days, wishing he'd never attempted contacting her, telling himself he was loathsome, impatient, stupid. He told himself she probably had another person she was interested in and had no intention of ever returning, and if her parents meant more to her than he did, well, that was fine.

But he still missed her.

He decided to go alone, after imagining himself with Skye Larkin or Amy Forge, which only made him feel an overwhelming weariness. He simply did not have the heart to try. Besides, he'd have to reinvent himself into a classy English person to be with Skye and a fleet-footed skinny person to be with Amy, which he certainly was not, either.

So, he'd be a plodding bachelor, dull, simple, beset with the mental capacity of a twelve-year-old.

But he made plans, washed his truck, took Champ to the dog groomer, got a haircut, bought a pair of hiking boots and three pairs of wool socks. He bought a pup tent, an oversized backpack, and felt a sense of purpose, if a rather weak one.

He would be gone a week, and Lila clapped her hands excitedly, saying it was the best thing he could possibly do. She and Nancy and Amy Forge were going out to eat every evening, she said, like a naughty schoolgirl, and when he got back they'd all be fat.

Anna no longer worked for Lila, having terminated her job after breaking up with him, and was replaced by a small Portuguese woman named Della, who was in her sixties but appeared to be half her age. Lila, of course, loved Della, and if her cleaning was inferior, she would never mention it, although Nancy lowered her bulk and swiped unhappily at baseboards and the base of floor lamps, saying she guessed they didn't bend over to clean in other countries, with Lila winking at Amos.

They waved enthusiastically as he drove away, Champ beside him on the seat, which made it much easier to leave. The day carried the decaying smell of summer's end, with foliage on the trees not quite turning just yet, the air brassy, shimmering with heat.

He drove slowly, turned up the radio, the windows down, taking back roads into the Appalachians, his destination a state park with a good hiking trail. If he decided to do something else, he could do that, too, as he was free to change his mind. Perhaps he'd drive to Maine, find the Atlantic Ocean, or stay right here in Pennsylvania and find the Appalachian Trail.

He was into his third hour of driving when he felt an uncomfortable tightening in his chest. He rubbed the palm of his hand across the front of his T-shirt, grimaced.

The discomfort eased, and he turned up the radio, sang along with his favorite song. Champ pricked up his ears.

He felt better on most days but he still struggled with control of his thoughts. He'd gone to see his counselor again and came away wondering if he was the one with the problem. "Repressed childhood trauma," the counselor had said. Amos thought it was hardly repressed—he'd been wrestling with his childhood trauma for years.

Why couldn't he just let go of his traumatic youth like a snake sheds its old skin and grows a new one? Who knew if his mother was to blame? Perhaps God had created him for the purpose of rising above the circumstances of his life to the glory to Him.

He had to rise above jealousy at a young age, the way she fawned and fussed over Cathy, then Lavina, which he felt he'd achieved time after time. Really, he'd forgiven his mother, and he didn't hold a grudge against his sisters.

Or so he thought.

But as he drove along, he remembered the things he'd cried about as a child when he lay in his small room, on the old mattress covered in plastic and heavy bed pads because of his constant bedwetting. Christmas had been the worst.

It was the glitz and glitter of the girls' packages, the streams of Barbie dolls and cars and houses, the pink bathrobes and fuzzy slippers, decorative socks and Dove deodorant, explained with a wink, that her girls were growing up and at certain times in life it was necessary to use antiperspirant. As if growing older contained a wonderful secret, but only for pretty girls.

For him, it had been the horror of discovering a growth of hair in places never spoken of, accompanied by a skunky smell of which he was informed with thumb and forefinger pinched over upturned noses and bellows of "He stinks, Mom. Make Amos take a bath." A certain cluck of disdain, and he was sent to the shower with instructions to scrub his underarms with soap. Growing older for him had been one more step toward being more repulsive.

It was Lavina, in her quiet lisp, who handed him the small antiperspirant, told him their mother had bought it for Dat, but she wondered if perhaps it wouldn't be helpful to him.

And it was, much to his relief. He had been so afraid deodorant was only for thin people, and the overweight ones had to smell bad all their life, which was the punishment for being big. Why had his father never informed him of these things? Perhaps he had never known to say anything, or his mother found him so insignificant it simply didn't matter.

Church had been at Ephraim Yoder's that Christmas, Sarah Yoder's place, in the semi-clean basement with the unpainted walls, the smell of overripe fruit and stray cobwebs in corners, one battery lamp and barely enough light for the minister to read Scripture. He'd sat in the row of boys watching poor Naomi, a baby on her lap and a child tugging on her skirts, noses running as she heaved herself up and down the steps. He remembered the "skunky" smell as she moved about the room, serving coffee at the men's table, and felt a sense of sadness for her.

There was something about Ephraim that bothered him. He had those small, ferret-like eyes. He reminded Amos of a lizard, or a snake, although he never told anyone.

They'd moved away into another district when he was eleven or twelve.

There was gossip about Ephraim Yoder, with hints of abuse on animals or children, even the wife, some said. Who was to prove it, though? And you had to be careful these days, insinuating things, making assumptions. A false accusation could ruin a man's reputation.

He wondered what had become of the family, and whether they were all still at home.

In the later afternoon, he became empty, his spirits sinking. He was never hungry these days, which he chalked up to his weird mental state, but knew he should probably get something somewhere. Champ needed out, so he pulled into the nearest Sheetz, filled up the tank, clipped a leash on Champ, and walked him to a patch of grass. He watched vehicles, drivers and passengers, the sun hazy with heat, the concrete giving off shimmers of it. Champ's tongue lolled as his breath came hard and fast.

He didn't feel like walking into the crowded store, but he needed the biggest bottle of water he could purchase, so he walked across the parking lot and put Champ in the truck, returned to the store and made his purchases. Then he got Champ out again, tied his leash around the leg of a metal picnic table, and sat at a table beneath an umbrella to sip the refreshingly cold water.

He people-watched mindlessly as Champ lay in the shade. He wasn't aware of the time passing, but eventually he noticed the sun was getting surprisingly low, so he put his trash in the garbage, grabbed his drinks, and moved off, following the route his GPS showed to the nearest hiking trail.

He hadn't slept well, and his eyes burned as he drove toward the sun. Somehow, he simply did not have the heart to throw a tent and sleep on the ground in a sleeping bag. He'd look for the nearest motel. A cheap one, maybe a Super 8. If he slept okay, he'd begin his hike in the morning.

This cheered him, the thought of sleeping well in a clean bed, refreshing his body and soul for the days ahead. He pulled into a Super 8, paid for his room, fed Champ, showered, and collapsed into the spotlessly clean white sheets. He fell into a dreamless sleep for the whole night.

He started awake, could not believe it was six-thirty. How had he slept so well away from home? In a strange bed?

No time to dwell on that now, he had to get moving.

He stocked up on water in both canteens, checked his water purifier and supply of dried food, found his destination on the GPS and followed it, marveling at the endless, ragged tops of the Appalachians. Magnificent mountains, and he was eager to begin.

The pack was heavy, too heavy to carry on his back, he thought as he tried to straighten up with its monstrous weight. But after he walked around the parking lot, spoke to a few hikers, picked up the map for the trail, he felt comfortable, a part of something he couldn't name. Courageous? Eager? He didn't know, but he felt better than he had in days.

He started out, refreshed, marveling at the grip of the soles beneath him. Good hiking boots were worth every penny. He took a deep breath, expanded his chest, put one foot in front of the other, resolutely eating up the length of trail he planned to cover. He'd do twenty, twenty-five miles a day for almost three days, then walk back to the truck. Get a taste of long-distance hiking, maybe do the whole trail someday.

The leaves above his head fluttered, the thick green forest damp and cool. He noticed the stately oaks, the biggest trunks and the healthiest bark, the lichens and rotting logs, chipmunks on tree stumps and bees hovering above wet places. The blue sky above, puffed marshmallow clouds billowing together, breaking apart, the sun becoming hotter as the day wore on.

He shifted his pack, grimaced as his shoulders felt the compression of the straps, walked up a long steep incline before leaning against a tree to catch his breath.

Chapter 12

Anna Riehl was getting dressed to go to the hymn singing at the neighbors', Aaron Zooks. The day was hot, too hot to be stuck upstairs putting on a *halsduch*, the neck cloth that had to be worn on Sundays. It was meant to promote modesty, but it was hot and uncomfortable beyond description.

She had showered but was still perspiring, complaining to her sister about August, Amish clothing, and *rumschpringa* in general.

Barbie was checking her hair in the mirror as she replied. "Dat said he's planning on installing mini splits as soon as he upgrades the solar panel system."

"Can you imagine AC?"

"I cannot imagine."

"The smartest invention ever."

"Exactly. Meanwhile, we swelter. Anyway, are you ready? We may as well head out."

"Yeah."

"Can you muster some enthusiasm here?"

Anna sighed, rolled her shoulders, then reached up to fix a straight pin.

"Not really. I just don't have the heart to join in again, to think of looking for someone, or to have someone looking for me. I miss Amos."

Barbie eyed her with a keen eye.

"What's so amazing about him anyway? He's a groundskeeper for some old lady. And from what you've said, he's got a whole lot of baggage from his past."

"In fact, I find him very handsome, sweet, and humble. He's perfect. Except for one little thing."

"He's not Amish."

"Precisely," Anna said, in mock acceptance.

"You'll be fine. There are other fish in the sea, as they say."

"For you, maybe."

"And for you."

They clattered down the stairs to find their parents in front of respective battery-operated fans, glasses of cold meadow tea at their elbows.

"You're off to Aaron's?" their mother asked, lowering the footrest of her recliner. "Anna, you have a pleat in your apron belt. You pin it too tightly. Come here and I'll loosen it for you."

"It's alright. Leave it alone, Mother."

Her mother was irritated, but let it go.

"Bye," Barbie trilled.

"Be good," Dat called after them.

THAT WAS THE night Anna was introduced to Samuel of Mohawk Valley who had come to Pennsylvania on a whim to spend a weekend with his cousin, Daniel Lapp's Mark. Tall, brown-eyed, with neatly cut brown hair, he was an ordinary guy with that hidden something proving to be a magnet to Anna's struggling heart. She resisted, felt herself still in love with Amos, but nevertheless felt his draw. She loved the way his voice was soft and low, the confidence he possessed, the trait she so admired.

She saw him again at the next singing, and by the third time, he was occupying a great deal of her thoughts. She found herself smiling around him, tossing her head a little bit flirtatiously. She had loved Amos, maybe loved him still, but it all seemed so simple to accept someone her parents would approve of.

There was always a blessing in giving in, in laying down your own will for your parents, your spouse, and most of all, for the God you promised to serve.

Raymond and Lydia Beiler sat together, numbed into total silence, after Sam and Cathy left, the sunny Sunday afternoon turning gray and merciless for both of them.

They were leaving the Amish, moving to Florida to be with his uncle's family, in late September. "Don't worry," Cathy said, "we're getting married on the way down, so it'll be legal. Don't try to stop us." Lydia spewed bitter words, which led to a horrible exchange with Cathy shouting and Sam sneering and cowering by turns.

From the road came the sound of clopping hooves, the rattle of steel wheels on macadam, the chatter of children in the buggy. Someone broke out in song, the melodious voice like a steel-toothed rake across their weary chests, the hearts underneath completely shattered.

Oh, but they had failed as parents. If only they could turn back time, be on the road with the horse and buggy, children in the back, enjoying the lively talk of them. And how had they failed? Many, many ways. Lydia felt her first real pang of remorse, the pain spreading through her like a poisoned arrow. She saw Amos, his ungainly bulk, his pimply face and sour odor, recognized the shame she felt to call him her son. Yes, shame when he walked into church. The size of him. The irritation—no, revulsion—she felt when he ate so fast, so . . .

She couldn't bear to think of it. But how could she have changed the way she felt even then? Should she have simply pretended not to be bothered by his size and disgusting habits?

And here was Cathy, disobeying in the same heartbreaking way. Why? Why were their children like this?

Florida was a thousand miles away, dear God. Well, they'd be back. That Sam didn't look as if he amounted to a hill of beans.

A sob broke from her gulping throat. She pressed a Kleenex to her mouth.

"Raymond!" she gasped. "Help me."

He cast her a wild-eyed look and quickly brought her a cold drink, which she sipped, eyes brimming.

"*Ach*, Raymond. Where have we gone wrong?" she asked mournfully.

"Maybe we haven't, dear. Maybe God gave us this cross."

"Don't talk like that, Raymond. You know there's something wrong. We didn't raise our children to be like this."

Raymond lifted his eyes to his wife. "Didn't we, Lydia?" And her eyes fell before the truth in his.

What followed in the days ahead could hardly be written in only a few pages, with Cathy working long hours to save money for the trip, brushing off her mother who clung to her like flypaper wherever she went.

She begged and pleaded, spouted Bible verses and the threat of hell, but saw it was useless. They tried to summon Amos, who would not answer his phone. Wild with anxiety, they called the big house, to have Lila's sweet quavery voice tell them Amos had taken a vacation, hiking the Appalachians with his dog, which sent Lydia into a tailspin. She was suddenly anxious about his well-being on top of worrying about Cathy's rebellious departure to Florida.

"Why Florida?" she begged at one point, her eyes brimming yet again.

"Why not, Mom? It's full of rich people, and Sam and I plan on making some serious money. We'll take care of you when you're old, so chill."

What followed was a long and pitiful plea. They were old long before their time, their children out in the world, and someday they would pay handsomely for their outright rebellion.

Lavina, however, stayed out of the bitter arguments and listened without comment to Cathy's plans at night. According to Cathy, Sam was perfect for her, there was no doubt. He was kind and funny and sweet, although he had a hard time keeping a job, but that was because his coworkers were jealous of how smart he was and made trouble for him. He drank a lot, but that would stop once he settled into a job he loved—he got so stressed out with unreasonable bosses. She trusted him completely. He was coming from an Amish family, after all.

They were moving away to get rich, live in a nice house with palm trees, and go to the beach on the weekends.

Lavina was soft-hearted, with a gentle spirit, so she told Cathy she would miss her terribly, and wished she wouldn't go, but if this was what she wanted, then she would certainly wish them blessings.

"You're the best, Viney," Cathy said, "You could join us."

Lavinia shook her head, figured someone would have to be here for her mother, who was unstable on the best days, morose on others, and completely maudlin in between. As she headed down the stairs, she put a hand to her forehead and breathed a long sigh.

Raymond had gone to his shop to tinker and obtain a bit of peace in the eye of the storm. Lydia had ranted on about making Cathy go on an Amish retreat to recover her faith. When Raymond let out a barely imperceptible chuckle, she berated him.

"Lydia, we have never been able to make her do anything. Don't you think it's better to let her go peacefully? If God wants to teach her a lesson, then He can do just that."

"Oh, that's so like you, Raymond. Just let it go, pretend nothing's wrong. We have to let her know how hard this is for us."

"She knows that, Lydia."

"No. No she doesn't."

The end of September looked a long way off for Raymond.

THE NIGHT WAS a surprise for Amos. He pitched his tent with great difficulty. He thought the term "pitching" was the perfect verb—just pitch it in the trash and sleep beneath the stars, a canopy of leaves for a roof. But eventually, he managed to get it set up. The fire crackled cozily, his sleeping bag was definitely good quality, and he felt safely cocooned inside the plastic tent walls. He slept till almost daybreak, refreshed and alert. He found himself whistling low under his breath as he built up the fire, used water sparingly to cook his oatmeal, relishing the taste of the sticky concoction.

A granola bar, a drink of powdered juice, and he killed the fire, packed up, and was on his way, still whistling soft and low.

He had not experienced any bad thoughts during the night and he found himself saying *thank you, thank you*, with each step.

Perhaps this was the best thing he could have done, to get away and experience new things, see different sights, get his mind off things that made him anxious, like the inheritance.

He could not understand this change, could not see through the murky darkness around him for now. He figured he would need to stop trying, learn to accept this, if it was a chastening from the Lord, and felt a trickling of comfort.

It was the inheritance, he reasoned. He was unfit to gaze into the future and have enough confidence to follow his dream of opening the home to troubled boys. What did he know about any of it? Without Anna by his side, he felt there was no point. His thoughts could barely contain the idea of life without her to boost his morale, to supply the confidence he would need from day to day.

He shouldered his pack, looked to the trail ahead, and began to walk at a pace he knew he would not be able to maintain. But he needed to hear the blood pumping in his ears, his breath coming in short, hard puffs.

He came to a lookout, a flat area jutting out over the side of the mountain, the sun rising above the vista below. He stood in awe at the emerald green, the dark pockets of ravines almost black, an endless undulating landscape of untouched wilderness. This area was immense, but only a tiny portion of the world—and him, alone, less than a speck.

He became aware of a voice and turned to look back the way he had come to find two figures walking together. He waited, curious, as they drew closer. An older man, with a young boy, smiling at him as they approached.

"Hey, there. Up early?" the older man said, eyeing him with interest. The young boy simply stood, watching him with a frank gaze.

"Yeah. Sleeping bags don't do much to soften your nest," Amos answered.

"I know what you're talking about. I'm Jim, and this is Craig, my grandson."

"Hi. I'm Amos. Amos Beiler."

"Good to meet you."

"You, too. You're the first people I've seen."

The small boy said nothing, and Amos detected a sense of animosity, a certain rebellion. He looked to be eleven or twelve, with eyes much older.

Amos turned his attention to him.

"Aren't you lucky to be out here rather than in school," he said playfully.

The boy didn't answer, but turned away, shuffled his feet to unearth small stones, swung his foot to kick them away.

The older man, Jim, shook his head, mouthed the word, "Suspended."

Amos raised his eyebrows but said nothing.

Without another word, they moved away, and Amos was left wondering. He shrugged and followed them, but overtook them within a few minutes, passed them with a friendly wave, and hurried along the trail. He would never know Craig's story, could only guess at the reason he had been suspended from class, but found himself thinking again how his eyes seemed old, as if he'd taken in much more than was required of a child that age.

As he walked, he was overtaken by the selfishness of his vacation, walking alone, with Lila and Nancy keeping the big house without him. He had not been raised to indulge in pleasures such as this, to simply go off and do something for oneself. He had to fight the voices in his head telling him he was childish, a baby, cowering in the gatehouse, thinking only of himself, tied up in knots with anxiety.

He stopped. It was only midmorning, but with startling clarity, he knew he had to retrace his steps, get in his truck, and return. Immediately. He turned on his heel, walked as fast as he could comfortably, lifted a hand as he passed the man named Jim and the small boy with accusing eyes.

Champ whined, tugged on his leash, but neither one acknowledged the dog. Suddenly, the brightness of the day, the liquid trill of birdsong, the intense green of his surroundings turned cold and gray, the sound of birds like irritating claps of sound. He increased his pace, dashed headlong down the trail, his heart pounding in his throat.

When he became so exhausted he was forced to stop, he sank to the base of a tree, wiped the streaming sweat from his face, pushed Champ away when he tried to lick his cheek. He had to get home, the urgency the foremost thing on his mind, as he burrowed his face in the crook of his arm.

It had been the child. There was something about the child being suspended from school, a misdeed he had done.

He lifted his face and gazed off into the distance, calm now but seeing nothing. What had triggered that sense of panic, the rush back down the trail? He had never been suspended from school, had he?

His mind wandered back through the years, going to a different parochial school, but could not remember being asked to leave the school on account of misbehavior. He had friends back then. Not real friends, but boys who were nice to him, included him in games. It hadn't been all bad.

There were good days in school, especially at lunchtime when he sat at his desk, opened his lunchbox to find freshly baked cupcakes, a thick sandwich.

His teachers had never shown an aversion to him the way some of the boys did, so he supposed he had a few good memories to hang onto.

He just didn't know why he had been overtaken by a sense of urgency, to get away, to go home. Was there a hidden event of his childhood?

He shrugged, got to his feet. He'd ask his mother sometime, or Lavina. He could not enjoy the walk back, his eyes darting from tree to tree, his mind on full alert for any sign of danger, a quick surprise. He felt as if the canopy of leaves would drop, close in on him, suffocate him, but he tried to shake off the ominous sensation.

It was time to go home, get on with the work, the caring for Lila and the vast amount of work surrounding the big house.

He'd be okay. These strange onslaughts of panic would subside, his prayers would be heard, and life would go on.

Had Anna, or the thought of her, anything to do with these strange attacks? He hoped it wasn't so, that he was such a hopeless child, so immature and spiritually empty he couldn't deal with a solid no, a taking away of his hopes and dreams. Yes, she still permeated his thoughts, his longings were sometimes unbearable, but he was an old veteran of disappointment and refusal.

When he finally reached his truck, he was exhausted, caked with sweat, and smelling ripe. He grimaced as he threw his pack on the back seat, told Champ he'd been great, ran a hand over his upturned face, ruffled his ears, and got into the truck, checked his phone.

Twelve missed calls? He hadn't had service for a while. He checked, found his parents' number every time. Why hadn't they left a message? There had to have been an emergency. He backed up, drove away, fighting down the lurking panic. Something was wrong.

He stopped the truck after he was out of the mountains, called his parents' number, relieved to hear the voice of his mother.

"Mom, what's wrong?"

"Oh, Amos." There was silence then, broken only by muffled sobs, gasping intakes of breath.

"Mom, what is it? Is Dat okay?" Amos felt his heart hammering.

He heard her blow her nose.

"It's Cathy. Cathy and Sam. Amos, they're going to Florida, to live there. They're going English. Amos."

Her voice rose on a high wail of anguish.

"Mom, listen. I'll be over, okay?"

"Amos, they're getting married, and they aren't Amish. I can never make a wedding for them."

"OK. I hear you. I'm about three hours away, but I'll be there."

He went to his own place first to check in and take a quick shower. Lila and Nancy were surprised to see him back early. He said he'd missed them.

Lila laughed her sweet breathless sound, and Nancy punched his shoulder.

"Oh, your mother called," said Lila. "She sounded a bit anxious."

Amos nodded, said he was going to see his parents now, that his sister had made a poor decision and they were worried.

He drove away, knowing love would always await him at the big house, would envelope him in its warm arms and make him feel safe. Was that the way God's love wrapped around him, too? He didn't know for sure.

He felt his heart accelerate as he approached his parents' house but knew this strange panic would present itself at every turn if he allowed it.

Help me. Help me.

His parents stood at the door, side by side, and he ached for them in a way that felt physical, as if his chest contained a cement block of sorrow, for their sake. They had both aged, their faces drawn, eyes red-rimmed. He wanted to reach out, hug them the way he was now used to doing, but he had never hugged his parents or told them he loved them, which would be awkward now. So he stood and looked at them.

"Hello, Amos."

His father's voice was gravelly, as if he was beyond exhausted.

His mother began to weep, turning away as if she was ashamed of her display of emotion. He saw her bowed head, the covering a bit crooked, a hairpin almost loosening itself in the roll of hair beneath, her plump back and wide hips, the pleats of her dress wrinkled.

Ach, Mom, was the only thing he could think of.

"Sit down, Amos. Coffee?"

"Not this time of day, Dat. But thanks."

He sat, his eyes going to his mother again. He raised an eyebrow at his father. He shook his head, so Amos waited.

When she came to the table, her eyes were swollen, her face splotched, a Kleenex to her nose. She lifted streaming eyes to Amos.

"It's your fault, Amos. She's following your example."

He should have known, he thought bitterly, but lowered his eyes and said nothing. His father opened his mouth, then closed it, watched his wife with an unfathomable expression.

"I'm so sorry Cathy ran off, Mom."

"Sorry is not going to fix it."

"Lydia, I don't think it's fair to blame him," his father said, in a hushed tone, as if he was afraid of his own voice and its consequences.

Amos steeled himself for the painful onslaught following.

But there was none—only a long silence, the only sound the ticking of the cheap battery clock on the wall.

Finally, her voice broke through. "But why? Why is she doing this?"

"Because she's Cathy, Mom. She has a mind of her own."

"We tried to raise her right, same as you. And you both left."

He could tell the anger was drying up her tears, so he allowed her to flay him with her bitterness, one lash following another, as his father bowed his head in submission. She finished with clear instructions. He must come back to the Amish, which would help her see the right way.

Amos spoke quietly then, but truth permeated every word. "How can you claim that your way is right when all the years growing up, I never experienced love? It wasn't until I left home that I discovered that I was lovable—by God and by other people. I know you love Cathy, but you always let her walk all over you. You never gave her any boundaries or taught her what it really means to follow God, and now she's going to have to learn the hard way."

At this, his mother berated him until her face was flushed with anger. He rose to his feet, saying there was no point in conversation.

"I can't carry the blame for Cathy's choices, Mom."

"I think he's right, Mom." Raymond said, soft and low. He felt unfit to be a parent or a husband, and so his voice could barely be heard. A truly humble man, he found family disagreements a terrible thing to bear, a burden larger than he had ever imagined.

Cathy had always rested proudly on the ornate pedestal of her mother's adoration, had expected the same kind of worship from her peers, and if she didn't receive it, felt puzzled, then angry. She lost her girlfriends one after another and ended up with the wrong crowd of young men, who soon recognized her for what she was.

Then there was Sam, born and raised in a hardworking family of ten, decent, God-fearing people who raised their children to respect the rules of the church, to drive a horse and buggy in the spirit of *deh-mute*, the proper humility. Sam never saw a reason to drive around in one, nor wear suspenders and broad fall pants, and so set off on a path of his own, the trail pocked with rebellion.

He left the farm, got a job with King's Seamless Spouting, but didn't get along with Jonas Miller, who thought he knew everything and bossed him around as if he was a ten-year-old. It was the same thing at the welding shop, plus he never got any sun there, so that job was history. He tried working as a framer, a roofer. Mason work had been the worst, being a mud boy. Getting that mortar right had been impossible, but that wasn't his fault, either. Dan King's Elmer expected him to be perfect, so one miserably hot day he told him what he really thought and then walked off the job.

Now here he was, going to Florida with Cathy. He knew she was raised to work, so he wouldn't have to make all the money himself. That was the reason for marrying a girl raised in an Amish home. They were hard workers, and that would come in handy.

And so, together, they made plans for a getaway, to the land of constant sun and pleasure.

Seated with Amos and her husband, Lydia was surprised, shocked to hear him siding with her son.

"Well, Raymond, whose side are you on? No wonder we can't raise our children, the way you won't work with me," she accused him in a sorrowful voice, and he felt remorse, then pity.

"I'm sorry, Lydia."

"You should be."

"Mom," Amos began, but caught himself, took a few deep breaths. "Try to be reasonable. Seriously. It's not fair to blame me for Cathy's choices."

For a long moment, Lydia gazed at her son, a wedge of doubt entering her solid deciphering of Amos's life. Here he was, a tall, almost handsome young man, who had, by all accounts, made something of himself. He went to church, kept a job, came home when asked. She could hardly compare the obese, slovenly, untalented boy she had raised with this man. Yes, he was a man, sitting before her.

But still. If she couldn't lay blame on him, she would have to shift the blame to Raymond. But with her conscience making her so miserable, she couldn't even manage to do that.

Raymond had always been kind. He had. No matter Amos's appearance, his eating habits, and slow, cumbersome ways, Raymond had accepted him for how he was. His son. And for the second time in her life, she felt the stab of self-blame and mentally writhed beneath it.

She could see Raymond, walking with Amos, an arm around his shoulders, when she herself found him repulsive, always sweating, that onion smell exuding from his body. And he was her own son.

But she had done the best she could.

Amos watched his mother's face, saw the way shadows came and went as she remained quiet.

"Well, I better get home," he said, rising from his chair. Raymond got up, put a hand on his son's shoulder, said, "Remember us when you pray, Amos." Amos choked up, nodded.

Chapter 13

Lavina was awakened by the chirping of her alarm. She rolled over, punched it, and sighed deeply before reality began to sink in to her consciousness.

Even as she lay there, her stomach clenched with anxiety, but she closed her eyes, whispered a prayer to let the Holy Spirit lead her in the way she should go. She prayed for Sam and Cathy, her parents and Amos, then checked the time. Three thirty-five. A market day, so she better get moving. She walked across the narrow hallways to the tiny bathroom she shared with Cathy, saw the closed door of her room.

All day she moved about the enormous bakery doing her job, which was the yeast breads and rolls, quietly instructing the younger girls who worked alongside. She was proficient in her movements, accomplishing more than necessary, always making the work easier for those around her.

She was, by all accounts, a remarkable young woman, with her tanned face and dark hair, her luminous eyes the color of cinnamon, darkening with emotion from time to time. She had the gift of discernment, growing up in a tumultuous house with parents who were not always in the role God created for them, which she always acknowledged with a great mercy, knowing they did the best they could.

They were her parents, no matter how incompetent, and she loved them. It was a gift to be able to love, even if there were times she felt so much anger at them both.

She learned as she grew to be a diplomat, to sow the seeds of peace, to placate hot tempers, to stay in her allotted space with the heightened awareness of the maelstrom of ill feelings circling around her like an approaching storm. Always on the outskirts, but forming her own opinion on many subjects, she was mature far beyond her tender years.

At fourteen years old, she began her searching. She read her Bible, used a highlighter, clung to promises from Psalms, Matthew, Hebrews, loved the prophets and patriarchs of old. At sixteen, she obtained her cell phone, read articles and blog posts from a wide range of Christians, and grew into a love of Jesus and all He represented. She loved the Amish church, cherished the quiet way of being plain, but with Cathy's influence, deviated from the path she had set for herself. But only for a short period of time.

It was the light in Amos's eyes, the peace on his changing features. Somehow, he had quieted, deep in his spirit, and she realized how far she herself had strayed, how she longed to have what Amos possessed. She had repented and turned back to the narrow path, longing to know a more fulfilled life, to have the genuine peace that Amos seemed to.

She joined another group of youth, absolved her friendship with girls like Cathy, and felt she'd come home.

She noticed a young man who only showed up occasionally, a quiet, shy person with a shock of brown curls, deep blue eyes, and a quiet laugh. She never approached him but found her eyes on his face repeatedly.

One summer evening, however, he spoke to her when they wound up on the same side of the volleyball net, and she found herself groping for the proper words.

"I've seen you around. You're Lavina Beiler."

She only nodded, had to look away from the bluest eyes.

And he leaped to hit the volleyball, sending a vicious spike across the net, putting an effective end to the beginning of a conversation. The remainder of the evening, she was aware of his presence, sorry to see him seated way down the line at the hymn singing table.

The following weekends, he was always there, but he never spoke to her, even at the volleyball net. She tried to let him go, told herself if he'd been interested he would have continued the conversation.

And then, Sam and Cathy sent her into a vortex of fear and doubt, her mother weeping copiously, spouting threats, admonishing at every turn. Lavina was left with a churning stomach and the assurance no decent guy would ever ask her out with the dysfunctional home in which she lived. Word had already gotten around that two of the three children had left the Amish.

Today at the bakery, her eyes felt gritty from lack of sleep, her future uncertain, but she remembered a verse from the Bible—to find contentment, no matter the state of her life. To be patient, and of good cheer.

She slid huge pans of bread and rolls in and out of ovens, smiled, and talked with coworkers as she thought of their needs as well as her own. Here at work, she was away from the house of sadness and disappointment, could pull the cheerful mask effectively over her face. Life went on, whether she wanted to or not.

She was always tired by the time Saturday evening came around, so she decided to stay home from the birthday party she'd been invited to. The girl was barely an acquaintance, so there was no sense in thinking she'd be missed.

It was when Sam came into the house, hurried upstairs to Cathy's room, and her mother began the tirade that wearied Lavina's bones, that she decided to call a driver and go to the birthday party, if only to get away from the chaos.

She dressed hurriedly, grabbing the nearest dress of sky blue, tied a black apron, and slid her feet into sandals before running downstairs. Her mother looked up, stopped shouting long enough to ask where she was going, nodded when Lavina told her. She saw only a glimpse of her father's slumped shoulders, his eyes downcast, before she told them goodbye.

There was a crowd of youth in the well-lit shop as she entered alone, but her eyes found him immediately. A surge of joy billowed over her like a hot air balloon, lifting her spirits, taking her away from the troubled home she had left.

Her friend Miriam came through the crowd, her face alight.

"I was seriously thinking you might not show up," she trilled.

"I wasn't planning on it, but Sam came over and . . . you know."

"You poor thing, Lavina. It must be terribly hard."

She slipped an arm around her waist, and Lavina could only nod, unable to speak around the unexpected lump in her throat.

"Hello, Lavina."

She looked toward the source and found him standing nearby, his eyes on her.

"Oh. Hello."

"How are you this evening?"

"Good. Doing good. And you?"

He only nodded, his lips smiling a bit, his eyes serious.

"Would you mind if I asked you to accompany me on a walk?"

She heard the question but could not quite process what he meant.

"You mean, now?"

"Yes."

Miriam made a face and moved off silently, quickly.

"Uh, yes. We can."

He motioned toward the door and she followed, grateful to see it was still partly twilight, the mountain darkened with a red orange glow above it, birds chirping and calling to each other as they flew to their nesting place. An owl hooted, another answered, as they walked side by side out the short gravel driveway lined with buggies, the shafts pointed skyward as if to stand at attention as they passed.

"You think I'm being bold, likely."

"No, not really."

"You probably don't even know my name."

"I don't."

"I'm Matt Beiler, also known as Charlie." She laughed, asked why Charlie, and he spread his hands and shrugged his shoulders, said he'd been Charlie since he was born. In school, where nicknames were prohibited, he was Matthew Beiler, but at home Charlie was ingrained too deeply to erase. His family had a great sense of humor; he had a sister named Fluff.

They discussed the reason, which turned out to be her hair, a profusion of curls, like his, but hers were impossible to tame. Thus the moniker, Fluff.

"Why not Fluffy?" Lavina asked.

"We have a cat with that name."

Lavina laughed again, really laughed, wondering how long it had been since she found anything funny.

"Does your family have a humorous streak?" he asked. He was watching her face and was shocked when she turned away from him and remained silent.

"I'm sorry, you don't have to say. Maybe I'm being too personal."

She shook her head. "No, it's okay."

She laughed, or tried to, but could only produce a shaking exhalation. "It's, it's a bit complicated. Maybe you don't know of us. Raymond and Lydia are my parents."

"No, I can't say I'm acquainted with the name, although eventually, if you dig deep enough, you can figure out who anyone is in Amish world."

"I'm glad if you don't know."

"Now what's that supposed to mean?" he asked in a lighthearted voice, and she understood he knew nothing about their family, and she would guard the truth.

"Oh, just . . . well, I can't really say, if that's alright."

"Mysterious!" he said, with something like a wink. "But seriously, that's fine. I get it; you don't know me yet. You probably wonder why I asked you to go for a walk. Well, to come right out honestly, I think you are an amazing girl, and I've been watching you for longer than you know. I tried plenty of times to grab your attention, at least say hello, but it's too hard, in this crowd. So, out of desperation, I came up with this plan."

She swallowed, her thoughts scattered.

"I know this is unusual, and may take you off guard, but I would like to get to know you better, and so this is phase two of my plan. You ready?"

He stopped, turned to face her. She had no choice but to stop and face him as well. His eyes were very blue and very kind, the crinkles around them deepening as he smiled.

"Remember the hurricane in North Carolina and Tennessee?"

"Yes?"

"Well, there's a Melard bus leaving Lancaster next week—actually, the week after, I think. The twenty-second, whenever that is. A group of older guys and girls, and four young married couples. I think there are twenty-seven or eight. Would you accompany me for two weeks?"

"You mean, to clean up and rebuild?"

"Exactly. I love work trips like this. The work isn't always pleasant, but the rewards in your soul are phenomenal. It's a great thing, helping these people."

She took a deep breath, her eyes sparkling with interest.

"I would love to go. But I'll need my parents' approval of course."

"Sure. I expected that." A smile lit up his face. "Lavina, this makes me so happy. We'll have hours on the bus ride to talk."

"We will we sit together? I mean . . ."

"You won't know anyone else. We don't have to be like a couple or anything—we're simply getting to know each other. I mean, if that sounds OK?"

She nodded, smiled, allowed the blue of his eyes to settle into her spirit. He took her hand, pressed it gently for only a moment, then released it.

"Thank you for saying yes, Lavina. I knew you might think I'm crazy, but once I had the idea in my head, I couldn't shake it. From now till the twenty-second seems like an eternity."

And how was she supposed to answer with all that unexpected happiness welling up inside of her, with her thoughts taking their own liberty and her heart turning cartwheels? So she reached out and touched his sleeve, lightly, and smiled into those blue eyes.

The remainder of the evening was spent among others, greeting friends, eating ice cream and cake, soft pretzels and cheese dip, tiny wedges of homemade pizza, potato chips, fresh veggies. The sweet sixteen-year-old named Ruby Mae glowed with the festivities surrounding her.

"Isn't she just adorable?" Lavina asked her friend Miriam.

"She is. I love her name. Ruby. If I ever have a little girl, I'm going to name her Ruby. Ruby Jo. Isn't that cute?"

"These little pizza slices are super."

Miriam slanted her a look. "How was the walk with what's-his-name?"

"Good, actually. He asked if I'd go to Tennessee. He said they need more volunteers. You know, helping rebuild after the hurricane."

"I bet they do."

"Don't laugh, Miriam. It seemed almost spiritual. Serious."

"Oh, wow. It was like that."

"It was."

Miriam squeezed her hand. "Congratulations, darling."

The disappointment was cruel, crushing Lavina with its weight of unfairness, after her mother pronounced her leaving for Tennessee impossible the day before Sam and Cathy were leaving for Florida.

She paced the kitchen as she talked, saying Lavina was all she had left, and what was she supposed to do at the hardest time in her life with no one to talk to? Her father was no help, sitting there like a stump when she needed him to support her with all they were going through.

"Mom, please let me go. It would mean so much."

"Absolutely not. There is no way. Can't you take your mother's feelings into consideration?"

It was not like Lavina to give in to the rebellion threatening to release a vocabulary of harsh, truthful words, so she bowed her head and toyed with her coffee cup.

"If this Matt, Matthew, whatever, wants you, he'll be back. Now listen, Lavina. Put this trip out of your head."

She brought up the subject at the supper table, telling Raymond in detail how selfish Lavina was being, thinking about going to North or South Carolina, wherever the flood had gone through, and did he know a Matthew Beiler from Lancaster?

Raymond swallowed his meatloaf, laid down his fork, crossed his arms, and took a careful survey of his wife's face, saw the crushing defeat in Lavina's. What he felt was unfathomable, but it surged through him. He felt his veins expand, felt his heart breaking into hundreds of pieces for his youngest, long-suffering daughter, realized he had been pushed to his limit. He opened his mouth and began to speak.

"No, I do not know this guy, Lydia, but if he asked Lavina and she wants to go, then she is allowed to do so."

There was an audible gasp, then a shriek.

"Raymond, I don't believe it. You're working against my decision."

He met the outraged disbelief head on.

"Yes, Lydia, I am. The unfairness here is too much. Lavina has never given us any trouble, and . . ."

Here Lydia broke in, reminding him of her departure to Amos's house, her voice strident with righteousness.

He held up a hand. "Stop. Just stop."

Amazingly, she did, her mouth open in shock.

"Lavina had to do what she needed to do to escape her life here at home, which Cathy had turned into a fiasco."

Lydia opened her mouth, but Raymond went on, his voice level and full of truth.

"Lavina has no responsibility where Cathy is concerned."

"But, Raymond, I need her to be with me. That's the day before they leave. I can't have them both gone."

"But you will. Lavina is going with my blessing. I'm sorry, Lydia, but it is grossly unfair to expect her to stay home in this situation."

Lavina found her voice, "Dat, it's okay. I don't want to get between you and Mam."

He shook his head. "No, Lavina, you tell this Matthew you will be glad to go. Your parents said yes."

"Dat, really . . ."

"Lavina, you're going. It will be good for you to get away."

The dishes were collected from the table in cold silence, the sound of water running from the spigot loud in their ears, dishes earsplitting, the scraping of leftovers into containers deafening. Lavina asked her about whether to save the gravy but found only an obstinate silence. So she went to her room, where she clenched her hands into fists as tears squeezed between closed eyes.

Why was her life so far from ordinary? Now, instead of the joy she should be experiencing, she was caught in a sticky web of her mother's disapproval. It would be easier just to stay home, a crutch for her mother in her darkest hour, having to watch Cathy leave with Sam. But her father had given his word.

She heard Cathy come home much later, heard the light knock on the door of her bedroom, lifted herself on one elbow and asked her to come in.

She pressed the button on the battery lamp.

"Hey, sweetpea," Cathy trilled. "You better take a long look at me, cause it's only a week and a half or so till I'm outta here. You should take a couple pictures of me in Amish clothes, cause once I leave, that's it. Hey, what do you think about asking Amos for a loan? Sam says he won't have quite enough for the security deposit on an apartment, says rent is terrible high in Florida. You think?"

Lavina shook her head, threw back the covers and set her feet on the floor.

"You can always google it."

"I did. But that's in Sarasota. We won't need a condominium."

She sighed, popped her gum, then stuck out her tongue and released the chewed glob into the palm of her hand, pitched it into the waste can, and ran the hand across her skirt.

"I think Sam might be a bit financially unstable, so I might have to take control. He drinks too much and that's where a lot of his money goes. He promised to quit though, and I trust him. He's such a sweetheart. He says now we don't have to get married till we're settled in an apartment, but don't tell the parents. Mom would have a stroke."

Lavina lifted imploring eyes.

"Cathy, I'm not sure going to Florida is a good idea for you and Sam. Why don't you give your relationship another year or so?"

"And risk losing him? Nuh-uh. Look, I'm not getting any younger, and I know I pretty much ruined my reputation among our group. What choices do I have?"

"You'd have plenty, really, if you gave it some time. You could make some changes, straighten up a little. People forget faster than you'd think."

Cathy snorted. "And be stuck with some pimply do-gooder whose idea of fun is filling a mortgaged house with children?"

Lavina's stomach jiggled with laughter in spite of herself. *Ach*, Cathy, so painfully honest, and so not cut out to be a content housewife and mother.

"Cathy, seriously."

"You know it's the truth. Look, I need money. Should I ask Amos?"

"You could. Or what if you told Sam he has to save up enough money before you'll go?"

"I can't lose him."

Cathy picked at the quilt, her eyes downcast, and Lavina felt a pang of empathy. There was no doubt in her mind, Sam would not come up to her expectations, but was there a way to tell her?

Ach my, Cathy.

She folded the corner of the quilt, folded it gain, then threw it away from her, as if a certain thought struck her as unnecessary.

"Lavina, do *you* have money?"

"I still give Mam most of my wages."

"I'm scared to ask Amos."

"Call him first."

"I'm scared to do that."

"Call him now."

Lavina watched as she pulled up his number, biting her lip. She was still so pretty, in spite of being older and the rough way she spent her weekends.

She put up a thumb and Lavina heard her brother's voice.

They said all the proper brother and sister things, before Cathy asked the loaded question, bluntly.

Cathy blinked, turned away from Lavina, checked her image in the mirror, pressed four fingers together, raised and lowered them with her thumb to represent his talking mouth, frowned, went back to the mirror, ran a finger along an eyebrow.

"I asked for a loan, Amos. A loan means I'll pay you back."

She listened, rolled her eyes.

"Sam has a job. He's just short this month. No, we'll pay you back as soon as we're on our feet. What? No. We have enough money to get us to Florida. It's for the security deposit. You know, they won't let you get an apartment if you don't have it."

There was another long silence, then she sat down hard, crossed her legs and swung her foot, picked at the side of her mouth.

"Well, after we both have a job, we can easily pay back a couple hundred a month."

She took a deep breath, got to her feet.

"Okay, okay, Amos. I'll tell him. No, he's not drinking anymore. Okay, good. That's fine. We'll be there. Okay, great. Amos, you're absolutely the best. Sure, we will. Thank you. Thanks a bunch. Love you, bye."

She swung around the room, her arms outstretched, her face lifted to the ceiling.

"We're going, we're going! My dream is coming true."

How the tides have turned, Lavina thought. Who would have imagined that mighty Cathy would be begging from the brother who she once proclaimed a "smelly, fat loser"? How often Cathy had reminded Amos that he couldn't hold down a job, that he was no good, would never amount to anything. And now he was the one with the power to make her dreams come true.

Chapter 14

On the twenty-second of September, Lavina stood in the cool darkness of early morning with her new lavender roll-away luggage, a brown shoulder bag, and a Stanley drinking cup filled with ice water. Matt was beside her, which created a sort of thrill throughout her being, although she could not quite shake the shroud of knowing she had disobeyed her mother.

She had met his family the evening before, a normal, very ordinary family of eight, living in a two-story home with a barn, a few outbuildings, and a welding shop where his father made a living to support his family.

There was humor, teasing, lots of noise, and an easy acceptance into the family structure, the meeting between them a seamless exchange of greetings amongst gawking younger siblings.

She had felt shy only in the beginning, and soon found herself drinking iced tea on the porch, listening to his parents, Chris and Betty, as they asked about her family, the community in Rochester. Bravely, she answered questions, dodged around the most difficult ones, but represented family life much the same as any other Amish household. She said Amos had never married but avoided mentioning he'd left the Amish. She said her older sister had found herself floundering for a short time but was now dating seriously.

Now here she was, wanting to be closer to Matt as they waited for the bus in the dark, hoping she would not disappoint him in the next two weeks.

They were the last stop, in Gap, the southernmost pickup, so she looked up expectantly as each vehicle went past, headlights piercing the night. Finally, the shifting gears and heavy whine of the large bus bore down on them, and Matt grabbed her suitcase, asking her to wait while he loaded it for her.

The steps were higher than she thought, but he was there, guiding her with a hand on her back, and through the aisle between colorful shirts and straw hats, white coverings and friendly greetings called out.

A group of single men, hatless, calling, "Charlie, Charlie."

A chorus of questions followed. "Who is she? Why didn't you tell us? Aren't you the sneaky one?"

She smiled and kept on smiling, realized the seats were narrow, and felt secure, tucked in, and yes, so very happy to be seated with Matt—or Charlie—for eight hours.

And now that her life had taken this unexpected turn for the better, she knew what a grateful heart felt like. To be away from the pain of her parents when Sam and Cathy left was a gift from God, straight from Heaven, a wealth of blessings no one deserved, a grace and mercy.

She'd had a tearful goodbye, wrapped in Cathy's arms. Almost, Cathy had broken down and wept, but caught herself at the last minute, said, "Call me," and left, her head held high.

When the sun rose, she could view the rolling farmland through tinted windows, heard the distant rumble of the engine beneath her, the presence of Matt beside her. She asked how soon they would stop for coffee.

"I should have thought to bring our own. I have a few Yeti cups, scratched and dented from falling off trusses and roofs."

"I'm sure we'll survive."

When the bus turned into a truck stop for breakfast, it was almost ten o'clock, the journey almost halfway over. They stayed in their seats till everyone was off, then Matt stood and extended his hand to help her.

When he smiled down at her, she realized how much his kindness meant.

"I feel as if I have known you all my life," he said quietly.

She felt the same. They had spoken of every subject possible, except for her family, which she managed to skirt every single time he brought it up.

She was aware of Matt's friends' curiosity but just smiled as she was introduced over and over.

"Well, Charlie, I'd say you got lucky, old man. If there's a recipe for catching one like this, I'll need a copy," a short redhead said openly, his face beaming with good humor.

Lavina was not used to being the center of attention, and she enjoyed it. She felt cherished, accepted, a part of something soft and comfortable, and soon learned it was the easy way Matt had with his friends. Everyone knew him, seemed to know him well, and banter flowed as full and smooth as a deep river.

After breakfast, she dozed after arranging her pillow and woke to find Matt watching her. She reached up to smooth her hair, straighten her covering, then asked if he'd slept. She stopped when she saw his gaze on her face, the seriousness with which he spoke. For only an instant, he brushed her cheek with his thumb, then whispered, "I will never do anything to cause you to be sad, or hurt, or disappointed."

She lowered her eyes, felt the color rise in her face, and wondered if that was how her father felt about her mother at one time.

"Let me ask you something, Lavina," he went on.

"Okay."

"Sometimes when we're talking, you go away from me. You sort of disappear into yourself for a while. Is something wrong?"

She shrugged. "I don't know what you mean."

"It's alright. I just think there's a mystery somewhere. Like why you don't like to talk about your family."

She hesitated, then plunged. "It's a lot. You may not want anything to do with me if I tell you about them. Or 'us,' I should say. I'm a part as well."

"It can't be that bad."

"Believe me."

He searched her face, but she kept her eyes lowered.

It was the odor of rot and dried mud, the putrefaction of dead animals and spoiled food, of overflowing septic systems, upended propane tanks, and flood waters all rolled into a stench she could taste on her tongue. Debris rose along embankments, sturdy houses pushed off their foundations, broken rusted vehicles and splintered mobile homes. People everywhere, living in tents and storage units, muddy and without hope.

Yet they were greeted with opened arms, tears, and quivering faces. "God bless you," "Praise God," over and over, as they were shown the shelter and kitchen for the volunteers. On either side, the mountains rose steeply, the narrow valley an unimaginable disaster of over thirty inches of torrential rain and howling winds, the aftermath leaving one speechless.

For only a moment, Lavina panicked, felt she could not stand the stench, the decay, and would need to claw her way up the side of these mountains to get away, to grasp the rope of normalcy.

"Are you okay, Lavina?" Matt asked, a hand on her shoulder. She thought she was, but his kindness released a pent-up sob, and she turned, went into his arms, her whole frame shaking as she wept. He stood quietly and held her, reached for her chin, finally.

"Look at me, Lavina. If it's too much, I can arrange for us to go back."

She shook her head, apologized, regretted her weakness.

More of the women and girls had the same response, with husbands providing comfort, which Matt was quick to point out.

The images of destruction would forever be imprinted in her mind—the doll's head with its brilliant blue eyes staring from between two rocks, the twisted lawn chairs, a refrigerator with one door torn away, couches and chairs, splintered porch posts and skeletons of dogs and cats, a macabre collection of bleached bones with gaping teeth and patches of hair.

As they walked among the ruins, there were signs of hope, too—a group of men shoveling mud into wheelbarrows, skid loaders with scoops of debris, dripping with stinking, slimy mud. The smell hung over everything, producing a gagging reflex until one was accustomed to it.

Yet the old men lifted a hand, grizzled faces alight with welcome, filthy bill caps pulled low over squinting eyes.

"Yeah, brother. God is good. He sent you guys. Praise the Lord." Others glared suspiciously, but eventually welcomed them.

The community center was only damaged in parts and volunteers had done enough renovation to enable safety and a night's rest, a place to prepare food and serve it. They met two more groups of Amish and Mennonites, were introduced and shown their sleeping quarters, the shared bathrooms.

Lavina recognized the fact she needed to dig deeply, to force herself to keep from despair, to face these two weeks with courage. Matt could not always be by her side, so she needed her own strength to sustain her.

At night, she could not go to sleep, thinking of Sam and Cathy, by now on their way to Florida, leaving her mother and father alone in the small white house permeated with sorrow, the disappointment following them like wafting white ghosts, in and out of walls, without reprieve. She lay on her hard bunk, her eyes wide, and prayed over and over for healing, for love and mercy. *And please, will you stay by my side tomorrow?*

She rose, bleary-eyed and disoriented, but after a cold face wash and a good laugh with a girl named Rosetta Martin, she got dressed and was told to leave her white head covering behind, that there were plenty of black *dichlin* (kerchiefs) for all the women. At breakfast, she found Matt, who searched her eyes, smiled.

They were assigned together, as she had hoped, and climbed onto the back of a rusted blue Chevy pickup with wooden racks and benches built along the sides, with nine others, packed in and ready for their workday.

Everywhere, there were uprooted trees, branches, and pieces of buildings, concrete slabs wedged into embankments. Broken windows, a piano lodged in the crook of a tree, endless glass bottles, tin cans, soaked cardboard, and discolored plastic.

The truck came to a stop at a rural intersection where a group of houses were simply no longer there, the only remaining thing the jutting foundations filled with stinking silt and a flotsam of debris. Anything you could imagine was wedged into this putrid, quivering mass, and the only way to begin was with hand shovels.

Matt looked at Lavina. "I think this is only for the men."

Lavina's heart sank, but she listened closely as the leader told them of the next stop around the bend, where the houses were back from river, and still intact, which meant work for the ladies.

How to describe the wreckage? With plastic gloves and masks, they scraped and shoveled, unearthed linoleum, bare wood floors. The men arrived and drywall was replaced, sanded, and smoothed.

Lavina found the work enormously gratifying, a group effort with women of different ages all sharing a common bond, that of volunteering their services for people in need.

Every evening, Matt would leave the others to their card games or basketball and find Lavina, who was always waiting for him at a designated spot. They often sat and talked, but sometimes wandered together down the road. Bit by bit, she released bits of information about her family in a small, brittle voice, as if each word cost her dearly.

"Where is your brother now?" Matt asked at one point.

"He's a groundskeeper in another town."

"He's not Amish?"

"No."

"So, is he, like, an alcoholic or on drugs? Is he in trouble with the law?"

"Of course not. He's, well . . . he's a Christian. He worships God. He goes to church."

"So, what's the problem?" Matt asked with sincerity.

"Well, you know, he's not Amish."

"He doesn't have to be. It's not for everyone."

Lavina looked at him, her mouth open in disbelief. For a long moment she said nothing, then shook her head. "Tell my mother that" was all she said.

"No, seriously, he sounds like a great guy. Really. I can't wait to meet him. We'll arrange it when we get back, okay?"

She nodded, smiling. She told him she'd been smiling so much around him that he must be getting tired of seeing her teeth. He laughed, assured her there was nothing wrong with her teeth, it was her mouth that bothered him.

She put her hands up, her eyes wide, and knew he was teasing.

"Oh no you don't, Charlie Beiler."

To be with him was like being found. Around him, she became a normal, pretty Amish girl content in her own skin, happy in this small world of two. He completed her. To be in his company was enough.

She shoveled mud, washed walls and cabinets, filled contractor's garbage bags with spoiled, rusted tin cans of food and broken dishes. Her hair went every which way, her black *dichly* lost the pins and slid off her head.

One evening after work, she lifted a mud-stained face to Matt and he kissed her, gently, then rubbed the mud off her nose with his thumb. She told him he was not allowed to take those liberties, and he called her Jane Austen, which was so sweet she savored the words.

They held a "sort of" church service, an impromptu Bible study and hymn sing, a handful of the locals attending with them. It was the most beautiful thing, and Lavina found her faith increased.

They made friends everywhere, sat down to dinner in repaired homes with television sets blaring, cigarettes, and Bud Light a way of life, and without guilt. There was a warmth, an all-encompassing gratitude, no matter where they went.

Especially Hetty Grimes, a widow in her eighties who lived in an old stone house that stayed erect through the storm, but the rain had soaked the floors and plaster walls, destroyed her furniture, and drowned her cats, all four of them. James, Crappie, Hector, and Biscuit, dead and gone.

She'd been airlifted by helicopter, said it was a good experience, knowing how things below looked as she ascended to Heaven to be with Oscar Poe, her dead husband. At least she hoped he made it; if he did, it was through a double dose of grace and an outpouring of divine mercy. Now there was a character, Oscar was. Didn't work hardly a day of his life straight through. Drank and smoked himself to death, but she stayed with him through it all. He had an eye for the ladies, too, but when she found that out she got down the ice pick and told him how it was.

She was simply genuine, a product left over from the forties, after the war, when everything was all hallelujah, spit, and vinegar. Folks went crazy, after that, she said. Genuine mountain wisdom, complete with folklore and myths handed down from one generation to the next.

Before they left, they hugged her, stood with her for pictures, said goodbye, and felt as if they'd lost a treasure.

The two weeks were rich with experience, times they would never forget, both physically and spiritually. Each night, they were so tired they could barely drag themselves into the shower, falling into hard bunk beds and sleep.

When the bus wheezed to a stop, they stood in a collective group, thinner, stronger, and strangely reluctant to leave. Many of the locals were there to see them off, tears running down ruddy faces, battered spirits given a lift.

Everyone was quiet, pondering the gravity of the situation, the monumental task remaining, the incompetence of government, which was a shame. But, someone said, the natural disasters were coming so thick and fast, how could any organization keep up? Matt would nod, or shake his head, but was always slow to speak his mind unless asked.

Lavina told him of what she would face at home—the loss of Cathy, and the truth about her mother's opinion on her trip to Tennessee. He listened, without comment.

"So now you know everything—or almost everything. I haven't told you everything about my mom."

"She seems to be an interesting character."

"You can always tell me you'd rather not have me after all. Sort of like returning an item after you bought it."

"Lavina, you just don't get it, do you?" he asked quietly. "I'm not scared off by your family."

Lavina said nothing, but he detected the shadow across her face.

"Are you dreading going home?"

She shrugged, turned her face to the window.

"I just need time, and courage to do the right thing. Being with you has felt so easy. I feel like I have to put back on my armor before going home, to protect myself from the worst. And I need patience to keep trying to help."

"Why don't you just move out?" he asked, taking her hand.

"I did, but they came and got me."

The sadness was unbearable, her voice thick and gravelly, as if loose stones kept her throat from clearing.

"If there's anything I can do . . ."

"There isn't, but thanks."

To EMBARK, TO step off the bus, was almost more than Lavina could face, leaving the cocoon of safety and warmth with Matt. Time after time, a wave of despair slapped her face, washed through with a physical sensation. She could not imagine greeting her mother, the house empty and quiet, the atmosphere stuffed with resentment, like a sticky humidity sucking the strength and good humor from her body.

Inevitably, she arrived at her home, alarmed how her hands shook as she paid the driver. Taking a deep breath to steady herself, she walked up the steps and into the house, calling out hesitantly, "Mom?"

There was no answer. The house was immaculate, as usual, floors Swept and polished, dishes put away, the stove sparkling.

"Mom?"

She peered out the back door, hoping to find her in the garden, but it, too, was empty. She checked the time, thought her father would soon be home, carried her luggage to the washer.

When his time to come home from work came and went, she became concerned and called the shop, to have a friendly answer with alarming news.

They were in Michigan, at a facility for people who needed rest. The words were spoken gently, choosing words carefully.

Confused, she thanked him and hung up. Why? Why had no one contacted her? She had no one to call, had no idea where in Michigan they might possibly be, so she sat on her mother's recliner, her shoulders slumped, and stared into space.

She took up her phone and called Amos, who had also been kept in the dark, astonished to find out his parents had actually done this by themselves.

He offered to come over, said he'd bring something for their supper, and she accepted gratefully, thanking God for her brother, the thoughtfulness and kindness he always showed toward her.

When he pulled in, she welcomed him warmly, taking the paper bag of sandwiches from their favorite burger place. They shared the food and all their thoughts and fears, the bond of sibling love a rope that would never be broken between the two.

Cathy and Sam had shown up at his place for the money, and Amos felt an empathy of sorts, in all honesty. But when he caught the scent of alcohol on Sam's breath, he realized what a mess Cathy was getting into. He still gave her the money, but not without a carefully worded warning about the decision she was making. He said if she ever found herself in trouble, he was only a phone call away.

"Lavina, I had a hard time believing that was my sister. Dressed like that, with all the makeup. But then, I suppose that's how Mam felt when I came home that first time, so I can't judge anyone else, as far as bringing heartache to loved ones."

"Mom would never admit it, Amos, but she's proud of who you've become."

"I find that hard to believe."

"In her way, Amos, she is. Sure, some of it is just that you're handsome now, which she respects, but it's more than that."

He shrugged. "Does it matter, really?"

He wiped his mouth on a napkin, leaned back. and searched her eyes. "Tell me about your trip."

So, she did, in detail, and he heard every word, making her happiness complete when he congratulated her about Matt.

"Beiler? We're not related, are we?" he asked.

"Probably way back somewhere. You know how it is, thousands of Beilers and Stoltzfuses and Kings and Zooks."

Amos laughed, and then turned the conversation back to their parents, wondering what exactly had happened and how they'd find out where they were in Michigan. Amos took out his phone and googled "Amish mental hospitals Michigan" and "Amish recovery homes Michigan," but nothing much came up. Most Amish facilities didn't have websites or online listings.

Both of them were used to drama, but this was another level. They felt adrift, without a map to navigate the uncertain waters.

It was almost two whole days before Amos received a call from an unknown number, answered quickly, then exhaled when he heard his father's voice.

"Amos."

"Yes, Dat."

"I'm sorry about everything."

There was a long pause, and he knew his soft-hearted father was fighting for control, so he stayed silent.

A sigh, then a long, drawn-out expulsion for breath, then his nose being blown.

"Amos, it's an awful thing to see your loved one go through what Mom did."

"Is she OK? Lavina and I were so worried."

"I imagine you were, and I do apologize. She didn't want anyone to know."

"I understand that . . ." Amos answered, holding back the words he wanted to say about it being ridiculous to leave Lavina to gather scraps of information from their dad's boss.

"She . . . well, what happened . . . she couldn't take the circumstances in her life. She hasn't been strong in the past, and this thing with Cathy is more than her nerves could take. She had a mental breakdown and refused the help that's available here."

"You mean the ER?" Amos asked, trying to piece things together.

"Yes. I had to get help from somewhere, so I asked Chris Zook—he's the oldest minister here in this district, and quite kind. He brought the deacon, and they did what they could, which at that point, wasn't much. But Chris spent days on the phone, trying to get her into an Amish home. He finally found an opening in Michigan, but the hardest part was trying to convince her she needed to go, and stay. Oh, Amos, we went through something."

He paused, and Amos heard the broken sigh.

"To see the love of your life go through such a dark place is devastating. I do love her, I always have."

"I know, Dat. You were always good to her."

"I tried my best. I still blame myself for going against her and allowing Lavina to go to Tennessee. I should have seen that her nerves were already too fraught to handle an additional conflict."

Amos said nothing, saw Champ scratching at the door, and went to open it, trailing a hand across his back.

"It was too much, Amos, too much. I regret my words now, as it seemed everything came together to send her straight over the edge, as the saying goes. It's my fault."

So, nothing had changed, only escalated. Even in the midst of a mental breakdown his mother continued to manipulate, shrewdly knowing exactly what she was doing to keep her husband in check. A helpless rage tore through Amos, and there were no words to reassure his father, only quick, hard breaths of contained anger and disgust.

"Are you there, Amos?"

"I'm here. Dat, you can't blame yourself. She's always been this way. She's a troubled soul, and I hope the counselors will be able to help there, wherever you are."

"I believe so. And Amos, keep us in your prayers, please."

Amos said he would.

Chapter 15

Life returned to a degree of normalcy for Amos, who took note of the October sky, the colors bursting on trees everywhere, the shade of blue above him creating an intimacy with the Creator as he begged for help on his family's behalf. He sought the face of Jesus in a way he had never experienced, which brought him peace and banished the anxiety attacks he realized he had brought on himself.

He needed to reevaluate his thoughts, turn to the Man who walked the earth as a human, accept the love and mercy, the grace so freely given. He just had to keep His face always close, graciously thank Him for the gift he had been shunning.

He put the roses to bed, mulching, trimming, marveling at one brilliant red rose blooming perfectly among dying leaves. Everywhere, nature put on a final hurrah before winter's harsh winds assaulted the property. It was one of his favorite times of the year.

He spoke to his father a few times a week, who had finally come home and left Lydia in the care of trained staff. She was on medication now, sedated to the point of having a long restful night after weeks of fitful sleep, so that was good.

Always, Amos heard the words but heard, too, the deep sorrow and crippling self-blame, handicapped with the weight of immense wrongdoing, which no words would ever assuage.

He went to his church, requested his mother's name be added to the prayer list, listened to a guest speaker teach on accepting others for who they were, and not for whom you thought they should be.

Now he whistled again, sometimes broke out in song, standing in the orchard with the scent of rotting, fallen apples, picking the almost ripe pears Lila loved.

The world seemed brighter, full of promise, as he spent his days pruning, trimming, and mulching, the great expanse of these grounds his domain.

And some day they literally would be his. Really, they were his now, and he would take a day at a time, place his trust in God to show him the way, to allow the Holy Spirit to guide him.

Lila watched from her seat by the window, wearing a pale pink sweater, her white hair like a gentle summer rose, her blue veined hands in her lap. Increasingly frail, she barely tipped the scales at a hundred pounds, her eyes sunken into hollowed cheeks, although they retained the brilliance of blue that shone with the same lively spark.

She watched as Amos used the chainsaw to sever a half-torn limb from the aging sycamore tree, smiled to herself as he lifted the roaring saw as if it were merely a butter knife. That boy was so strong, she thought proudly, chuckling to herself as she bent to lift the mug of honeyed tea to her mouth.

When she looked again, there was Skye Larkin and her dog, Amos shutting off the chainsaw, laying it aside and turning to greet her. Lila grimaced as Skye went in for the embrace, stepped back and faced him, hands on her hips.

She became increasingly agitated as the conversation went on far too long, rang for Della, and asked her to bring the binoculars from the hook on the back porch.

Taking them in trembling fingers, she steadied herself and adjusted the glass, then found Amos, took note of his expression, which seemed open and friendly, then trained the glass on Skye Larkin and grunted loudly.

So, she was at it, what Lila had feared most. Flirtatious, weaving her web of seduction around her Amos. Well, not if she could do anything about it. Setting her jaw, she lowered the binoculars, picked up her phone, and dialed his number, peering through her bifocals with determination.

He answered on the first ring.

"Yes, Lila?"

"I need you here at the house as soon as you can," she answered.

She watched as he lowered his phone, spoke a few more words before backing away, lifting a hand as she turned to leave. Quickly, she hid the binoculars, surprisingly agile for one her age, sat up straight, and clasped her hands primly as he came up past the garage.

When he appeared at the arched doorway of her sitting room, lifted eyebrows as he questioned her call, she pointed to the chair opposite. Joseph's chair, but now the one Amos often occupied.

He sat, waited.

"Amos," she began, "the only thing you needed to come up here for was to get away from her."

Amos widened his eyes, a painful blush spreading across his face.

"You know what she wants, don't you?"

Lila watched his face shrewdly, her bright blue eyes discerning.

He shrugged, his face color deepening.

"She wants this property after I'm gone. She and her parents know you're going to inherit it, and their only hope is marrying her into the estate. I want you to listen carefully, dear boy. She has been married before, and it hasn't worked out. With your conservative values, I don't believe you need to keep company with her at all."

She stopped, her thin shoulders erect.

"I know them as good neighbors, but I also know their deep disappointment of losing this home. I also know they will ruin it—and you—if they get their hands on this place. If you're willing to keep your distance from Skye, plans will continue as before. But if the Larkins worm their way in here through you, we can change matters by one phone call to our trusted attorney."

Amos was speechless. This dear, frail person, more of a mother to him than anyone had ever been, to put on this display of power.

Aggressive, even.

"I . . . well, I hardly know what to say, Lila," he stammered.

"But you do understand the seriousness of the situation."

"I suppose, if you say so."

"The Larkins are nice enough, as neighbors go, but they are also very worldly. Skye wasn't like her parents for a while, but their greed has overtaken her as well, and I could never rest in my grave thinking I had left Joseph down. I trust you will consider my words."

From that moment on, Amos recognized the steel beneath the soft perfumed frailty that was Lila, and he gained a new respect, never having thought his respect could grow larger. She was still the owner of his dream, and had lived to a ripe old age and seen countless foibles of the human race, so who was he to scoff at her authority?

But it proved to be only the beginning.

Raymond Beiler went back to work with an air of true sorrow, his whistling silenced, his mind hundreds of miles away, where Lydia was kept in comfort, in good hands, this he knew. But it didn't make the whole thing less complicated.

Who would be able to crack that iron will?

Oh, she was formidable, she was. A silent adversary he was frightened of. Was any counselor strong enough? And so, his whistles were silenced, his open face remained closed, creating deep scowl lines around his mouth, furrows across his brow. Often, his eyes misted over with emotion.

He disregarded curious glances from coworkers, kept to himself, and spoke very little at lunch hour. He had committed a terrible sin, and the only grace he could seek was hidden from his troubled view.

He came home to an empty house, Lavina often staying at a friend's house or coming home late from market. He liked the taste of Wheaties and corn flakes, he really did, but thought of Lydia's meatloaf, the chicken and rice casseroles, his favorite.

He was halfway through a bowl of corn flakes when he experienced such a deep well of regret, he put his spoon on the table, pushed his bowl aside, and put his face in his hands and wept.

He wept loudly, with rough grating, feral sounds, that were the result of years of pent-up sorrow and disappointment, the cereal gone soggy in the bowl.

But it was not in Raymond's nature to pity himself or blame others, so he asked God for his forgiveness, accepted his paltry lot in life, and kept going, buoyed by occasional evening calls with her counselor.

Contact with her was forbidden, which was a gigantic pill to swallow, but he was told to be patient, it was for the best.

His one ray of sunshine was Matthew Beiler, the young man Lavina had chosen to accept. From Raymond's viewpoint, he was a likable chap with a great sense of humor, and an all-around nice guy.

In his opinion, Lavina was better looking as far as that went, but Matthew wasn't bad. Not bad at all.

He enjoyed having him in the house on the weekends, his heart swelling to watch them walk together, talk as they cooked breakfast. He went to church with Matt seated beside him, Lavina in the back seat, listening as they kept up a lively chatter.

"You are two old ladies at a quilting," she told them.

"Come on, Lavina. Give us a break."

"Here now, Viney," from Raymond.

As is the Amish custom, Raymond was received into church services with empathy. A handshake held longer with kind eyes filled with brotherly love, a word of encouragement—it was like an ambrosia to the soul.

If there was gossip from a few women who preyed ferret-like on hapless souls, Raymond would never know, content to glean the goodness so readily available.

He wiped furtive tears as the ministers asked the congregation to keep Lydia in their prayers, was questioned by well-meaning friends after church dinner had been consumed, could only relate the sparse information the counselors would allow, but drove away with the comforting knowledge of being blessed with a tremendous support system.

He was suffering, was going through a deep dark valley, but God was with him. He pictured a whole flock of sheep, himself among them, the white-robed Jesus with his loving staff leading them on across bright hillsides, beside still waters, and through eerie shadowed valleys.

AND THEN, ON a dull November day, Amos flipped the zero-turn mower, pinned his right leg underneath, and experienced bone-crushing pain. He cried out for any available help, and knew there was none.

It was on the steep slope he always respected, clinging to the left side of the fast-moving machine, experiencing the thrill of mild danger as usual. But this time, it was over in a split second, his world erupting in a volcano of spewing pain. He knew he was pinned, lying on his stomach with no way of lifting himself to heave and tug at the mower.

He smelled oil, could hear the engine sputtering, thought of flames.

He called repeatedly, grimaced and ground his teeth in pain, but still he remained unheard. His phone was nowhere to be seen, a wave of guilt steadily growing. He'd been checking his texts, not a good thing on that slope. He kept calling, hoping.

It was Champ who bounced up on the porch steps, paced and whined, propped himself on the windowsill with his forefeet, put his nose against the window and yelped. Lila took notice, summoned Della and Nancy, and they wisely knew something was out of whack, in Nancy's words.

Pulling on windbreakers, they followed the dog to the slope, heard Amos calling, and ran as much as was possible for their age and substantial size, gasping and calling his name.

"You alright?" Nancy asked, bent over him, breathing like a locomotive.

"Does it look as if I am?" he breathed, squeezing his eyes as waves of pain overtook him.

"Me and Della can't lift this thing," she gasped.

"Call an ambulance. Quick," Della gasped.

Champ whined, licked his face, then settled down beside him as if to stay as long as needed. Nancy unearthed her phone from the deep folds of her housekeeping apron pockets, couldn't remember the address, which Amos supplied in hurting gasps.

Lila was alone, so Della hurried back, out of breath, flapping her hands in distress as she crossed the room, relating the accident in her heavy accent.

Amos was never so grateful, hearing the far-off wail of the ambulance, the blue-clad men lifting the mower, efficient in all their movements. The leg was put in a splint and he was rolled on a stretcher into the back of the ambulance.

The ER in Rochester was overcrowded, an array of the sick and wounded in hallways and waiting areas, harried nurses and doctors with squawking pagers prowling the area.

The wait seemed interminable, but eventually a nurse in green arrived somewhere above his head, said shortly, "Hey bud," and pushed on the wheeled stretcher. He saw the ceiling, fluorescent lights, blue curtains and beige walls. He was turned, noticed a blood pressure cuff on the wall, a small sink and cabinets, before the nurse came into view, saying nothing as she took his vitals.

"Mm. What happened?" she croaked, her voice like falling pebbles.

"Rolled the mower."

"Mm."

He looked at her, a faint recognition afterward. Where had he seen her?

"Doctor'll be in," and she left.

He thought bitterly, nurses like her should be fired. The least she could do was present some semblance of manners. Where had he seen that close-cropped grayish hair?

He waited, and waited longer. A computer on wheels, lights and clicks, with a semi-friendly nurse with long dark hair tied into a low ponytail, her glasses far down on her nose.

His name, address, phone number, driver's license, insurance. He longed for painkillers, anything, but none were offered.

The nurse came back.

"X-rays," was all she said, and he felt himself pushed out and down the hallway again, passing talking people, other nurses, and into the X-ray room, where finally, there was a person with empathy, ready to hold a decent conversation.

And back to his curtained cubicle to wait again, to review the angle of his foot for what seemed like the hundredth time, hoping he would not need surgery to correct it.

He was hungry and thirsty, needed something for pain, but supposed none of that was possible, so he settled himself for the duration.

She glided in soundlessly, and he slanted his eyes on her name tag, wondering if he should complain about her to her supervisor.

He wanted to, in the worst way.

Sarah Yoder.

He remembered the Sarah Yoder of that awful gift exchange from his childhood, but there was no way. Yoder was an Amish name, though.

"You need anything?"

"A drink and some pain meds."

"Sorry."

"What's that supposed to mean?"

"Can't. Doctor needs to check out your X-rays."

She glanced at the white band on his wrist, then looked at him. She hesitated, then walked out.

Amos waited, tried to relax, and dozed off, but the pain kept him awake, so he thought of many different times in his life when he was in pain, only it was not the physical discomfort he experienced now.

She returned, asked if he needed a blanket. He looked at her name tag, pointedly.

"What?" she growled.

"I used to know a Sarah Yoder."

She walked out. He raised his eyebrows. Half an hour later, she was back, crossing her arms and drawing herself up to her full height.

"Who are you?"

"Raymond and Lydia Beiler are my parents. I'm Amos."

She narrowed her eyes, rubbed her nose, turned sideways, opened her mouth and closed it again. She blinked, looked toward the opened curtain as if planning her getaway. But instead of leaving, she said, "Ephraim and Naomi Yoder."

The words seemed to be garbled, as if she half swallowed them with shame.

"You are their Sarah?"

She nodded, her face a mixture of defiance and embarrassment. She was thin, her eyes lined heavily in black, her nose prominent like her family's, but her face was almost pretty. Not beautiful, yet it had a certain magnetism, drawing his eyes to hers repeatedly.

"You left, too?"

"I did."

"Is that all you're going to say?"

"Probably."

The curtains were pushed aside, a tall, stoop-shouldered doctor greeted him affably, and Sarah Yoder disappeared.

He was taken to the third floor, prepped for surgery to repair crushed bones and torn tendons, the words of medical jargon rolling around in his head before he knew nothing, then woke in a recovery room blessedly free of pain, groggy and disoriented.

He called Lavina to arrange a driver to take him home, was rewarded by the sight of her and his father, serious and loving, so glad to know he would be okay.

Crutches, swathes of foam and elastic bandage, but no hard cast because of the swelling. Papers were signed and he was on his way home.

Lavina insisted she was staying. His father agreed wholeheartedly, making the necessary sacrifice when the need arose, the way he'd done his whole married life. Selfless love, family.

Were there ties that could compare?

He slept very little, was nauseated and cranky the following morning, wished Lavina gone with her sweet, optimistic outlook. She cleaned and cooked, clucked like a biddy hen about all the dog hair, and why did he use this ancient sweeper? No one used an Electrolux.

"I don't care what you say, it works," Amos said defensively.

"Alright, no need for testiness here," she said, laughing.

The day was dull as tepid dishwater, too warm and wet for October, bunched clouds lowering above brown fields. All Amos could think of was all the work to finish before the snow arrived.

Lila insisted on hiring a landscaper to finish up, and Amos breathed easier knowing the shrubs and trees would be properly trimmed.

That Saturday afternoon, Matt Beiler arrived, and Amos was properly introduced. They clicked immediately, without a trace of mistrust, shook hands and began to talk, stopping only long enough to include Lavina from time to time.

At one point, Matt said he couldn't see how he flipped the mower on a slope he'd been on a hundred times, and Amos said he was texting and driving, the cardinal sin.

Matt howled with laughter and Lavina joined in.

He felt at home, as if he'd been on a long journey and finally was among two people who genuinely knew him. He felt so at ease, he told them about Sarah Yoder. Lavina shook her head, unable to remember a Sarah, although she did remember the smell of Ephraim Yoder's basement when church was at their house.

"She's so, well, I don't know how to describe her. She doesn't say anything. I was thinking of reporting her, she was so rude. A nurse shouldn't do that, especially when you're in pain. And then I saw her name tag."

"She told you who she was?"

"Yeah. She did."

"I wish I could see her," Lavina mused.

"Let's see if we can find her."

They found a Sarah Yoder online, then a few more, and unexpectedly stumbled on to her picture. Yes, it was her, Amos said. This was the one.

Lavina recognized the facial features, the children her age bearing a resemblance.

"I don't know what it was about that family, but something was just off."

Lavina nodded.

They discussed Anna Riehl, and Amos having to go through the wasteland of a breakup, that parched area no man should ever have to navigate, but often did.

Matt listened with interest, genuinely caring about the long painful journey Amos endured. Was still enduring from time to time.

"Her parents simply have that control, and she thought it necessary above all else to be obedient to them. I just never thought a liberal-thinking family like them would be so opposed to her leaving the Amish," Amos finished.

"Sometimes, they are the ones with the most pride," Matt added.

Amos nodded, his dark brown eyes remembering the pain still.

"She was like a breath of fresh air. So energetic, so kind, confident. I was so sure we were meant for each other."

He shook his head, then asked if anyone heard anything about Cathy. No one had.

"I'm concerned, Lavina. There is a sea of red flags for that relationship, and I'm not trying to be judgmental."

"You are, though. Just a bit," Lavina said softly. "We can give them the benefit of the doubt. Perhaps he will quit drinking and surprise us all with his ability to keep a good job."

"What a marshmallow you are, Lavina," Amos countered, a bit sheepishly. "Sweet and soft."

THE WEEKS WENT by, marching in slow succession, punctuated by trips to the orthopedic surgeon, a hard cast, the ever-present crutches.

He ate too much, out of boredom and inactivity, became soft and irritable, yelled at Champ and wished Nancy would stay at the big house with her endless train of bars and cookies and cupcakes.

Scott and his pastor came to see him, which brightened the endless month of November. They urged him to come back to the gym and church services as soon as he was able.

His father visited, with a sad update on his mother. She had only begun treatment, and she may have to stay for up to a year. His shoulders drooped with the weight of it.

"But does she actually have a diagnosis?" Amos asked, his patience short these days.

His frustration with his mother was like a rash all over his body, laying dormant until he chose to scratch it. He couldn't shake the feeling that this was just her latest stunt, a grand manipulation to keep his dad under her control.

"They're still doing tests, I guess. We'll know more soon."

He said goodbye to his father that night, knowing he could not change his feelings about his mother. The forgiveness would have to come from God; by himself, it was quite simply not doable.

The bills from the hospital began to arrive, a tangle of numbers and totals, what was co-pay and what the insurance picked up, when this amount was due and when that amount. He called the hospital to try to make sense of it. He was told to go to the billing office in a month or so. So after the hard cast was removed, he did what they said, got everything squared away, and walked across the parking lot with a new spring in his step.

Finally, he was free, even if he stepped gingerly and wore an outsized moccasin on the injured foot.

He noticed the blackened bare branches of the trees, the scudding gray clouds blown by the stiff breeze, checked his phone, and walked directly in the path of a low-slung sports car, whose driver put a palm to the horn in the middle of her steering wheel.

Chapter 16

He moved as quickly as possible to escape collision and Sarah Yoder rolled down her window.

"You have a habit of that?" Her voice scratchy, abrasive.

He stopped, shrugged. "Maybe."

She didn't smile or laugh, merely eased away and left him by the side of the parking area, feeling as if a stiff breeze had blown through and left an icy chill. He watched her circle the building, but she did not reappear.

He drove home, celebrated the removal of his cast with a homemade German chocolate layer cake with thick nutty coconut icing between the layers and down the sides, Nancy's specialty. They toasted his health with lifted cups of tea.

Lila wasn't feeling well that evening. She refused cake and had only a few sips of her tea before lying back in her chair and closing her eyes. Amos stayed for the night, settled himself in the guest room, and found Sarah Yoder's profile on his phone.

On a whim, without expecting an answer, he messaged, "Safe at home." He lay awake after that, waiting for the ding signaling an answer. He peered bleary-eyed, saw 10:45, then 11:30, and was drifting off when he heard the signal.

He rose on his elbow, blinked when he saw "Good job." Hmm. He sent a "thanx," and fell asleep.

The following morning, Lila felt better, but was shockingly pale and a bit disoriented, asking for Joseph, saying it was time for his coffee.

Amos and Nancy conferred in the kitchen and decided to take her to her family physician, to be safe. Lila did not want to go but gave her consent after they promised her lunch at the Orchid, her favorite place for minestrone and sponge cake.

She walked in on Amos's arm, the doctor's face showing only a certain professional concern. But after blood tests, the doctor asked her to spend a few days in the hospital for IV transfusion to help the dehydration and stage three renal failure.

"Oh, I don't like to do that, but if it will get me feeling better, I suppose I must."

She smiled her quavery smile, her old blue eyes dulled and not quite focused. Amos and Nancy breathed a sigh, relieved to know she would be under professional care.

He visited the following afternoon, tapped lightly on the door before entering, and found her asleep, her thin chest rising and falling steadily, her breathing soft and barely noticeable. He stood with his bouquet of ferns, baby's breath, and six pink roses, watching her angelic face in repose.

Surely God would welcome her into the legions of angels hovering around his throne, this dear saint who had lived for Christ all her life, loving Joseph so well, a true vessel of love and kindness.

As she slept on, there was a faint rap, the whisper of rubber-soled feet into the hushed room, and he found Sarah Yoder with a fresh IV bag, her face impassive.

"It's you" was her way of greeting.

He felt a five-hundred-pound oaf holding flowers that drooped and smelled like old dandelions. She could have said hello, at least hi. Instead, she was an ice queen, completely unapproachable. Who did she think she was, anyway? He watched her fluid, efficient movements, noticed the long, tapered fingers, the cap of unusual hair—blond, white, and gray all swirled together.

Lila never opened her eyes, just lay there, so weak and thin there was barely a ridge beneath the sheet. He set the flowers on the windowsill and stayed there, leaning against it, his arms crossed on his chest.

Sarah Yoder's back was turned, but he heard, "What's she to you?"

He wanted to say the typical "none of your business" type of thing but instead said, "I work for her."

That must have been sufficient, as she never bothered to answer or comment. She stood for a minute looking down at her before leaving. Amos watched her back, could not imagine this girl being the Sarah Yoder he remembered.

Lila's eyelids flitted, the blue veins wrinkled, and her blue gaze met his.

"Amos. It's nice of you to come for a visit. Did you bring Nancy?" she asked softly.

"She and Della will be in later."

He bent to kiss the soft leathery cheek, then held her hand, smiling down at her. "How are you feeling?" he asked.

"Much stronger. It was the best thing to come in for fluids and rest. You know, Amos darling, I'm going to stop being brave. If you don't mind too terribly much, we're going to situate your bed in the library across the hall. I do believe I would rest easier knowing you're close by. I don't think it will be long. I can feel the angels approaching closer every day. I like to think I can hear the whisper of their wings, don't you think?" she asked, sighing.

He could only nod, his throat choked with emotion.

He looked up to find Sarah Yoder again, her dark-rimmed eyes almost unnaturally large in her small face. She was carrying a yellow pitcher of ice water, replacing the one on her stand.

She looked up and their eyes met. Her eyes were not gray or green, but an unsettling color between brown and yellow. They were hard, unfeeling, challenging him to say something, anything, and if he did, she would throw it to the floor.

He lifted his chin, stared, slowly lifted the corners of his mouth in a half-smile. She looked away, swiftly, and walked out, leaving Amos to wonder about her life from the time she turned sixteen to now.

He drew up a chair by the side of Lila's bed and assured her he would do anything she required.

"We have a spare bed. It will take a few of you to carry it down the stairs. I know it will make extra work, but hopefully by Thanksgiving we'll be settled."

"I'll do it tomorrow, Lila. I can do it by myself."

Lila nodded, drifted off to sleep, somehow seeming too weak, too easily done. She was released the following morning. Amos was told quietly about hospice services again, which he promised to speak to her about, but knew the subject would not be welcome.

CATHY CALLED LATE that evening, his phone jangling his nerves after he was almost asleep. Her voice did nothing to create a more generous mood, but he answered civilly enough.

"Hi, Amos. What's up?" she trilled, obviously delighted with herself and her status in life.

"Nothing much, Cathy. How about you and Sam?"

"Oh, excellent, excellent. Got a furnished apartment and we both have jobs. Florida is loaded with opportunity. Loaded."

"Glad to hear it. What did you find for work?"

"Cleaning hotel rooms. Making money like crazy. Some days it's like forty an hour."

"Good. Glad to hear it. What about Sam?"

He caught the hesitation, but she said he had just started working for a roofer.

"It's been tricky with all the Spanish speakers. He says they're all talking about him behind his back, but he'll get used to it. He was home today with a terrible sunburn on his back."

"Is he working on his drinking problem?"

"That sounds so old school. What an old fuddy-duddy you are, Amos. He just drinks sometimes. Mostly beer."

"Sometimes?"

"Well, yeah. A few here and there. Stop it, Amos. He's nice to me."

"I'm glad."

"How're the others?"

"Well, Mom had a nervous breakdown and went to Michigan for help. They say she needs to stay for up to a year."

"What? You're kidding. How's Dat taking it?"

"You know, doing the best he's capable of, like always."

"You need to pack up and come for a visit."

"Not now. Lila isn't well."

"The old lady?"

"Yes. She was in the hospital."

"She'll probably push off one of these days. Leave all that money to some university. The way rich old ladies do."

When he hung up, he was shaking with restrained anger. Her level of audacity was startling. The sheer volume of selfishness. But who was he to judge? Who was he to measure her with a stingy evaluation? He had hurt his parents many times, still did, so he leaned on the kitchen counter, clasped his hands, and prayed for God to deliver him from the jaws of anger and judgement against Cathy, to keep them both from evil.

They're in your hands, Lord. Keep them in your care.

But he knew he would have a hard time letting go of his worries and concerns. They were, after all, his family, no matter what had occurred in the past, tied by the bonds of blood, a connection that tethered their hearts together always, for better or worse.

In November, Lila was back in the hospital with difficulty breathing. Amos and Nancy stayed by her side. She was taken to the ICU after a few days, when the breathing became more labored. She woke only occasionally, her blue eyes dulled by medication.

Only one person was allowed in her room, yet Amos could not bear the thought of leaving her, so he sat in the waiting area, staring dully through large windows looking out over the parking area, seeing nothing. He felt heavy in his spirit, crushed like a crumpled piece of paper. Who was he to obtain the inheritance she would leave him?

He felt his own inadequacy, the torment of never having done anything right, no matter how he told himself he had left his demons behind.

He needed Lila with her steady faith, the owner of the house and goods, the one who made decisions. How would he manage without her? He had his own set of responsibilities with his parents, Cathy and Sam.

He had to take time to visit his father.

He watched as vehicles came and went, a variety of people walking across the parking lot. Then he spied her with that long, swinging stride, her head held high, sending the message that no one could approach her. He felt as if his crushed spirit was being smoothed, straightened. There were no words, only the comfort of a mystery he could not yet reach, but the assurance God was here beside him, in this hospital room.

Nancy was with Lila till late in the afternoon, so he thought he might as well go see his father, who had the week off, his boss telling him he needed to rest for a while.

Making his way to the elevator, he saw her bending over a chart, her gray-blond hair like a cap, dressed in the blue uniform of every nurse.

He stopped. For a moment, he thought she would ignore him, but she looked up.

"Hey."

"Hello, Sarah. We keep running into each other."

"You mean you keep getting almost run into? You should watch where you're walking."

"That's fair." He laughed, remembering the parking lot incident. She didn't smile, but he noticed her smooth complexion, like tanned porcelain, the way her eyes resembled green cut glass with prisms of brown. Almost yellow. A generous mouth, but definitely no smile. No warmth.

"Lila Smith is in the ICU unit," he offered.

"That's not my job."

"Oh." Then, "I'll see you around, probably."

She nodded.

He walked away, wondering why he'd bothered.

He found his father in the barn, leaning on a gate, watching his flock of turkeys. A moving mass of white feathered creatures with long necks and small heads, beady eyes and no beauty.

"Amos."

"Hi, Dat. How's it going?"

His father lowered his face, shook his head. When he faced Amos, he was trying to keep his emotion in check. "She's not responding well."

"Mom? Did you talk to her?"

"Her counselor called. They're taking her to be evaluated at a facility. I guess medical, which is unusual. They're thinking she may have bipolar disorder or something."

Amos said nothing.

His father continued, "She won't take her medication. They found a whole stash of it somewhere. I don't know how these things work, but she's not well."

His father appeared to have aged dramatically, his eyes sunken in his lined face, his beard peppered with white. He was too thin, his shoulders stooped, his shirt collar wrinkled beneath his worn coat. Amos saw the worn Red Wing shoes, a hole in the toe. His throat seized up.

He remembered his mother's complaints, how fast he went through work shoes, and did he realize how expensive they were? Why did that one toe always wear out? His father would look down to see, as if he should apologize for wearing shoes at all. Yet he knew the amount she spent on Cathy's sneakers, to keep up with her friends.

The old bitterness rose like bile.

His own sneakers, pushed away from the soles by the weight he bore, burst one pair after another. Taken to Walmart, she purchased the cheapest she could find, sucking her teeth about the width of his feet. She had never known anyone with a size ten in sixth grade, she said, shaking her head the way she did when she lost her wallet or she saw a dead cat on the side of the road. An occurrence in her life that was unwanted.

His face red, straining over his large stomach as he pushed his damp feet into the shoes, now enormous, a rowboat. His mother wrinkled her nose, told him his feet smelled and he didn't wash between his toes properly, bringing fresh heat into his face.

To this day, he disliked buying shoes, even thinking of shoes.

"Let's go to the house, Amos. I'll make coffee. Getting downright chilly in the evening."

The house looked in need of a good cleaning. There were bits of mud and gravel strewn across the rug by the door, dust on furniture, and rain-streaked windows. Amos noticed crumbs on the table as he sat. He wondered about Lavina but thought it better to remain quiet—the poor man was visibly struggling.

His dad poured two cups of coffee, pushed the Oreo package in Amos's direction, an underlying tremor in his veined hands.

A space of silence before he collected himself.

"Amos, you are the only person I can confide in."

Amos lifted his eyebrows.

"I have failed your mother. I should have known there was something wrong. But I have never been intelligent enough to pick up on these things, the way she was."

Amos waited.

"She was—I don't know—a bit unstable when we dated and right after we were married. Out of nowhere, she would become terribly angry, throw things—glasses, vases, boots or shoes—then weep for hours. Great heaving sounds that were hard for me to hear. I would try to comfort her, but she never wanted me around at those times. When Cathy was born, she struggled to keep the depression at bay, soldiered on by herself, refused any treatment.

"I tried hard to keep the worst of it from you children, but I know you were victims of some of it."

"You didn't fail her," Amos said softly. "She failed herself."

His father shook his head.

"I wasn't weak when we were married. I knew where I stood, had my two feet on the ground. But over the years, I became a coward, did anything to avoid the sheer volume of anger. I did it for you, for Cathy and Lavina, but perhaps it was the wrong thing. I don't know."

He hung his head miserably, his calloused fingers wrapped around his coffee mug. Amos saw the broken nails, the brown stain on the old mug, his favorite, and wondered if he ever had a moment in which he indulged in pleasure of his own. He loved to go fishing, dreamed of fishing trips on remote lakes and rivers, but would never ask his wife if this was possible.

They'd discussed it at times, the rare moments when his father's face lit up, and he'd talk about fly fishing in Wyoming, catching walleye on Lake Erie, the way Dan and Melvin Beiler did. Stayed at a lodge, went for a week.

Amos looked up to find his father studying his face, as if he held the final answer before self-condemnation was complete.

"No, Dat. You did the best you could. I've told you that. It had to come to this. You know all things work together for good to those who love God, and perhaps what seems hardest of all—Sam and Cathy going to Florida—was an event God allowed to finally make Mom see she needed help."

"*Ach*, Amos, that sounds a bit off the wall."

"It's true, Dat. God's ways are not our ways, and we don't always understand, but to have Mom at a facility where she'll finally get help after all these years is a blessing."

"How can you say that?"

"We . . . our whole family has suffered. You have suffered, and I know I suffered most of my childhood. Why not thank God that something might finally be changing?"

His father shook his head. "I cannot do it. She's suffering, too. I can hardly bear the thought of her out there in Michigan, staying at a place she doesn't like."

Amos nodded, even as the audacity of his thoughts frightened him. *Let her. Let her suffer a while.*

Time after time, he'd carried the weight of being a repulsive human being to her. And his father spoke of *her* suffering.

Caught in the churning rapids of his past, he leaned back in his chair, thrust his feet beneath the table, knowing his father was talking but absorbing nothing. Grimly, he relived the actual feeling of her hands with the scissors, cutting his hair, stepping back with a sound of disgust. His head smelled, his hair was greasy, and he had a layer of dandruff an inch thick. What was wrong with him? When had he washed his hair? Two weeks ago?

A snicker from Cathy.

"I need a different shampoo," he'd mumbled, the heat rising in his face.

He couldn't get rid of the dandruff, sat in church with flakes of white scales falling like snow on his black mutza. He'd wanted the floor to open up and swallow him. It was Lavina who brought him the blue and white bottle of Head and Shoulders, the medicated shampoo a boost to his battered ego. Every day, he stood beneath the stream of hot water, scratching at the miserable flakes, until one day, like a miracle, the problem had cleared.

He felt so much better about himself, walked downstairs, his brown hair thick and lustrous, to find his mother and Cathy, hands over their mouths to keep from laughing.

With the remnants of a snicker, Cathy asked what was wrong with his hair. His mother could not contain herself and laughed outright.

"It's so thick and woolly," she garbled.

He went to the mirror in the laundry room, saw the reflection back at him, small brown eyes, spotted skin like a lizard, and yes, the bushy hair of a buffalo. He turned away, felt the need to remain calm, to grow a thick outer shell around his heart, protecting the onslaught of hurt and despair.

And his father spoke of *her* suffering.

"It's for the best, Dat. Believe me."

The stream of words continued, a torrent rushing from opened gates, the loveliness of her when she was a teenager, the good times, the moments when their love was complete. There were many of them, and for this, he would always tell himself their marriage was good. They had no real problems, so that was something, the way no one in the church knew things were not the way they should be.

Incredulous, Amos listened.

"Look, Dat, I better move along. I'm staying at the big house with Lila, since she was in the hospital for the second time, and Nancy will be appreciative if I don't get back too late."

"Ah, I was hoping you could stay longer."

"Where's Lavina?"

"She's staying at a friend's house."

"I'll try to be back as soon as I can."

"Good. You do that."

Driving home, though, he didn't know how soon he would return. The way his father polished his childhood only worsened the situation. *No, Dat, no. It wasn't like that. It was like walking on a vast, grassy field with buried explosives, and if you stepped on one, serious injury followed, with no one to help the healing of it.*

How would he ever heal completely? He had come so far, but the fact that he was even a little glad his mother was suffering meant his heart was still a mess. He wasn't overjoyed, but had to admit there was satisfaction, a silent refusal of empathy.

He needed a good workout, something to take his mind off his father's denial of reality.

He entered into the brilliant lights of the gym, machines whirring, all manner of bodies running, walking, pumping iron, straining to pull, push, lift, squat. He felt the adrenaline as he changed into gym clothes, wondered what his total lift would be today.

He pushed himself to the limit, then beyond. He finally felt fully recovered from his injury, so he didn't hold back. Perspiration ran down the sides of his face, glossed his shoulders and arms, soaked his socks, and still he kept going, feeling better as the minutes went by.

An hour, fifteen minutes more.

Scott lifted a hand, came over for a resounding high five.

"Man," he said, whistling low, "you just blew it out of the water."

Amos grinned, confidence surging. "Thanks."

"You need to lift at a professional level."

"Someday. But thanks. Thank you, Scott. For everything."

Their eyes met. Both understood.

He felt his throat constricting with emotion, turned away.

She was there. At the desk, her foot tapping impatiently, dressed in jeans and a black puff jacket. It was absolutely her.

"Customer," he told Scott, then followed him to the desk.

He didn't know his own appearance as he stood close to her and said, "Hello, Sarah." She looked over and said nothing for a long moment. He didn't notice the hesitation, or the soft coloring of her face, or the fact she became rattled to the point she needed to do something with her hands and so swung her backpack off her back, lifted the flap, and rustled the belongings inside.

After which, she mumbled "Hi," then asked Scott in her graveled voice what you had to do to get service around here.

Chapter 17

He received an invitation to his father's house for Thanksgiving, Lavina saying she was cooking, and both sets of grandparents were planning on being there. Just the grands, him, Dat, and her, a small get-together, but she'd be so happy if he showed up.

He told himself he wanted to be there, but in truth, he knew it would be awkward. His grandparents were kind, but there was no doubt they grieved him leaving the Amish. And with Cathy in Florida and their mom at a mental facility, there would be an especially dark cloud over the gathering.

Sure enough, the day dawned gray and cold, the clouds bunched in dreary layers, as if determined to make tangible the mood of the day. But Amos tried to be cheerful as he left the gatehouse and walked toward the big house. A brown layer of crisp leaves covered the driveway and the lawn beside it, but he'd let the wind take care of them. He looked up the hill to the big house, content to see Lila's rosebushes circled with staked burlap, her precious plants put to bed for the winter.

She'd told him only yesterday she might not be here to enjoy the peace roses in June, the favorite peach-colored ones rising in profusion over the trellis. He always felt a plunge of his heart when she spoke of dying, both because he truly loved her, and because he didn't want to face the property alone.

He had thoughts of selling it to the Larkins, had actually picked up his phone to place the call, but in the end, lacked the courage.

Skye visited on occasion, which he always enjoyed, but only to a point. He was appreciative of her beauty, especially the tumbling mane of beautiful hair, enjoyed the perfection of her face, but felt only a vague sense of humor as she tried her best to entangle him in the snares she so carefully set. Always, Lila's stern warning played in his mind.

Sometimes he thought of Anna Riehl, but the overwhelming sorrow was eased, like a raging fire burning itself out, leaving ashes, cold and gray. He sifted through them occasionally, but could barely conjure up her face, let alone the vitality her small frame exuded.

He had loved her, with the hope of a future together, but it had not been right, not meant to be. That, or he'd been selfish, unwilling to return to the Amish way of life for her.

He watched the clouds changing and shifting, the raw November wind bending bare branches, leaves skittering across the drive, blowing behind shrubs and into corners. Champ ran from one end of the yard to another, leaped and frolicked like a puppy, his pink tongue lolling as he panted.

He picked up a stick, whistled, and threw, watching as he became a black blur, driven by flailing legs, and came back to him with the stick in his mouth. They played this game the whole way up the drive, until Champ had to wait on the porch while he visited with Lila.

He found her in her chair, dressed in a brown sweater and slacks, reading, her glasses perched on her thin nose, a cup of tea by her chair.

"Good morning, Lila."

She put her book on her lap, open-faced and upside-down, and turned to him with a brighter than usual smile.

"There you are, Amos. Happy Thanksgiving, my dear boy."

She reached out a hand, and he held it in his as he bent to kiss the powder-soft cheek.

"Happy Thanksgiving, Lila."

"Thank you. Nancy tells me we're having the Larkins today. Oh my. I'll find it quite exhausting, I'm afraid, but I can see no way out, as I have improved. I suppose Joseph will just have to wait a while longer up there."

She chuckled softly.

"And I'll be at my parents' house."

"Yes. And that is such a good thing. Give them my best."

"I will. Is there anything you need before I leave?"

"Yes, Amos, there is. I don't know how strong your broken and mended leg is, but the chandelier in the dining room has two missing bulbs. It's dangerous business for Nancy or Della, so I would like for you to take care of it, if you would, please."

"I'll do it now, before I leave."

"You must tell me about your day when you get back."

"I will."

He set up the folding stepladder, replaced the small bulbs, and went to the kitchen to pester Nancy, who was cooking a feast for Lila and the Larkins, her own family waiting for her return for the holiday.

"Hey, darling," he called out.

Nancy made a sound, rolled her eyes, then smiled at him.

"Anything for breakfast?" he asked, lifting lids, checking the oven.

"No. Not today. You'll have a big dinner." She slapped his arm. "Get away from there. No, leave that lid on."

He laughed, made sheep's eyes at her, slipped an arm around her shoulders, saying, "Please?"

"Okay, but only an egg sandwich. That's it."

But she was smiling, pleased to have Amos in the kitchen to tell him about Tom's ongoing recovery, Denise's divorce finalized, and how if she had a windfall of cash, her life would be downright peachy.

He drank orange juice, ate his egg sandwich, and listened, noticing his first thankful thought of the day. This kitchen, the warm friendship he and Nancy had developed over the years.

"See Amos, that's what I like about you. You're one of the few men I know who actually listens. Some girl is really missing out, and I mean it. That little Anna Riehl made a big mistake."

"You think?"

Amos wiped his mouth, got to his feet.

"I do think. I don't know why you don't get a girlfriend. There's a bunch of single girls all over the place, but do you even make an effort? Ever?"

"You might be surprised one of these days."

"Would be a surprise."

Della came banging into the kitchen, dragging the vacuum cleaner, a dustcloth over her arm, her eyebrows drawn down in a dark V.

"Amos Beiler," she barked, in her heavy accent, "you throw those lightbulbs in the laundry room trash bag, they break, and I cut my finger."

"I apologize, Della. Sorry. Is it bad?"

"Bad enough."

"Oh, let it go, Dell. He didn't do it on purpose."

Della confronted Amos, a finger wagging in his face. "Next time, put them in a plastic bag, wrap up good, then throw them out."

"Yes, ma'am. I won't forget."

But she was harmless as a housefly, and he knew she was pleased by his apology. He stopped to say goodbye to Lila, noticed the old blue light of her eyes, and kissed her again, held her hand longer than usual.

"Goodbye, Lila. I'll be back tonight."

"Have a good Thanksgiving. I'll be here when you get back."

He let himself out, collected Champ, and went to the gatehouse to dress for Lavina's dinner.

On the way to his parents' house, he had a sense of well-being, gratitude for small things in his thoughts. For Champ, for Nancy making his egg sandwich, for Lila teaching him about love and acceptance.

He drove along the hills of northern Pennsylvania, passed slow-moving horses and buggies, windows closed against the November gale, lifting a hand in answering waves.

Did he ever want to return to that? It was hard to imagine himself driving a horse, wearing a straw hat and suspenders, but his life might take that turn. Who knew? He didn't need an immediate answer, figured it was like the unraveling of a spool of yarn.

He was greeted kindly enough by his elderly grandparents, seated in the small, bright living room. His grandfather on his mother's side, coming all the way from Lancaster, averted his eyes completely, but the remaining three were cordial enough. His father came in then, drew up a chair, and visiting commenced.

They spoke of the November weather, the weddings they had attended, who was marrying whom, the bumper crop of high-yielding corn, and then Lavina called Amos to help mash potatoes.

He stood in the steam of hot, boiled potatoes, wielded the masher round and round while he kept up a lively chatter with his sister, mostly about Matt, who would not be present, to be respectful to the old folks.

"That wasn't done years ago," she whispered, rolling her eyes.

"All dating was in secret."

"Mom and Dat, too?"

"No, not as much. You done with that?"

"Almost."

Seated around the table, Amos realized how he missed a traditional Amish meal, complete with *roascht*, the delectable stuffing with the turkey cut up in pieces and distributed through bread, celery, onion, butter, and broth. It was a way of stretching meat, a practice going back to the nineteenth century, and was still served at all Amish weddings and many festive occasions. Moist, peppery, and savory, it was delicious served with mashed potatoes and gravy.

Creamed peas, buttered noodles, red beet eggs, coleslaw, pepper slaw, applesauce, dinner rolls, and strawberry jam rounded out the meal. Everyone fell onto loaded plates with a good appetite. Seconds made their rounds, more *roascht* and gravy, a bit of coleslaw to go with it, then dessert.

Mommy Beiler had made the pumpkin pie, high and custardy, quivering with perfection. And there was a carrot cake in three layers, fruit salad, and a golden caramel pudding.

Amos ate with abandon, felt stuffed and loosened his belt, and Lavina glowed in the praise from her grandmothers as she told them she followed her mother's recipes.

Serious faces, then, at mention of their daughter. But the two old women only spoke in hurried, secretive whispers as the dishes were being washed. These things were not spoken of, except in soft tones. When they inquired openly how she was doing, they were answered with "Goot. Sie iss gute" ("Good. She is good.") Heads in large white coverings nodded, knowing this wasn't the whole truth. But what was behind them would be left behind, swept with a deft twist of a Scriptural broom.

To place a hand on the plow and look back was not fit for the Kingdom of God, so this they would not do. Lydia was finally getting some help, so they would leave well enough alone.

Although they didn't hesitate to go about their grandmotherly duty of reprimanding Amos.

"Amos, it's high time you let go of your worldly things and come back to the Amish where you belong."

"You'll soon be thirty. Amos, it is not good that man should be alone. You know that. You need to come back, find a nice Amish girl, and settle down. What if Jesus came back in the clouds and you were driving your truck?"

"It would be too late," from the other grandmother, sighing with the heaviness of his lost soul.

"But I have accepted Him in my life. I am a believer." He knew he could not tell them Jesus had "saved" him, as the Amish preferred another phrase. "I have a living hope in my soul."

"But your truck and English clothes . . ." one lamented.

"You watch television. It's the devil's device," the other warned.

"These things don't bother me. I am not Amish, so I'm not disobeying my church. They are only material things that will pass away."

"Oh now, you watch it, Amos. That's a mouthful."

This was spoken with a righteous sniff and a crocheted handkerchief to her nose. In her opinion, Amos needed to be snatched off the broad way and plopped back on the narrow road of self-denial.

But they rested better after their duty had been performed, adjusted the footrests of the nice couch, pulled a warm throw across their laps, and told each other where there was life, there was hope, where Amos was concerned. Their stomachs filled to capacity with the buttery *roascht,* they both yawned, sunk their chins on their chests, and nodded off, tilting sideways toward each other.

Amos thought wistfully of the football game at home, then went to find Lavina, who was putting dishes in the cabinets.

"Anything left?" he asked.

She smiled at him. "I'll fix you some leftovers."

"I'm not going yet. I ran the gauntlet with my *mommies* (grandmothers), now it'll be the *doddies* (grandfathers) raking my wayward soul in front of the judgment seat."

"*Ach*, let them, Amos. They're old, still see things in black and white. They're doing what they believe is right."

"I wish, though, they'd understand."

Lavina shook her head. "They never will, and they don't have to. What does the Bible say about eating only herbs? Some do. Others eat meat. You know what it means."

He nodded. "Tell me about Mom."

Lavina shook her head, her eyes filling with a bright wash of tears. "She may have to be institutionalized. Imagine. They might . . . well, they're talking of shock treatments."

"Why that?"

Lavina shrugged, "Past trauma? Who knows? But it's terrible hard on Dat."

"What is it exactly?"

"Look it up. It'll tell you."

She started to say something, hesitated, and stopped.

"What?" Amos asked.

"Nothing. Just ready to suggest something stupid. Let's go sit."

Raymond came through the kitchen after them, followed by both grandfathers, and they all settled on comfortable chairs, sharing memories of a simpler time, back when the Amish were real Amish and shucked wheat, put up hay without a baler, roasted their own corn for cornmeal, milk from the cows went in cans, and a man could pay off a farm like that. Even purchase two more.

"Yes," quipped the sleepy *mommies*, freshly wakened from a wonderful nap, bright-eyed and ready to voice opinions. "Yes indeed. We didn't live the way they do now. Pancakes and bacon for breakfast. We shelled corn, dried it, ground it, and cooked it with water and salt. Fried mush for pennies. Washed diapers and patched our clothes. Patched over patches. We were lucky to have two Sunday dresses; now they have twenty."

"More than that," shouted Mommy King.

"Quiet down," Doddy rumbled.

"Remember when buying an ice cream was a major purchase? No one had money in those days. Eli's Check's Abner, the other side of Bird-in-Hand along *da alt* 340, went to Zimmerman's on a hot day in summer and was short three pennies, so he took off three pants buttons and added them to the stash."

"Did he get away with it?" Raymond asked, then roared with laughter when there was a resounding no, and the fact poor Abner went home with no ice cream cone and three missing pants buttons.

The visit was an elixir for Raymond's weary heart and mind, and when his parents' driver showed at the front drive, he appeared a younger man.

Hands were gripped solemnly, promises of prayers offered, kind invitations for Amos to come back, praise for Lavina's cooking, and then they were down to the large van, a small stool placed carefully for the *mommies* to step up on the running board. And away they went, leaving Raymond with his two children, his eyes still shining with remembered words of encouragement.

Thankful for parents. Thankful for children.

Thankful for health and strength to work.

"Pie!" he shouted. "We shall have pie!"

They cut wide triangles, heated the coffee, Amos made tea.

Had anyone heard from Cathy? Amos winced, but went ahead and related the phone conversation.

Lavina gripped her cup in both hands, shaking her head. "I can almost guarantee no good will come of this. Sam is likely on vacation with Cathy's money. It's maddening that she remains so blind."

Hopeful as always, Raymond wondered if it was that bad, and Amos didn't say much more, knowing his father had enough to worry about.

The overcast day turned into night early, and for the first time ever, Amos was reluctant to leave.

Upon arriving home, he let Champ out, changed, and went to the big house to sit with Nancy and Lila a while before going to bed in the guest room across the hall. He heard Nancy's car start, heard her drive slowly away, then turned on his side, arranged the pillow, and prepared for a long night's rest.

But sleep eluded him. The old house snapped and cracked around him. The wind scraped branches against the window. Far away, a dog howled, then another. He flipped on his back, thought of the grandmothers. Should he return? Marry a readily available Amish girl? But this was his life. This was who he was. He belonged here with Lila. He sincerely felt this was the path chosen for him. He could not see clearly, not yet, didn't profess to understand all the pieces of his life, but he was at peace.

He was meant to be here, meant to keep his dream alive, no matter how hard Satan tried to take it from him. He was almost through his classes, the panic attacks had disappeared.

Since Anna, he'd decided he didn't need a partner. He would take his time, wait on the Lord until he could fly, like the Bible verse about the eagle he loved so much. Yes, he would do that, wait upon the Lord, he thought, and it seemed as if the whole house was filled with hope, soft and light and cozy, a place of trust and rest.

His bell rang.

Lila. Throwing back the covers, he padded across the hallway.

"Amos!"

He heard the desperation.

"I can't breathe," she whispered.

He pressed the needed numbers, went to her, and lifted her by sliding an arm along the back of her pillow, elevating her heart. So light. She was barely more than the weight of a feather.

"Try to relax, Lila. I have you. Just lie back."

But the breathing rasped as she labored, working hard to ease one breath out and another in.

"You called?"

"I did, Lila. I think they'll be here soon."

She nodded, closed her eyes, the thin blue-veined hands plucking at the hem of her blanket.

"I'm just trouble, is what I am."

"Don't say that, Lila."

The distant sound of wailing sirens, lights across the ceiling, washing across the walls, men and women in blue, and then Lila was whisked away into the waiting hands of trained attendees.

Amos sat in the emergency room cubicle, the green curtains drawn as Lila breathed steadily now, lifesaving oxygen pouring through prongs in her nose, a saline solution through her veins.

He watched for her, hoped he'd see her, but every intrusion through the curtains was someone else.

"Was she on hospice?"

"Not yet."

Questions, answers, a repeat of two times prior.

She had to be admitted, tests performed on her heart and kidneys. He accompanied her to the third floor, watched for Sarah Yoder, but she didn't appear.

When Lila slept, he decided to stay, positioned himself on the vinyl recliner and dozed fitfully. He awoke to find his sweatpants pushed up, one sock half off his foot, and a horrible crick in his neck. His head felt stuffed with cotton, his mouth was dry, like cracked, parched earth, and his teeth felt positively hairy.

He looked up after he ran his fingers through his hair, and there she was, tall and thin, the big, unsettling eyes mocking him.

"You here again?"

"Afraid so."

She sniffed, turned away. "You look like crap."

"Thanks. Hey, is it possible to acquire a toothbrush?"

"Yeah."

She adjusted, smoothed, read numbers, then left. She wore the green cotton trousers and tunic, loose and wrinkled. Crocs on her feet. He watched every move, the plane of her cheek, the curve of her prominent nose. He wanted to know her story, wanted to hear the words of why she was here, how she had survived the journey.

She stood in the doorway, held up a toothbrush in a plastic wrapper. He got to his feet and made his way around the bed.

Held out his hand. She deposited it, met his eyes, his soft and brown, holding warmth, hers cold, hard, dark with enlarged pupils.

She lifted her chin. Her eyes slid away.

"Thanks."

She turned. He called after her. "Do you want to grab a coffee when you have a break?"

She stopped without turning, shook her head no, and walked away.

He shrugged, went back to Lila, stroked her cheek with the back of his hand, but she slept on. He loved her with all the love he kept from his own mother, and at a time like this, it was an endless well, a fountain bubbling.

What was that about love begetting love? It seemed fitting. It seemed pure, from the source all love was first formed, and he was only a speck to receive and give a drop of it.

He patted her hand, then made his way down the hall to the elevator, following signs to a small cafeteria.

He ordered a coffee, a bacon, egg, and cheese muffin, considered a coconut doughnut before deciding against it. He grabbed a paper, added it to his tab, and sat, reading and drinking piping hot coffee.

He felt a presence, looked up to find her, arms crossed, defiant.

"Hey."

He was clearly pleased.

She stood, saying nothing.

"Sit," he said, smiling.

"No room."

"Sure there is."

She sat tentatively, perched on the edge of the seat, as if she was prepared to take flight at a moment's notice.

Chapter 18

He couldn't believe she'd changed her mind but knew instinctively it would be better to let it go, stay quiet, calm, slow, the way his father had taught him to get a calf to drink.

"You want a coffee?"

"I'll get it."

She slid out of the booth, as fast and liquid as water, and he folded the paper, creased it with his palm, opened the wrapper of his sandwich. She returned. Black coffee, nothing to eat.

He asked if she wanted half of his sandwich, she said no. Not "no thanks," just "no."

He took a bit, chewed, swallowed coffee, looked at her. She looked back, frankly, curiously.

"Sarah," he said.

She lowered her eyes. Loads of mascara and black eyeliner.

"I was hoping you'd be working."

She said nothing. He decided to dive right in.

"I'm curious, if you are the Sarah I remember, how you got here."

She kind of snorted. "It was hard. Really hard."

"I would love to hear it."

She bit her lower lip, pleated a napkin, twisted a bracelet on her arm. When she let go of the bracelet, she pulled on a dangling earring, then rubbed an eyebrow. Finally, as if coming to a decision, she shook her head.

"Not now."

"OK. Another time?"

She shrugged.

He pressed on. "Are you seeing anyone?"

"No."

"I need a ride home. When is your shift over?"

"Eleven."

"Do you mind?"

Suspicious.

"Where do you live?"

He told her, and her brow wrinkled as she shook her head.

"Never heard of it."

But she did take him home, in the low, purring sports car, her hand lightly on the wheel, remarkably thin against the seat. She seemed ill at ease, kept her eyes on the road, followed the GPS on her phone as he tried to keep a conversation alive, making small talk, asking too many questions.

But he did find out where she lived and asked if he could drive over some day. She shook her head, said he probably didn't want to do that.

When they drove up to the gatehouse, she said nothing at first, just sat waiting for him to leave. Reluctantly, he turned to look at her. She stared straight ahead, her eyes never leaving the big yellow brick house, the wide black shuttered windows, and the imposing front door.

"The old lady live there?" she croaked, then cleared her throat.

"Yes, she does."

She raised one eyebrow.

When there was silence, he blurted out, "Sarah, look. I would like to know you better. Can't we, like, get together for dinner or something?"

She shook her head. "You don't want to know me."

"Why do you say that?"

"Believe me, you don't."

"But we come from the same background, I remember your parents."

"You don't know anything about me, okay? Drop it."

"I'm not going to. When I sit here in the car, I feel this is where God is leading me. Why would we keep running into each other? Sarah, come on, give me a chance, just to hear why you left."

She lifted one side of her upper lip in a sneer, a derogatory move angering him.

"God. Really? Who is God?"

"Stop, Sarah. You know who He is."

"No, I don't."

Amos sighed, lifted the handle on the door.

He realized he needed to restrain himself from saying more, so he said he'd likely run into her tomorrow. She nodded. He thanked her, offered some money for gas, but she shook her head. He closed the door and walked away without looking back.

Champ punished him for staying away so long by barely acknowledging his presence, brushing past him to get outside. He trailed a hand across his back, but his thoughts were not with the dog, but on the mysterious Sarah, the shell of herself, what was left of her. How had she lost all the weight? Why was she so cold? He thought of a parade of drugs, pills, addictive substances causing a person to become thin, rotting teeth, pocked and riffled skin, strange eyes. He decided no, she displayed none of that. She was closed, sealed away as securely as a locked container, a safe with a combination lock only she knew how to open.

He let Champ back in, then searched the refrigerator for something to eat, thinking of her as he made a sandwich. Her parents, Ephraim and Naomi Yoder. He remembered there'd been some gossip about Ephraim, but nothing confirmed. He was a bit narrow-minded at school meetings. He remembered this, his father bringing up the subject at the supper table, how Ephraim Yoder thought it would be best to separate the girls and boys in singing class, the way they stood too close. Things like that.

Sarah had been heavy, a full-figured girl, self-conscious but talkative, even a bit noisy, in an odd way, as if she needed to be seen and heard, but had no idea how to acquire the attention she sought.

Ill-fitting clothes, her hair never done the way of the popular girls, she was accepted only by the kindhearted ones, the girls who were taught to include everyone, no matter their appearance.

He had fared worse than she, openly mocked and belittled, cast out by a devilish unkindness. A freak. He was mottled by acne, puffy skin, obese, shuffling through his weekends with his eyes on his shoes, his shoulders hunched as he tried to appear smaller.

His past was often too painful to consider, and these days he often felt it was not worth looking back. He had his hand on the plow handle now, as the Bible verse taught him, and he would never find happiness till he quit turning back.

He carried scars, but was it wrong picking them open time after time? He had needed to talk about these things, had talked about them with counselors, but ultimately, the decision to forgive was his.

His mother, far way in Michigan, undergoing treatment for who knew what? Who, really, could understand her motives, the dislike of her only son? How long was he going to hang on to that runaway horse, ending only in disaster, that renewed sense of vindication?

He hoped he'd see Sarah again tomorrow. He had no intention of giving up on her. She fascinated him in a different way than Anna Riehl or Skye Larkin or any other girl ever had. She wasn't beautiful like Skye, wasn't perfectly cute and delightfully confident like Anna, but an unnamed emotion assaulted him every time he was with her.

He fully planned on peeling away the hard shell in which she existed.

The following morning, he awoke with a renewed sense of purpose. The day rose bright with a cold November sun, the browned grass ruffled by a fickle wind puffing in different directions, blowing brittle leaves under any crevice available. He stood on the porch, inhaled deeply, raised his heavy arms to the sky, and was immediately awash in thankfulness.

Gratitude was an emotion, but the source of it was the Holy Spirit within, so he whispered for guidance, for the way he should take. For

Lila, for his mother, for Matt and Lavina, and a special prayer for Sam and Cathy. For all his loved ones, the ones he had caused pain when he left the church, a circumstance he could never completely put behind him.

He went to the big house to share his breakfast with Nancy, who always pretended to be too busy to sit with him but held that special smile in place as she set down his mug of coffee.

"How is she, Amos?"

"She sleeps most of the time. She's on oxygen and an IV."

"You'll let me know in plenty of time, will you?" Nancy asked, her mouth trembling slightly.

"Absolutely, Nancy. I know she's like your mother, same as mine."

Nancy nodded and Amos recognized the absence of speech as a sign of emotion. Moments passed before she told him Skye was looking for him yesterday, in the morning. She gave him that shot of silent warning, and he ducked his head, grinning.

"You know she's gorgeous," he said.

"Of that I am aware. She also wants this place. She and those parents of hers."

Amos laughed, peeled a tangerine, and popped half into his mouth, then the other. He chewed, nodded, and asked if she'd work for them if they bought this place, which brought on a wave of denial, ending in a rebel yell.

Still laughing, he got off his barstool, told her he'd call after he got to the hospital.

He found Lila awake, sitting up, her breakfast on a tray, dwarfing her thin form. She smiled, waved, and said a resounding good morning.

As he bent to kiss her cheek, she rolled her eyes and said he was looking sharp in that leather jacket, now wasn't he?

"You're feeling stronger?"

"Oh, probably for an hour or so, then it's all downhill after that."

He helped her spread the napkin over her lap, spooned brown sugar into her oatmeal, and buttered her toast. She ate a few bites, sipped her juice, but laid down the spoon and shrugged her shoulders, saying she'd had enough.

He was sent out by a small, thin woman with the bulging eyes of a chihuahua, saying it was time for her bath and to give them thirty minutes. So he rode the elevator to the cafeteria and read the paper, observed people, and kept an eye out for Sarah Yoder, who occupied a large part of his mind.

He considered a bagel, but chose iced coffee and a banana muffin, both too sweet, then ate a package of cheese crackers, thought of the calories, and regretted his choices.

He took the stairs to the third floor, easily, and found his way back to her room. He was elated to find Sarah bending over Lila with a needle, drawing blood from a fingertip. Lila's eyes were closed, a smile on her lips. A pang of grief, or something like it, made him aware of the shortened time he would have her with him.

Sarah straightened, turned her back to the apparatus on wheels she had brought into the room, adjusted, typed, then turned to him.

For the first time, her eyes were not cold. There was warmth and a subtle welcome.

He had taken extra time to dress, to brush his teeth and comb his hair, choosing colored shirts and replacing them, finding just the right pants and shoes. He could not go wrong with the brown leather jacket, and as a final touch, he'd pumped the small glass vial of men's cologne.

"How are you?" he asked, already knowing the idiotic grin was on his face.

She nodded, then a smile tugged at the corners of her mouth. She stayed, and the smile widened, reached her eyes, and he kept his on the soft light in hers. What passed between them was a beginning, a tentative step forward, like a bare toe extended in a lake to test the water, but it was there.

He felt his own masculinity, his own ability to be attractive, and he stepped forward, a hand touching her shoulder lightly as he said softly, "Good to see you, Sarah."

She caught her lower lip in her teeth, her eyes falling away, then turned and wheeled the cart past him and out the door.

None of this escaped Lila, who watched Amos with bright, birdlike eyes, her thin face wreathed in smiles.

"She is special, that one. She talks to me. Did you know she's from the Amish people, just like you? She went to college on a scholarship and worked two jobs to make her own way. An amazing feat, don't you think?"

He said it was, absolutely, and she watched his face, a knowing look in the kindly blue eyes. He told her he'd known her family when they were younger, and that it was nice to run into her here.

He read passages from the tattered Bible she'd brought, while she laid back and closed her eyes, her lips moving with his words. They talked about the big house, the maintenance and cost of the real estate taxes, but she seemed to wither like a plucked rose and fell into a deep sleep, her soft snores rising and falling with the humming of the monitors.

He saw, watching the dear old face, the lines smoothed in sleep, and thought about life and death and the reason anyone was born.

He wondered, then, if his mother was glad to know she had a son when he was born, if she looked on his new face and felt affection. Any kind of emotion. Had she wanted another girl like Cathy, with doll-like features and wisps of blond hair? Or did she turn away from the sight of his oversized, bloated face? Once, he'd heard her tell a friend, "It was a jolt, I can tell you. After Cathy."

Those were her words, followed by a raucous laughter, the friend joining in. "A jolt." She had been shocked.

"Well," the friend had gone on, "boys are often not as adorable at birth, but they're still cute. All babies are cute."

Amos had slunk away, taking his plastic bucket of Matchbox cars out under the tree and running them over the exposed roots, wrecking them, one by one, gritting his teeth with the need to destroy.

The friend was a Mennonite woman with wavy hair stacked on top of her head, her small, netted covering on the back. Large flowers spiraled over her dress and her sneakers were pure white. He often wondered how she kept her shoes so white. Her name was Louella Bricker, and she loved "antiquing," going to antique shops and thrift stores with his mother, who brought home odd objects to decorate and redecorate the house.

They went to Olive Garden sometimes, which he imagined to be like the Mount of Olives in the Bible. He pictured restaurant tables beneath olive trees. Cathy hooted and yelled when he told her, and he ran off and hid in the hedges by the henhouse.

Lavina took the time to explain restaurants to him in later years, but somehow, Cathy's wild laughter stayed with him, and he cringed when he rode past an Olive Garden even now. That was the sort of thing he needed to work on, the counselor said, but sometimes, it felt impossible.

"Face your adversity. Take it on," he'd say.

He still harbored his dream, coddled and protected it. He was planning a website, found what would be required at the big house. But all in God's time. He would wait, then he would shoulder his purpose in life and find the reason he was born.

Another thing he'd wondered about was only three children. Why had his parents had three, when most Amish families had two or three times that amount? He heard it from his father one day, when he'd asked why he had no brother, and was given the reason in his faltering voice.

His mother suffered with depression after each baby to the point her milk dried up and they were bottle fed, often by himself at night, while she wept inconsolably in her bed. He knew long nights with crying babies, he'd said, but she couldn't help it, she had weak nerves.

He learned how to mix powdered formula, how to get those strangled burps up, how to arrange a diaper over his shoulder to catch the reflux, how to make his own breakfast and survive a day at work on a few hours of sleep.

This was all said in a lighthearted, offhand way, as if he'd actually been delighted to have the opportunity to care for each one in succession. It made Amos feel loved, warm circles created in his chest, and he looked up at his father adoringly, said he probably didn't cry as much as the girls.

"No, if I remember right, you were a good baby. You slept five hours at a time," he said, smiling down at him.

And Amos was proud of having done something right and walked a bit taller.

Sarah came back later, took Lila's vitals, brought apple juice and graham crackers, and ignored him completely. She erased her name on the whiteboard and wrote another name. She was on her way out the door when he caught up to her, saying, "Wait."

She did, but exuded reluctance like a fine sheen of perspiration.

"Would you want to do dinner some evening?"

"I don't do dating," she said, looking at the plastic black-and-white clock on the wall.

"It wouldn't be a date. Just dinner. A chance to talk. We do have some things in common."

"What?"

"You know, growing up Amish."

"I don't want to talk about that. Look, you're wasting your time."

"No, I'm not. Maybe we could just go for a drive instead of dinner."

Finally, she looked at him, her eyes without warmth, hooded.

"Not if you're going to talk about being Amish. No."

"Okay. I won't."

She tried to push past him, but he stopped her.

"Saturday afternoon, around four."

"I'll let you know."

He watched her walk away, sighed, and lowered his shoulders in defeat. His task seemed monumental and only for a moment, he considered letting her go. He might do himself a favor, actually.

That evening, a rapping on his door produced Skye Larkin, windblown, her well-cut coat collar pushed into the heavy mane of hair.

His stomach lurched.

"Hey there, big boy." She smiled up at him, knowing well the effect she had.

"Hello, Skye."

"Can I come in?" she asked, holding her head to one side, enough charm to weaken his knees.

She sensed his reluctance, but pushed past him, greeted Champ with exuberance, praising him for his fine taste in dogs. She spoke of the weather, Lila's health, Christmas coming, and said she was there to invite him to their annual Christmas party. Her parents missed him so much.

She finished with, "Aren't you going to ask me to sit down?"

"No, probably not," he said truthfully. "I was on my way out, actually."

"That's too bad. But you'll come to the Christmas thing?" She placed a hand on his chest, and said, "Please? For me?"

"I'll text you."

"Amos, why do you avoid me? Why are you never home?"

"I don't avoid anyone intentionally, Skye. Lila has been to the hospital twice, and it's been hard, seeing her fade away. My own mother isn't well—she's in rehabilitation in Michigan—my sister Cathy eloped to Florida with someone who seems to be unstable. It's been a lot."

"Oh, you poor guy. That is a lot. Certainly. Maybe if we got together, I could make it better for you."

She stepped closer and for one breathless moment he lost his resolve. He felt her nearness, the face so close to his, and knew he was only human, a man given to weakness.

He realized the sweetness of her before he thought of Joseph, the story of the temptress in the Old Testament. He placed both hands firmly on her forearms and propelled her away, his heart still pounding.

"No, Skye. You are a beautiful person, but how can I give in to you and go against God?"

He realized his voice was shaking, his mouth dry.

"Well, so you are Amish, after all?" she said, in a mocking tone.

Amos shrugged, felt clumsy, speechless.

She walked to the door, her head held high, swung around with accusing eyes, and told him she'd see him at the party.

Amos nodded, smiling to make her feel better, hating the hurt he caused her, unwilling to be an object of her scorn. He felt weak, miserable, and cruel.

She drove away, slammed on the brakes at the end of the drive, and roared down the road in a blur of headlights and red taillights.

So, this was the only courage he could muster, this weak milk pudding he substituted for a backbone. The usual self-loathing began, starting with Sarah's refusal, or near refusal, the inability to keep Anna Riehl, and who, really, did he think he was?

His phone began the customary tune. His father.

"Hey, Dat."

"Hi, Amos. Hey, I just received a message from Michigan. I'm supposed to go out there and can't really see my way through. It's going to cost a couple thousand with a driver if I go alone. I know some people would look down on me if I rode with you, but could you take me? I won't stay—it's just to have a session with the counselors."

Amos was caught between two obligations, but quickly told his father about Lila, then said he'd talk to her doctor in the morning. If he thought it was okay, he'd go.

"I'll pay for the gas, Amos."

"*Ach*, Dat." He said the Amish expression with a smile in his voice.

"You'll let me know tomorrow?"

"Yes. If at all possible. When's your appointment again?"

"Monday. We'd have to leave Sunday night, drive most of the night. Can you even do that?"

"For you, Dat, sure."

HE HAD A restless night, his dreams chaotic and unreasonable, plus Champ made a mess on the floor after too many snacks. Back at the hospital, Amos was sleepy, irritable, and not in the mood to tangle with the middle-aged nurse on duty. Skye's visit had twisted his sense of well-being, leaving him dangling like an empty noose, ominous.

The doctor breezed into the room, his florid face set off by an unkempt thatch of white hair, and spoke reassuringly about letting her go home as soon as her appetite and blood pressure were better.

Lila spoke firmly, her quivering voice willed into a semblance of control, and told him the sooner the better, her blue eyes shining. He patted her hand and said this young man could take her for a walk, how would she like that? He'd find a nurse to assist them.

Amos spoke with him in the hallway and was assured a few days away would be fine, but she would need round-the-clock supervision by a trained health care specialist. Yes, he said, he would see to that.

It was Sarah who helped her out of bed and to the walker, gently guiding her out of the room, Amos on the opposite side. Lila's thatch of uncombed hair pulled at his heart, the white scalp showing through the matted clumps. So vulnerable, and he knew she would be horrified; her white hair had always been impeccably set and coiffed.

She was doing great, her feet shuffling along, a smile on her face, greeting nurses, but Sarah kept one hand on the walker and another on her back. Amos realized the seriousness of this fragile lady and put thoughts of Sarah and her answer behind him, following Lila back to her room and safely into bed, then watching as Sarah tucked her in like a child.

She straightened, adjusted the IV pole, then turned to Amos and met his eyes. Taken aback, he merely raised his eyebrows in question.

"Does your offer stand?" she ground out.

"Of course."

"Okay. Here's my address. Four, then."

He could barely think to put it in his phone. He looked up to thank her but she had disappeared.

The remainder of the day was held in the light of a rosy glow, as if everything was liquified in pink lemonade, complete with prisms of sunshine, peppermint pinwheels, and bright red lollipops, like Cathy's childhood Candy Land game. He felt himself on the first block, and he'd move forward one step at a time, navigating the twisting path, always looking forward to the next card he picked up.

Who knew? Anything could happen.

CHAPTER 19

SHE LIVED ABOVE AN AUTO PARTS STORE, A STEEL STAIRCASE ON THE north side, the corrugated steel roof above it speckled with rust and pockmarked with holes, as if someone shot randomly at this unlikely target.

It was in a small town called Gainesburg, one town south of Rochester, on Bing Street, close to Route 433. The shoddy staircase led to the parking lot of the auto parts store, with a knobby cherry tree growing out of a patch of dirt and brown grass.

The blue-and-white NAPA sign swung on rusted hinges, the large windows smudged and half covered in broken plastic mini blinds. A few cars were parked in front, with children in bright puff jackets playing in the back.

There were yellow lights in the upstairs windows, but he decided to wait. She might not want him in her apartment at all. The wind rocked the truck, flapped at the sign, sent a small cardboard box across the macadam. A heavyset man in camouflage came out of the store, stopped to light a cigarette, then lifted the trunk lid of his car, heaving a bag.

She appeared, then, at the passenger side, dressed in a gray wool coat and jeans, sliding onto the seat in a lithe movement, fluid and unhurried.

He looked at her, noticed the cap of gray striped hair, the heavy eyeliner and porcelain skin. She smiled, but it was a tight, cautious smile. He smiled back, but genuinely, his brown eyes warm.

"Hi," he said quietly.

"Hi," she answered, just as quietly.

"Tell me where you'd like to go."

"Just drive. We'll figure it out."

"Sounds good."

They moved off, turned left, and followed Route 433. She crossed her legs, sat back, her hands clenched so tightly her knuckles were white.

There was no conversation, only the gray November twilight, with black mountains like ribbon ahead of them.

"There's this place, a sanctuary for butterflies, like a greenhouse, about twenty miles along this highway," she said, so soft and low he couldn't grasp the whole sentence.

"Just tell me when we get close."

She said nothing, so he kept his eyes on the road. Five miles, then ten. He was not uncomfortable, with the silence stretching between them, but still he was happy when she cleared her throat and asked if he'd ever heard of this place.

He admitted he didn't know of it, but he'd be glad to go.

"I go all the time."

There it was. Bird and Butterfly. Quite large, impressive, a dome rising above a brick façade with glass walls on steel grids stretching beyond. She was out of the truck before he could open the door for her. Tall, formidable, that unsettling helmet of gray hair, the long steps and certain strength in her walk. All this silence.

He missed Anna's trilling chatter, the soft roundness of her, the happy normalcy of their relaxing times together. Anna had been so restful, so cozy and easy, and he was accosted by a sense of loss, akin to sorrow.

He paid at the desk, then held the large double glass doors and allowed her to pass. A variety of people were coming or going as they passed through another set of doors and were enveloped in warm, wet, tropical air, an array of green date palms, dwarf trees, and an amazing variety of plants growing in verdant profusion. He became aware of brilliant moving objects, hopping and flitting, moving among branches and flowery shrubs.

Birds twittered, whistled, and warbled, while the silent butterflies hovered above flowers so large and beautiful they appeared otherworldly. He was struck silent.

He became aware of a hand on his sleeve, the other hand pointed to the glass dome.

He saw the brilliant colors of the parrots, the beauty of tiny yellow canaries like a constellation, and was in awe. He had no words, had never imagined a place such as this. She kept her hand on his arm, searched his face, and said quietly, "I knew you wouldn't say anything."

He took his eyes away from the birds, the lights on trees and flowers. She was watching him intently, and he still could not find his voice. She stepped closer. He felt the slim nearness, felt the connection between them. He looked down at her upturned face, which was not that far below his own, and smiled.

"It's magical. Like Heaven," he managed.

She nodded. "I found healing here."

He wanted to ask what she was healing from but decided against it. They walked slowly, then sat on stone benches, amazed to find bright butterflies within arm's reach, their wings moving up and down as they fed on nectar.

It was unreal, the brilliance of plumage, the gossamer majesty of delicate wings, fountains splashing among waxen leaves with spiked white blooms.

"I could come here every single day without tiring of it," he said softly.

"I'm glad you like it. I knew you kept the lawn and gardens at Lila's estate."

"It's nothing like this."

Sarah nodded. She remained quiet, then, and he did not speak at all, except to make an announcement when yet another specimen flew into view.

"How did you find this place?" he asked, shrugging off his coat, laying it across his legs.

"They had a fundraiser. Flyers plastered all over the town. So I drove over one afternoon and kept on coming back."

"I can see why."

"It sort of takes you away from stuff, you know? Stuff you need to deal with."

"Yeah, I'm a real winner in that category."

She looked at him sharply. "What is that supposed to mean?"

He sighed, waved a hand to dismiss her.

"I promised not to talk about being Amish."

"For me. You can tell your story."

"Not here. It's almost disrespectful to the birds and butterflies, don't you think?" She agreed, and they kept walking, marveling at the brilliant display. Then she did an unexpected thing, a gesture he would never forget. By a pool of clear water, she bent to pick a sprig of lily-of-the-valley and tucked it into the buttonhole of his jacket, keeping her hand there longer than necessary. He looked down, then he looked at her, asked why she did that. She said she'd felt like it.

Afterward, they stopped at a small Tastee-Freez, but it was closed for the season, in spite of the blinking neon lights. She shrugged, said there was an Arby's ahead.

That was where they began to talk. They sat for three hours on a hard red booth and told their stories, or at least pieces of them, as she sipped coffee and he ate a roast beef sandwich and curly fries. Periodically he slid the fries toward her, but every time she shook her head.

She never told him why she'd left home, and he never told her the most painful injuries, the deep mental anguish he endured.

It was a rosy version, one laced with distrust and lack of being vulnerable, but it was a start, one block on the Candy Land board.

"I hate my father," she said darkly.

"Strong words," Amos commented.

"Who cares? I'm not a Christian. It's not like I think there's a God keeping track of every word I say."

"I care. Sarah, I do. Don't do this to yourself."

"If there is a God, why does He allow . . . ?" She waved a hand. "Stuff. Why does He allow things to happen? Cruelty, suffering."

"I don't know. I don't have all the answers."

"Then why are you a Christian?"

"I have to have something, Sarah. Something greater than myself. When I met Joseph and Lila, I experienced love, the real kind that comes from God, and I never looked back. I am a believer in Jesus, the cross, the resurrection, all of it."

Her voice became very small. "At one time, so was I."

"What happened?"

"I can't say."

"You don't have to."

"So, I guess you won't want to do this again."

"Do what?"

"Ride around. Talk. Go places."

"Why?"

"Well, I imagine you have plenty of girls to choose from."

"I'm sure you've dated before," he countered.

"Never. No interest. Didn't really want to go out with you, either, but . . . well, you are different. You don't expect a guy who looks like you—you know, buff, good-looking—to be so sweet and gentle with an elderly woman."

"Looks like me? Sarah, you have no idea. You must not remember, but we knew each other when we were younger." He went on to remind her of the Christmas gift exchange. Her eyes grew wide, unbelieving. "When I left the Amish, left my home, I was over three hundred pounds. My face was like a muddy gravel road. Hideous. I had no friends, no talent, was slow and clumsy as a buffalo. I still battle with the demons of loathing myself. You have no idea," he repeated.

She saw the sincerity in his eyes.

"You're really that Amos, aren't you? I can't believe it. You're so different." Then, softly, she asked, "You never tried drugs? I mean, for the weight loss?"

"No. Just exercise, sensible eating. Honestly, pills make me nervous; I'm afraid of addiction. Actually, food was my addiction, until it wasn't. Scott at the gym helped me get healthy."

"In my profession, pills are easy. You learn about uppers and downers. Before you know what happened, you're addicted. It's how I lost the weight."

Much was left unsaid and a certain uneasiness centered around them as they drove through the night. Had they both allowed too much?

Would they want to see each other again? There was so much at stake, the bruises and scabs of mistreatment, the hard times, the lack of understanding exactly what had occurred in their growing-up years.

And so they rode in silence.

He walked her to the steel staircase and she did not invite him up. She kept her distance, put up an invisible barrier, and he did not attempt the goodnight kiss or a friend's hug, but said goodnight and walked away, started the truck, and moved off.

She plodded up the steps, inserted the key in the lock, and let herself in, then threw herself on the blue thrift-store couch and stared stonily at the cheap, water-stained ceiling. She rose, went to the medicine cabinet in the green tiled bathroom, picked up an orange prescription bottle, shook out three white tablets, and swallowed them dry.

She caught her ghoulish reflection in the cracked mirror and one bright tear rose to the surface, caught on the mascara of her lower lids, then slid down her cheeks, leaving a black streak behind.

Amos prayed as he drove. She had not denied an addiction, but had not confessed to one, either. Was she still using pills? He had never missed Anna more, the soft bubbliness of her nature, the way she made him feel—cherished and appreciated, without a thought of what he would say, what he would hide. It was simply all out to be inspected, hashed, and rehashed.

Sarah unsettled him, tilted his world on its axis. Something was gone awry with her, some score left unresolved. He realized he was backing off, moving away, unsure if he wanted to see her again.

And so, he kept talking to the Shepherd of his heart and soul.

"God, you know we're a poor match. She's damaged somehow. She's like handling sharp knives. What do I do now? Why did I ever imagine her for myself? I don't really want her. You know what I need. Please consider my cry. Why did I miss Anna so much tonight? I need you more than ever."

He slept dreamlessly, then rose refreshed and sat with Lila. Sarah was off on Sunday, so he rested on the vinyl recliner, read Scripture to Lila, and then spent the afternoon preparing for his trip to Michigan.

His clothes thrown in his black gym bag, Champ taken to the big house, the thermostat set at 60, and he was on the way to his father's house.

He found his father pacing the floor, watching anxiously in case visitors would show up and observe him climbing into his own son's vehicle, a line crossed then and there. He wasted no time getting in, shutting the door, laughing about the handiness of tinted windows.

"Dat, I'm not in the *bann*,*" Amos begged.

"To some, you may as well be," Raymond said quickly, his eyes darting guiltily till they moved onto the interstate at Rochester, away from Amish teams moving along roads.

It was the Amish way, Amos realized. Your conscience is ruled by a higher authority, never your own. So many things are held without guilt in front of God, but the brethren in the church are your judge, and guilt enters, tormenting your conscience.

As they moved smoothly along the four-lane highway, he could sense his father relaxing, becoming talkative, making himself comfortable. He was saving a bundle of money and spending time with his only son, and for this, he was doubly grateful.

---

* The *bann* refers to those who join the Amish church and then leave it and are therefore shunned by the community. Because Amos never joined the church, he doesn't need to be shunned.

He talked of his work, of Matt and Lavina, and Lavina's talk with Cathy. Amos pricked up his ears, anxious to hear.

"She's working six days a week cleaning houses. He started another job but got in trouble with the foreman."

"Doing what?"

"Framing houses, I guess. I don't know. He told Cathy it's too hot to work through October, but it may have cooled off by now."

"No, I mean, how did he get in trouble?" Amos asked, running a hand across the dash to rid it of accumulated dust.

"He swung at him, caught his ear."

"At the foreman?"

"He was let go."

"I guess he was. Now what? Surely Cathy is ready to admit he's a loser. Something isn't right."

"Well, but if she makes enough to cover everything, they should be doing alright. He'll grow up eventually, be a man and provide for her. I believe he's very nice to her, for the most part."

Amos sighed. There it was, his Dat wearing the perpetual rose-colored glasses, the world taking on the brilliance of optimism and unreality.

He would never change, moving lightly through dark times, convincing himself there were much better things to come just around the next bend.

Sam and Cathy were doing well, would repent and come back to the Amish, Amos would follow in their footsteps, and they would all be one big happy family, feet planted solidly on Amish soil.

Well, it was best not to pop that balloon, best to allow him the bliss of hiding behind the rock of deception, but he felt resentment rise like yellow bile in his throat.

His own mistreatment by his mother, all the unfairness he'd endured, wasn't so bad. Lydia didn't mean to hurt his feelings, after all.

"I hope we don't hit snow in Michigan," Amos said, lifting the sun visor to peer at gray clouds on the horizon.

"Turn your radio on. See what they say," his father instructed.

"We're still in Pennsylvania," Amos reminded him.

He laughed, said he was a *dumbkopf* (idiot). Amos couldn't help grinning, knowing his own father was so guileless, so completely erased of grudges and mean spiritedness.

Darkness enveloped them, like a silent black shroud. Amos drove steadily, speaking little, content to be in his father's company.

"Gas. Bathroom. Food. Three essentials," his father trilled happily.

Amos laughed, and his father told him exit thirteen.

It was a relief to stretch, to move around, fill the tank, and join his father at a table, where he was busily engaged in conversation with two men, rough-looking characters anyone else might have avoided.

"No, no, I'm not a Hutterite. No, there's a difference."

And he was off, explaining church doctrine in detail, which Amos could tell left them clueless. He tried inserting a silent stop sign, but Raymond was on a roll, glad to share his plain values with the heathen of the world. Did them a favor, ushering them onto the straight and narrow.

"Okay, dude, I get it. All I want is a hat like that," the tattooed guy teased.

Afterward, Amos warned his dad as gently as possible that it was better to stay away from strangers. But Raymond was far too delighted to have found out they rode Indian motorcycles, and some of them were made in the early 1900s, which he'd read in the paper not too long ago. Did he know they were a superior bike?

No, he didn't know that, which delighted his father even more. The fact that he knew that bit of knowledge and he didn't even have a phone. Just went to show the worth of a good newspaper.

The night was long, his father asleep beside him, the headlights poking into the gloom, his GPS the guiding light. An hour till the destination, a half hour, then he woke his father.

They were almost there, which shook him up badly, not prepared to meet the unknown before him.

Lydia, his beloved wife, was ill, gravely so, a mental condition of the mind, and this he had to face. No amount of denial would save him now.

He walked up the steps of the rambling facility, the brick façade surrounded by clipped boxwoods, well-maintained lawns and flowerbeds, old deciduous trees as thick and tall as he had ever seen. There were vans, smaller cars, a horse and buggy tied to a hitching rack on the gravel lot, and as Amos sat in his truck, another team came trotting up beside it.

So, there was an Amish settlement in Michigan. Probably more than a few. Amish people were scattered all over the United States and Canada, their population still growing rapidly due to the larger family units. It was a mother's duty to bear children, a father with many had his quiver full, and in most cases there was love, peace, and order, or a semblance of it in every household.

Here was his mother, suffering a mental breakdown, a thousand miles from home, among strangers. A wave of empathy rose within him, but it was short-lived, as he gave in to his own painful moments as a child.

Would his father be able to see her? He knew these places had stringent rules, but it would mean so much to him to talk to her, see for himself how she was faring.

He watched an elderly couple tie and blanket their horse in the stiff gale, the white-bearded man holding his head sideways to keep his hat on his head as he struggled with the buckles on the blanket, his wife waiting patiently, her shawl held together by strong pins. These bonnets appeared different, like a stiff bowl out the back, instead of a row of large pleats like his mother's.

He was glad he could know these things, this difference in Eastern and Western dress. He experienced a moment of pride, the feeling of being from the Amish, a part of them. There was so much good, so much fundamental common sense.

He had never admitted this to himself before, but watching the elderly people, he felt the love for the church of his youth. That was where he understood the fact there was a God, a figure on a throne he never doubted. Like a newborn, he'd been fed on milk. He had been nurtured by the Amish ministers and their German-Pennsylvania Dutch dialect, learning the difference between right and wrong, Heaven and hell.

He must have fallen asleep and woke up with his face on the steering wheel, shivering with cold. He started the truck, drove around a while to heat up the cab, marveled at the health of stately pines everywhere, the watery marshes leading to a lake eventually.

He'd love to bring Anna here. She would enjoy the scenery, would want to drive around all day, marvel at the sights like a child. The exuberance, the lively enthusiasm to experience sights and sounds, adventures. He could see her kayaking, plying that small fiberglass craft through unknown lakes, pointing out birds, hawks, falcons. She'd know the difference.

Why now, all these thoughts of Anna, this longing for her, when he had felt something for Sarah Yoder? Perhaps he was meant to be alone, and this was God's way of pointing him in the proper direction.

He passed a small gray building, paint peeling from the sign, as it swung wildly on a rusted chain. Nonni's Pizza. Anna would ask him to stop. She loved pizza. He remembered all this with a sense of failure, a milky fog of melancholy he could not dissipate. Did Sarah eat? Ever? He supposed she must.

He turned back toward the care facility, his mind churning as he tried to make sense of his longing for Anna, his lack of feeling for Sarah. Was Sarah a Christian, or did she actually not believe? Was that it? Their spirits could not unite.

He prayed, gripped the wheel with intensity.

He did not want to see her again, and he told this to God, also told Him there was something off with her, and he was not willing to deal with it. He had enough in his life.

When his father returned, the usual smoothness of an untroubled face was replaced by a drawn mouth, furrows along his cheekbones, as if some giant trouble had finally wrecked his sunny disposition.

He climbed into the truck, closed his eyes, and sighed heavily. Amos kept his eyes on the horse and buggy tied to the hitching rail and waited.

"Go, Amos. Just go," his father ground out.

Amos looked at him then, saw pain, failure, hopelessness, and a seething anger. He put the truck in gear and drove, his chest physically aching for his father. Slowly, in bits and pieces, the sad story of his mother's refusal to see Raymond came through, the lies of his abuse, the sickness so prevalent now.

Amos shook his head. "Did they give you hope?"

Momentarily, his face brightened. "They did. But why would she tell her counselors she was abused, when mistreating her has always been the farthest thing in my mind?"

"I know, Dat," Amos reassured him, and did know even now, his heart had always contained enough love for them both, and that was something.

Still, he had hidden himself away, handily lifted newspapers, did not have the backbone to assert parental authority when it was so desperately needed, leaving his mother wrestling with her own mental instability, the strong-willed Cathy, finances, and yes, him. His own disobedience, the knowledge of having an English son out in the world, while his father moved in an imaginary bubble.

Who was to blame? Perhaps no one.

God worked in mysterious ways to fit pieces of a perfectly designed puzzle, creating a masterpiece for his own special use. Amos pondered this as he drove, allowed his father time for quiet contemplation, and felt a new dawn on the horizon, a new view of the future.

Painful as circumstances proved to be, there was work being done. Hard work by trained counselors who would unearth the darkness of his mother's past, which he had always imagined to be troubling, at best. His father might have to finally step out of his self-imposed artificial bubble, face the cold hard truth, and be a man his ailing mother could lean on.

Chapter 20

They settled Lila back into her large living room surrounded by all the things she loved, the great wide windows with the heavy rose-colored drapes pushed back to allow the light to play on the papered walls, to catch a glint of gold-framed portraits and porcelain vases of silk flowers.

She shook her head, said absolutely no more hospital visits. She wanted hospice, was ready to leave the earth behind. She was frail and shivering as Amos and Nancy helped her onto the recliner, covered in clean sheets, a warm throw across her lap and a cashmere shawl around her shoulders. She assured them if there was difficulty breathing, then so be it. She gazed around the room at her beloved possessions, but waved a hand as if to dismiss the thought of earthly treasures.

Her time was coming closer, this Amos was aware of, but the thought of his inheritance always felt like a stone in his stomach, a heavy burden he could not shoulder willingly. How often did people around him joke about having a million dollars, or words to that effect? Wealth. Riches. Everyone sought after a life of ease, but for him, it brought a terrible responsibility, one he could not address without gut-wrenching despair.

He tried to rise above it, told himself he was ungrateful, childish, and had too many of his own father's attributes, but knew it was more than that. It was his own inability to feel worthy of anything, confidence to take on responsibility sadly lacking.

Could he give it away? Could he simply rid himself of the vast sum by contributing to worthy causes? But there was his dream of the house being filled with the sound of boys, boys like him, who barely survived bewildered lives of neglect, emotional and physical abuse, or worse.

Yes, his own case might seem laughable to some, but to him it was real, the sense of failing, having failed, and would always fail. He was handicapped, a quadriplegic of the mind.

He needed to rise above it, with God's help.

Christmas came, with a light sprinkling of snow and ice. Amos did not attend the Larkins' Christmas party, but they came to visit Lila with an abundance of gifts, Lila laughing shakily. Amos had decorated here and there—a vase of fresh greens, a wreath on the door—but there were no strings of lights, no Christmas tree, as Lila wished. She was just so weary, she said.

Amos felt the absence of Christmas festivities and cut pine branches, spruce, and magnolia to make garlands for the gatehouse, strung white lights along the porch eaves, the long windows, and around the door.

Why not?

He invited Matt and Lavina and his father, sent cards to Sam and Cathy, texted Sarah Yoder and wished her the best, but could not bring himself to invite her to his house. He put a ham in the oven, wrapped potatoes in foil, made a salad, and looked forward to his family's arrival. Tomorrow he would be at the big house, on Christmas Day, but today—today was his own.

His father had aged, though it had only been a short time, his face with undertones of gray, as if the blood had mostly drained away. His shirt was rumpled, his black vest in need of a good cleaning, his black lace-up Sunday shoes smudged and caked with dirt.

Matt was, of course, well-groomed in the Amish way, his hair cut neatly, quite the presentable young man, Lavina at his side in her festive red Christmas dress, a black apron pinned around her waist. They made a striking couple, and by all appearances, seemed well settled into their relationship.

The evening began with a chorus of hearty greetings, the gladness of Christmas with family foremost on their minds. Amos realized more than ever the value of retaining these ties in spite of lifestyle differences.

Matt, especially, put him at ease, made conversation easy, and Lavina moved around the kitchen, arranging cookies on a tray, heating her casserole of baked macaroni and cheese.

His father, however, worried him, seemingly without appetite, but doing his best at helping with the festive mood.

"I really miss your mother," he said at one point, after he refused dessert. "Seems as if I have a hole in my heart where she needs to be. I was dependent on her for so much."

"I suppose . . ." Amos began, then stopped.

He was aware of Matt and Lavina watching him closely, so he continued.

"I suppose, Dat, she was dependent on you as well."

His face brightened. "You think she was?"

"I do."

They discussed Sarah Yoder, at length, with Amos admitting his lack of enthusiasm, his ongoing feelings for Anna Riehl. Shamefaced, he admitted he was a loser.

Matt expressed empathy, saying he'd been there, more than once, and it did not make him a loser. The right girl would come by some day, but the journey was different for everyone. Since he had Lavina, he realized his past relationships all had a purpose, and Amos would certainly know if it was right.

Late one January evening, the weather turned beastly, a howling wind driving unhealthy branches clattering to the ground on frozen roadways and chopping board fences in two. He was in the gatehouse, knowing Della would keep watch over Lila. The mercury on the rusted outdoor thermometer showed eight degrees, the sheen of ice on top of snow-covered fields the only thing keeping the snow from whirling away, creating whiteouts.

Amos shivered, went to the wall and turned up the thermostat, then grabbed a fuzzy throw to keep the chills away, listening to the rise and fall of the Arctic blast. In his mind, he pictured homeless individuals, prayed they'd have a shelter welcoming them. He thought of deer on the mountain, their slender legs breaking through the ice, the edges like knives cutting through quivering flanks.

He was drowsy, but a certain sound above the sound of the wind wakened him. A loose shutter? These older houses had their share of odd noises, spouting, whirring, loose shutters flapping, cracks in windowpanes whistling.

No, there it was again.

He reached for the remote, turned the sound off, fully awake now.

Yes. A slight rapping on his door.

Throwing the blanket aside, he hushed Champ, slid the bolt, and opened the door. A thin figure, hooded in black. He flipped the switch for the porch light, illuminating Sarah Yoder's shivering form.

Her hoarse voice. "Can I come in?"

"Of course. Please do."

He stepped aside. She passed him like a plume of black smoke, moving soundlessly across the carpet, sank on the edge of the sofa, and put her elbows on her knees before dropping her face into her hands.

Immediately, he went to sit beside her, a hand to her shoulder, asking if she was OK. There was no response.

He noticed the thin wrists, the long, tapered fingers, like porcelain, the skin so white and delicate.

He decided to wait, but rubbed her back gently, allowing her to feel the mercy, the caring. Champ walked over and nosed her knee, then sighed and walked to his bed in the corner.

When a deep sound emerged, it frightened him, like the ragged edge of a broken saw. A strange rasping sound that was neither a sob nor an inhalation, but a painful sorrow from deep within. He drew her to him then, a heavy arm around the narrow shoulders.

A few minutes elapsed, until another raw, grating sound emerged, then another. It was like dry heaves after the worst stomach virus. He held her, said nothing.

Below, the furnace rumbled to life, the wind wailed and howled, a loose shutter reverberated against the stone. Still, he waited.

She drew away.

"Sarah, tell me."

She threw back the hood, lifted her face, and took a deep breath. She was completely dry-eyed. How, with those sounds from her throat?

"I came here to tell you my truth. I am an addict. I'm addicted to pills, all sorts of pills. Anything I can find."

Amos recoiled, turned his face away. So here it was, the reason he could not go on with the relationship, if it could be called that.

"Will you say something, please?" she asked, in a small scratchy voice.

"Sarah, I hardly know what to say. I mean, is it really that bad?"

She nodded, put her face back in her hands.

"I need help, but I don't know where to turn."

Amos was overwhelmed with the need to remove this person from his house. He did not want to get involved. Addictions sickened him, the mark of a weak character.

"I don't either, but I'm sure there are resources available."

She ran a hand through her short gray hair, grimaced, then turned to look at him.

"Amos, I know what you're thinking. You don't want me here, you don't want to get involved. Nobody ever does. Not really."

"But I do." He wanted to believe his own words.

"No, you don't. But I have no one else to turn to."

"I'm going to make tea, okay?"

He got up, filled the kettle, got down two mugs, the tea bags and honey, then went to sit beside her.

"First, you'll hear my story. If at the end, you want me out, I'll go. You are the only person I have met since I was Amish who is hearing me out, okay? It won't be easy, and you probably won't believe me."

The kettle whistled, and he brought back the tea, set it on coasters. She lifted a mug to her mouth, sipped, whispered, "That's good."

And in her low voice, she began to talk, her words punctuated by sighs, restless hands through her hair, then knotted in fists.

It started when she was eleven years old, her father coming to her room at night, then her brother, lasting until she finally broke away the day after her eighteenth birthday.

She gave herself up to it, after her father explained it was the highest form of love in plain churches, but to receive this honor, it had to be kept in secret chambers for God alone. She was chosen, special. It was only after she turned sixteen that she began to doubt the falsehoods.

She shuddered with suppressed sobs, but remained dry-eyed throughout the telling of it. Her mother knew, but felt she had to submit to the desires of her husband, a twist of Scripture.

She learned to survive on the strength of her hatred, denounced God and every form of religion, spiritual or otherwise, left home and worked two jobs while going to school. She knew nursing was the profession for her, the way she lived without emotion. She could do the job well without getting burned out with the patients' suffering. Ruined in soul and spirit, she was alive and burning for vengeance. She hated with her whole strength, hid away from prying eyes, learned how to make money, a ruthless form of retribution.

She stole things, lots of things, became addicted to pills after she passed her tests, walked through life with half-erased memories, dead inside, filled with the parasitic hatred only the pills could ease.

"I was at my worst, between ten and fifteen meds a day, when I met you. Since then, I have seriously considered suicide twice. It would be easy to overdose."

Amos choked when he tried to speak. Tears ran freely from his soft brown eyes. His mouth quivered when he saw himself, truly saw himself, for the first time. He was spiritually blessed with an abundance of grace, yet he could not share any of it. He thought himself far above this trembling shell of a woman before him, held on to his whole suitcase of love and grace he had received for his own forgiveness. Locked away by his own self-righteousness.

When he took her in his arms, she pulled away violently, threw herself across the couch, tucked up her knees and lowered her face into the fetal position.

"Don't," she rasped.

"Sarah."

He had no words, felt helpless in the face of this abomination.

"Sarah, listen. You are safe, okay? I'm not going to hurt you. Our first duty is to take it to the law."

She leaped off the couch, spat horrible words, raw abrasive language.

"I will literally not allow this secret to become public, ever."

"Your name will never be mentioned."

"I don't care. No. If I knew you would do that, I would never have told you."

"But it will be dealt with now. Your father and your brother can't escape justice."

"Oh, he will. He'll find a way."

Far into the night they talked, the storm intensifying, the furnace rattling repeatedly to life, warm air wafting the baseboard, the fireplace crackling as Amos kept piling on wood. He was drawn into her life despite his will, recognized many of her emotions, the outward appearance of normalcy over and over, year after year, until the sense of true identity was crushed beneath falsehoods.

At one point, Sarah kept blaming herself. If she had only been stronger, smarter, more assertive. She had been dumb, stupid, ignorant. She believed them. Both of them. Once, she had barricaded the door, but it did no good.

Her eyelids drooped, her shoulders slumped with dejection.

"Amos. I need to go home."

"You are not leaving. It's absolutely unsafe on the roads tonight. I'll bring a heavy quilt and sheets for you, right here on the couch. Tomorrow is Sunday, and we'll stay in the house."

She sighed, bit her lower lip.

"For one night, I'll be okay," she said, with so much sadness, he was hardly able to bear it.

She stood and he went to retrieve the sheets and blankets. When he returned, they stood awkwardly, facing each other, unprocessed pain between them, and he had no words to let her know his feelings—the ballooning grace, the kindness and empathy, the need to make it better somehow.

He took her thin shoulders in his hands, asked if it was OK. She shrugged, her face lowered. His left hand fell away, but he replaced it, drew her toward him slowly, gently, until the rumpled gray hair rested on his chest.

"Sarah, from this day forward, I will protect you. We will work this out together, in your own time. I promise never to push you into an agreement, or any action, until you are perfectly willing."

He heard her swallow before the sobs began, a heaving sound of immense sorrow, grief for the life she had been forced to live. Amos recognized the beginning, a small growth of what was to come. And he held her until she melted willingly into his arms.

Sodden Kleenexes, her dark mascara running in black rivers down her contoured cheeks, and still she wept.

Finally, she raised her face and asked if he'd said that because he felt sorry for her, or if he meant he liked her enough to try to help.

"I don't know, Sarah. You've been so honest with me, and now it's my turn. I have a girl named Anna Riehl who seems to be stuck in my mind. She broke up with me because her parents didn't want her to leave the Amish, and I was attracted to you, but first I have to deal with my feelings toward her."

"Well, I'm a lot to deal with. I'm a mess. You say you'll help now, but I'm sure you'll change your mind, and that's understandable," she said softly.

"I promise you, Sarah."

He never thought he would kiss her, but in spite of himself, his hand went to her chin, lifted her face to his, and gently sought her trembling mouth, touching his lips to hers. He felt himself soaring, his spirit alive. It was so much more than he had imagined.

She pulled away, said, "I'm sorry."

"For what? Sarah, that was all me."

And he kissed her again, soundly, honestly, the joy reaching new heights, and he drew away first, smiled into her eyes, and told her with a trembling voice she was safe with him and it was not simply a duty.

It was hard to leave her, hard to let her alone in the living room, so he made the excuse they needed to keep the fireplace going and slept beside her on the recliner, covered with every blanket and throw he could find.

In the gray light of morning, she showered, wore Amos's pajamas, which luckily had a drawstring around the waist. Shy, her guard up, she emerged from the bathroom, her hair spiked, dark, without a trace of the black eyeliner. She appeared much younger, vulnerable, even apologetic.

She waved in the direction of her eyes. "Nothing much to look at." But there was. There was a rising softness, the dark hard green of her eyes like a spring fed pool surrounded by ferns and lily pads, evoking an appreciation of the gentle nature hidden deep beneath layers of shame, guilt, revulsion, and hate.

So much better, the clean nakedness of her eyes, revealing a new beginning. He had to go slowly, had to exercise patience, open his own heart and allow grace to flow from God, without mentioning His name. He was no better than she. He understood all the helplessness, the absence of self-worth, confidence gone.

"Sarah, I love your eyes without make-up. It makes you look younger."

She shook her head. "I can't stand it."

He laughed, handed her a baking sheet to put the bacon on, and she smiled at him. Shocked to see a genuine emerging beauty, he turned away, busying himself with the coffee maker.

Everything was happening too fast, a blur before his eyes, a runaway horse. He poured a cup of coffee, handed it to her, allowed his fingers to cover hers, looked into those green, blue, yellow, hazel eyes, slightly swollen.

Breakfast was astounding, with perfectly scrambled eggs, bacon crisp and salty, waffles dripping with butter and syrup. He assured her he didn't eat like this very often, only his *trushiny Suntag*, that in-between Sunday he allowed himself on occasion. She laughed out loud at the Dutch word, remembered the Sundays with no church service to attend. Then her face closed and darkened, and he knew her mind had conjured some old memory.

"Sarah, I don't want you to go. I'm afraid your apartment will be cold."

"Oh, it is. My thermostat is set at ninety, but it never goes above sixty. I run an electric space heater, but it's a piece of junk."

Amos narrowed his eyes, an idea escaping his lips too quickly. "You know what? We're English, so we could move in together. No strings attached, right?"

For a fleeting movement, he recognized the hope in her eyes, but it vanished as quickly.

"You know we weren't raised like that, in spite of everything. I don't really want that for myself," she said softly, shyly. "I couldn't truly wear a white gown, but perhaps . . ."

Her voice trailed off.

He was actually relieved to know she felt that way, and told her so. They cleaned up the kitchen, she in the sagging pajamas, her hair with no sense of style, some standing straight up and the rest laying flat. But Amos thought her attractive at a whole new level, wondered why he had ever doubted.

But she did leave, after lunch, after more conversation, after an even deeper connection emotionally. He asked to see her again, of course, but she wanted a few weeks to process all that had taken place, saying the future was uncertain for both of them. Reality was ominous, if justice was to be served honestly. What if her mother were incarcerated for her piece in all of it?

He held her for a moment, then let her go and watched her drive slowly away without looking back.

He went to the big house, his Carhartt beanie smashed over his ears, the heaviest coat he owned, which wasn't all that heavy, the wind finding its way through the layers. Lila greeted him warmly, so weak she could barely lift her hand, her eyes filled with a radiant light.

Nancy told him she had slept very little, with Della prowling around all night, thinking Nancy was neglecting Lila, when in fact, she wasn't. Della drove her up the wall with that accent, her heavy shoes, and the constant tea drinking and running to the bathroom.

It was his turn tonight, she reminded him, and he needed to clean his room, the furnace filter needed to be changed, and the third story lightbulbs needed replacing. Plus, she wasn't sure the birdbath by the shed hadn't cracked in two during the night.

She crossed her arms, stepped back, and asked if he'd seen a ghost, or what? Was he sick?

"No, and no," he answered. "I'm fine. Winter bleaches a person's skin."

Nancy nodded and hurried off, her wide hips jiggling below her belt.

He read to Lila first, a whole chapter from Corinthians, watching her eyes droop sleepily as he read, her lips moving with his. Would he ever know the Bible the way she did? It was an inspiration to live the kind of life this beloved old couple had lived, although he probably had to settle for less, with all he'd experienced before this.

And now there was Sarah's past facing him. He knew without a doubt that the right thing was to report her father and brother to the police, but not before Sarah prepared herself. He relived the night, moment by moment, her words like thorns he had to step across.

Why did God allow this insanity? This ruining of an innocent child? He had to stop himself from his own roiling thoughts, the storm in his mind almost more than he could bear. Someone would have to pay. Sarah had already suffered so much, and it would take years of recovery, with no guarantee of being healed fully.

And what of his feelings for her? Had it been the night itself, or was he developing a new love? How did one know pity or sympathy from love?

One day at a time.

He finished his work, then drove to the gym, where he ran five miles on the treadmill, pumped iron till his muscles strained, drank a protein shake, and sat in the office with Scott, exchanging the weekly news. Scott was still a good friend, a trusted confidante, a loyal ally on his health journey, so they never ran out of things to talk about.

He chatted with lots of regular gym-goers now, but never on the same level as Scott, who had been with him from the time he'd stumbled in, weighing over three hundred pounds, flabby, calorie-laden, his face a minefield.

Now he felt at ease, laughed, joked, and discussed new fitness options. He felt good remembering the night with Sarah.

He asked Scott's advice, without naming names. He knew she sometimes came to the gym, though they hadn't run into each other there since that first time she came in for a membership. He asked Scott, what were the chances of a normal relationship after a woman had been mistreated to such a degree?

Eyebrows raised, Scott leaned back in his chair, rested his elbows on the arms, and formed a tent with his fingers. "I dunno about that one. I guess it depends on the person's disposition, the ability to forgive. It's risky, at best. Is she a believer?"

"No. Also, she's addicted to prescription meds."

Scott raised his eyes to the ceiling, let out a "Whoa. Whoa, man."

"I know. But she asked me to help her. She doesn't have anyone else."

"Be careful, Amos. This could take a chunk out of you."

"There's plenty to go around."

Scott laughed, brought his chair down, got to his feet.

"Bring her around. I'd like to meet her."

He clapped Amos on his rock-hard shoulder, and he drove home with a sense of well-being. Anything was possible. Anything.

And who knew, really, how love began? Wasn't each story different?

Where and when had he last seen Anna Riehl? Somehow, he couldn't remember. Could hardly remember her face, or the softness of her rounded shoulders.

Chapter 21

On Thursday morning there was a winter storm watch on the news for northern Pennsylvania, all of New York, and most of New England.

He called Sarah, but she did not pick up. He thought of her constantly and wanted her to stay with him again if the storm hit. He hated imagining her alone her cold apartment.

He checked fuel tanks, removed broken branches around the house, then looked up to see a minivan come steadily up the drive. He continued with his work, but straightened to watch a young Amish girl emerge, her white covering on the back of her honey-blond, streaked hair.

Anna. It was Anna Riehl.

She spied him immediately, waved, and called out, "Hey, Amos. How's it going?"

He didn't answer, but walked over, his heart beating like a gong in his chest. Was there still a chance? Oh, Anna. Her face, her hair, so short and round and adorable. He fell all over again, foolishly and absolutely.

She turned her pretty face up to his, proffered a small hand, and said it had been a long time. He smiled, nodded, said it had, yes.

It was then he noticed she was holding white envelopes. She lifted one and handed it to him.

"I have invitations for you, Nancy, and Lila. To my wedding the first week in April."

Her face registered happiness, but a certain trepidation—a shame, or embarrassment, perhaps both. He took it, looked at his name with her handwriting, and swallowed the rising bile of defeat.

"Who is the lucky guy?" he mumbled.

"Samuel Zook of Mohawk Valley in New York."

"Never heard of him."

"No, you wouldn't have." She hesitated, then forged ahead. "Amos, it's what my parents want. It's so easy. They're over the moon for me."

"And you're over the moon for yourself?"

"Well, yeah. Of course. Duh," she gushed, but could not help herself from meeting his frank appraisal. Her eyes fell away.

"Do you love him, Anna?" he ground out, the bitterness on his tongue like metal.

"Well, you wouldn't come back for me, Amos, so what does that say about you? Your character? I was between a rock and a hard place, and you know it."

There was no justification. She had spoken the truth. So he lifted the white envelopes, said thanks, and walked away, leaving her standing by the minivan. She turned and ran up the steps, which Amos observed, his chest wrenched by old memories, the breathless pleasure of seeing her running up those steps so long ago, a lifetime. A small brown wren, her quick movements, her short compact form he loved so much.

But here it was, the proof of his refusal to give in, the invites to her wedding. A part of him longed to run after her, fall on his knees, and tell her he'd go back to the Amish if she'd marry him. Almost, he attempted it, but he knew her vow to Samuel was made. The hardest part was forgiveness toward the parents who barely called themselves Amish, but would die of shame if one of them left the fold.

He shook his head as if to clear it. Time to calm down.

He met Anna coming down the steps, asked if Lila recognized her. She shook her head, tears rising quickly. "She seems so old."

"Yes, she won't last long."

"You'll let me know when she passes? Bless her heart. She was always so sweet to me."

"Yes, I'll notify you. Still the same number?"

She nodded.

"Amos, don't be bitter. It wasn't meant to be. I'll be very happy, living in Mohawk Valley. Milking cows on the home farm. They say it's beautiful there."

"I wish you every happiness, Anna. Nancy and I will be at your wedding. Thanks for the invitation."

She moved away quickly, a small round blur, a rush into the vehicle, and they wended their way down the drive.

He turned on his heel, thought about the strangeness of life, the ways in which everything was unpredictable. There went his helpmeet to establish a home for boys, so soft and kind, so perfect in every way.

Discouraged, heartsick, he stumbled out the drive in the February light and let himself in, sat at the kitchen table, and pouted like a child. He knew it was not mature, or manly, or any good thing, but he didn't care. It felt good to wallow in his hog pen of loss and self-pity, to indulge in every negative thought popping into his mind.

He was only human, no matter how his elevated view of himself turned out to be wrong. There was still Sarah, in all her incomplete healing, the thought of her too hard at times. Did he understand her at all? When confusion clouded over the brilliance of the Light, it was time to return to the source of all his stability, the Father in Heaven.

Cathy called later that evening, as he was preparing for bed, the big house groaning under the lowering snow clouds, the atmospheric pressure creating aching joints.

He tucked his phone in his shoulder, kept rubbing Deep Blue into one knee, grimacing.

"Cathy. How's it going?"

What followed was an astounding verbal assault, one of troubles piled as high as her ears. The weather was cold and rainy. Sam kept hopping between jobs, and their rent had risen twenty percent. She had a roaring bladder infection, and what was that thing Mam used to do with red beets and ibuprofen? She had no money to go to urgent care, and no health insurance, so if that red beet stuff didn't work, he might have to send her some money.

He recited the boiled beets: drain the juice, straight up magnesium, ibuprofen to relax the bladder. But he thought it was for kidney stones, not an infection.

"What's the difference? It hurts."

"Where's Sam?"

There was a long pause and he asked, "You still there?"

"Yeah. Sam is down at the Pink Flamingo. He's a bartender. Amos, if you tell Dat and Lavina, I'll be really mad. Look, I know it isn't good, but at least he makes enough money to pay for his own liquor. He's still good to me. Well, mostly. We had a whopper of a fight, though. I work all the time to pay for things. There's rent, food, the car, the light bill, and we don't have time to enjoy ourselves except going to the beach on Sunday. Amos. Keep this to yourself, but his drinking is out of control. He drinks five or six every night. He says he can quit anytime he feels like it, but I'm beginning to wonder. I have the blues tonight, in all this pain."

"Where's Sam?"

"I told you. He works till the bar closes at two a.m."

"And you're alone?"

"I am. Mostly. There's this poet—he's a famous author of poetry, who comes to visit sometimes. He's in his fifties, sort of like a dad. He makes pierogies, some kind of dough with cabbage and I think beef wrapped up. His name is Dominic Kelovsky. He's unbelievably brilliant. Made a lot of money on his books."

"Cathy, please be careful. I was always worried about Sam, but this sounds really messy."

"Seriously, there you go again, riding your high horse of self-righteousness. You're a jerk."

Click.

Oh boy, he'd done it again. He sincerely regretted warning her, felt bad, and tried calling her back, but knew she wouldn't pick up. It had to be hard. He felt no satisfaction in being right about Sam, only a deep sadness for Cathy.

He called Lavina, but she must have been asleep, so he let it go. Poor Cathy, poor thing. If he could reach Sam right now, he'd pound him. He called Sarah, was wide awake when she didn't pick up. How many pills had she swallowed today? Yesterday? Should he have taken her straight to rehab?

He stuck his head under the pillow and fell into a deep sleep, awakened by the insistent beeps of his phone.

It was Lila, asking for a drink of water, and would he mind helping her out of bed and onto the recliner? She believed her breathing would be easier there. She was so light, he could easily have carried her, but allowed her the dignity of using the rolling walker, her stockinged feet sliding slowly behind it. She sighed deeply when Amos adjusted the recliner, thanked him for the warm covers, and said wouldn't they enjoy the snow tomorrow? She smiled even as the thin, blue-veined eyelids closed.

He went back to his room, called Sarah again, and was rewarded with a quick hello.

"You're still awake?"

"I can't sleep, Amos. I tried doing without . . . well, some of the meds."

"Look, why don't you come over? I have to stay at the house with Lila, but drive over and make yourself at home before the storm. Please?"

"I'm not well. I get shaky. Fidgety. I'd be embarrassed."

"It's okay. Are you warm?"

"Sort of."

"Just get in your car and come over. The key is under the right urn by the door."

"But . . . what about tomorrow?"

"You'll have off. Or else I'll drive you with my truck. They're predicting up to eighteen inches."

There was a long stretch of silence. Then, "Do you want me to?"

"Yes, I do."

"Okay. But I'll bring clothes this time."

He thanked God with sincerity, a deep cup of overflowing gratefulness. She was trying. That was all he needed to know. He lay awake for a while, looking forward to the light of morning.

But it was nine o'clock before he could get away, with both Nancy and Della cancelling because of the storm. He was impatient but had no choice but to call Sarah and ask her to come up to the big house. He felt the hesitation in her voice, but she agreed, and he watched until he saw her dark figure through the swirling snow.

He met her at the door, a finger to his lips. Lila was asleep.

They moved silently down the wide hallway, past the open stairway, checking the living room where Lila lay asleep, then moving on.

Sarah missed nothing, the high ceilings, the large doors, trim work, the thoroughly modern kitchen. She was in awe, had never seen such a house.

What would happen to it when she passed?

Amos shook his head, let her believe the children would inherit it.

"I have to be at work by twelve," she said unexpectedly.

"Seriously? I was hoping you could stay. You can't drive."

"Well, I can't fly, either."

He laughed and she accepted his offer of using the truck, then left shortly after, leaving him alone with Lila, still breathing shallowly and slowly, but relaxed.

He went to fill the bird feeders, brought fresh suet cakes, and filled the heated bird bath, picking up the two pieces of the broken one and bringing them into the garage.

His phone rang. Cathy.

"What's up, Cathy?"

She was crying, he could tell, the stuffiness of her nose giving her away.

"It hurts, Amos. I'm in so much pain it feels as if my legs are falling off. They won't treat me without money. I don't have enough."

"They have to treat you, Cathy. Tell them your situation."

"Just give me your credit card number."

"I'd rather not. Drive yourself to the urgent care. Go immediately. You need antibiotics."

"I'm scared, Amos. I'm ashamed. It's embarrassing."

"Where's Sam now? Why can't he take you?"

"He's sleeping. He has to."

"This is eleven. If he got home at two, that's a good nine hours. Wake him up."

"Amos, you don't get it, do you? I don't wake Sam."

"Why not?"

"Don't pry. It's my life, my business."

"Just go, then."

She hung up on him, and he sighed, watched the falling snow.

His parents, Cathy, and now Sarah. Everywhere there was a churning, rushing river of care and sorrow.

There had to be a better way. There was a better way, that of mentally handing it over to God in Spirit, allowing oneself to rest.

He heard a weak call, entered the living room quickly.

"Amos darling, would you tie back the drapes on the left window? The snow is so beautiful and I'm missing too much of it. Have you fed the birds? I know there will be at least a dozen cardinals later in the day. Joseph and his entourage come for a visit," she chuckled.

He adjusted the drapes, asked what she would like for lunch, then heated the chicken noodle soup in a bowl and arranged it on a tray with a piece of toast and two canned pears. She ate with a good appetite, made small talk as she ate, and said she would try not to go today, in all this snow.

Amos smiled, patted her hand, said she'd be here for a while yet.

"In the spring," she said, "When the daffodils are all abloom, matching this yellow house. It will be beautiful but will not compare to the mansions He promised us."

She appeared eager, joyous, as she spooned the last of her soup, then started in on her pears.

"Yes, yes, I'll be here till the daffodils bloom. Don't you worry about the snow. I'm going to stay right here and enjoy my time with you."

She requested the Scrabble board, much to his surprise, but after a few words she fell asleep, her white head drooping to the side. He removed the game, put the recliner back, and covered her shoulders.

The day was achingly long. He wished Sarah would drive back as the snow heaved up. Nancy called, and Della, but he told them to relax, he was holding down the fort. He called Sarah, but she told him she was very busy, she'd be okay, the snowplows were everywhere.

At twelve, he was still awake, watching the road, the absence of moving headlights, a painful pit in his stomach.

At a quarter after one, a pair of headlights came slowly but steadily up the road, turned into the unplowed drive, and wallowed through knee deep snow straight up to the porch of the big house.

He met her at the door, pulling her into his arms, puff jacket, fur hood, and all. He held her, rocked her, and told her he'd stared a hole through the window watching for her.

She smiled, said he had a great truck, a good set of winter treads, and she had no trouble.

"Come on, we're going to make you a cup of tea. There's sourdough bread and cheese. I'll make you a grilled cheese."

She tucked her arm in his, asked what she did to deserve this.

Later though, when she drooped with weariness, she told him the battle was real, fighting against the need for a few uppers, or downers, or simply popping a few to take away anxiety about everything. The past, the present, the future.

"I told you, Sarah. Remember?"

She nodded, "I know."

He showed her the guest room, in spite of wanting to keep her. What was this? It wasn't love, not the love he had for Anna, or the youthful heart thumping excitement for Skye Larkin. He wasn't sure what this was called, like a circle, drawing closer, but barely noticeable, it was so slow, patient, and steady.

He went to the living room, watched the falling snow at night. The only prayer on his lips was "Let it be, Lord Jesus. Let it be."

THE STORM BLEW itself out the following morning, the world covered in a blanket of pure sparkling crystals, the air so crisp and cold it hurt his lungs as he went to the garage. He shoveled a path to the house, relishing the use of his arms, the way he could throw the snow, all a reward for the hard work he put in at the gym, changing his life.

Gone were the days of self-loathing, stuffing himself with high calorie food as a source of comfort, and for this he was doubly grateful. It had been hard work, changing his lifestyle, but it was so much better now.

He watched bluejays squabbling at the feeder and laughed to himself, the notion of human beings often displaying the same senseless arguments.

He kept smiling, thinking of his mother and Cathy, blue jays if ever there was a likeness. Strangely, he felt something akin to longing, as if he wanted to see both of them. His mother, the one he could not imagine wanting or missing, but he did. She was suffering, probably more than he realized, walking the path of illness, a hard road for someone beginning the journey of emotional wellness. And Cathy. His stomach lurched, anxiety welled.

Take her, Jesus. Take her and Sam into your care. Keep them in the palm of your hand.

All around him, the purity of fresh snow reminded him of the mercies of God, new every morning. The fir trees were weighed down with a heavy layer, and as he watched, a fickle wind caught branches, sent the snow whirling away in a thin, transparent cloud. He hoped the wind would pick up, create deep drifts. Keeping Sarah there at his place.

He bent to his task, his thoughts returning to Cathy. He missed her, and that was the truth. He needed to see her, try to get her to view her situation through the lens of honesty. He worried about the poet. She was so pretty, so vulnerable, likely feeling rejected over and over with Sam turning to alcohol for his own pleasure, self-medication, escape, whatever caused a normal young man to turn to that quagmire. Quicksand, a dangerous unseen enemy of the soul.

He straightened his back, squinted at the brilliant snow crystals, thought of Sarah and her dependence on meds. That was understandable. He could not begin to imagine what she had endured. She had made something of herself, reached a goal, likely the path to retaining her own sanity, but in the process had replaced her human heart with one of stone, denounced God. He knew she was a work in progress, and that perhaps he was wasting his time. There were moments, however, when he glimpsed a break in the wall she'd built around herself.

He couldn't shake the urgency of seeing Cathy. Should he go? Take Sarah? He couldn't. Not when Lila was unwell. He would never forgive himself if she passed without him.

He set his shovel against the railing at the steps, then went to the garage for the tractor, shoved snow off the drive, let Champ out, who lunged through the deep snow, his tongue lolling, panting, while Amos watched from the porch. *Crazy dog*, he laughed to himself.

After the driveway was cleared, he put the tractor in the garage, went up the steps to the house, straight to the kitchen to find a cup of coffee.

He found Sarah, hunched over the bar, her long fingers wrapped around a mug of steaming coffee, her legs crossed, one foot bobbing up and down in agitation. She would not look at him as he entered.

"Good morning, Sarah."

"Yeah, well, you shouldn't leave me alone in this house with the old lady. I looked in on her and she's still sleeping. What if she needed you?"

"Lila doesn't sleep much at night. She sleeps better in the morning after I'm up, or Nancy's here. Sorry, though, if you weren't comfortable staying alone. Did you sleep well?"

She shrugged, drank her black coffee. Amos filled his own cup, sat at the end of the bar and watched her, thought again how difficult, how damaged she really was. Like handling sharp knives. One slip up, and you hurt yourself.

"I need to go home. Take care of things," she said suddenly.

"Okay. But I doubt if the roads are passable yet. It's fine for you to be here, Sarah. Lila will want to see you."

There was no response, so he took himself off to check on Lila, walking carefully so as not to awaken her, knowing she'd had a restless night.

Lila lay on her recliner, her head resting on the pillows he'd arranged at 3:13, when she'd whispered her "Thank you" and fallen asleep. He wasn't surprised, seeing how comfortable she appeared to be, that a restful, deep sleep had overtaken her. He tiptoed over, touched the white hand, and stopped.

For a long moment, he knew. There was no warmth, there was no life in the dear old hand. Tenderly, he reached out, smoothed the soft white hair from her forehead, touched her cheek, and thanked God for taking her, the end of her life without pain and suffering.

He felt the loss, then, keenly. His shoulders heaved with a sharp painful sob that caught in his throat, and he fell to knees, bowed his head over her precious, lifeless form. She had been everything to him, had represented a pure form of love, had been a mother, a grandmother, an angel helping him through the rough spots in his life, and grief was a crushing stone.

Who could fathom the ways of the Lord?

She had wanted to see the daffodils one more time, but He had called her in the middle of a snowstorm. In his mercy, He had taken her.

His hands went to his face and tears fell between his fingers as he wept. He wanted to stay here with her, the hush and peace of His presence comforting him, even as the sorrow of parting engulfed him.

I have loved you, Lila. Your love created mine.

He became aware, then, of a hand on his shoulders, and found Sarah. In the stillness, in God's presence, he knew with startling clarity what Lila had been to him. He must take up the torch and be that person for Sarah. None of it would be easy, but he was here on earth for a higher purpose, and God would be there for him every step of the way.

THE END

About the Author

Linda Byler was raised in an Amish family and is an active member of the Amish church today. Growing up, Linda loved to read and write. In fact, she still does. Linda is well known within the Amish community as a columnist for a weekly Amish newspaper. She writes all her novels by hand in notebooks.

Linda is the author of several series of novels, all set among the Amish communities of North America: Lizzie Searches for Love, Sadie's Montana, Lancaster Burning, Hester's Hunt for Home, the Dakota Series, The Long Road Home, New Directions, Stepping Stones, Seekers, and the Buggy Spoke Series for younger readers. Linda has also written several Christmas romances set among the Amish: *Mary's Christmas Goodbye*, *The Christmas Visitor*, *The Little Amish Matchmaker*, *Becky Meets Her Match*, *A Dog for Christmas*, *A Horse for Elsie*, *The More the Merrier*, *A Christmas Engagement*, and *Love Conquers All.* Linda has coauthored *Lizzie's Amish Cookbook: Favorite Recipes from Three Generations of Amish Cooks!*, *Amish Christmas Cookbook*, and *Amish Soups & Casseroles*.

Other Books by Linda Byler

Lizzie Searches for Love Series

BOOK ONE

BOOK TWO

BOOK THREE

TRILOGY

COOKBOOK

Sadie's Montana Series

BOOK ONE

BOOK TWO

BOOK THREE

TRILOGY

Lancaster Burning Series

BOOK ONE

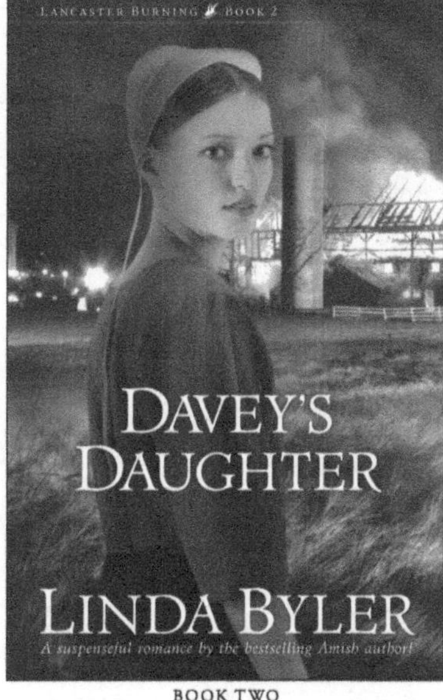

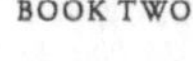

BOOK TWO

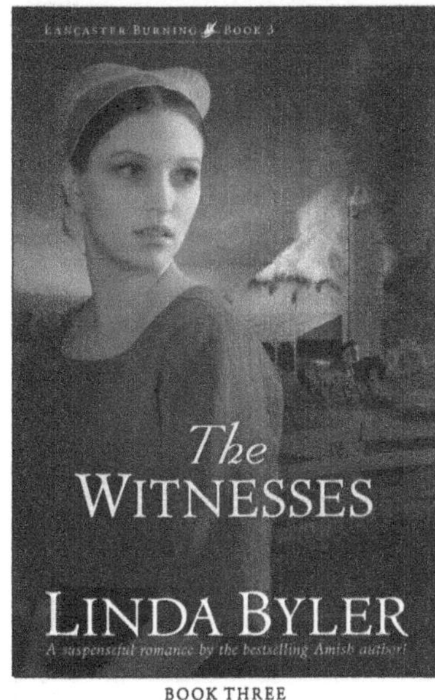

BOOK THREE

TRILOGY

Hester's Hunt for Home Series

BOOK ONE

BOOK TWO

BOOK THREE

TRILOGY

The Dakota Series

BOOK ONE

BOOK TWO

BOOK THREE

TRILOGY

Long Road Home Series

BOOK ONE

"A GIFTED WRITER"
—Publishers Weekly
A BEACON of LIGHT
An Amish Romance
The
LONG ROAD
HOME
–BOOK TWO–
LINDA BYLER

BOOK TWO

BOOK THREE

New Directions Series

BOOK ONE

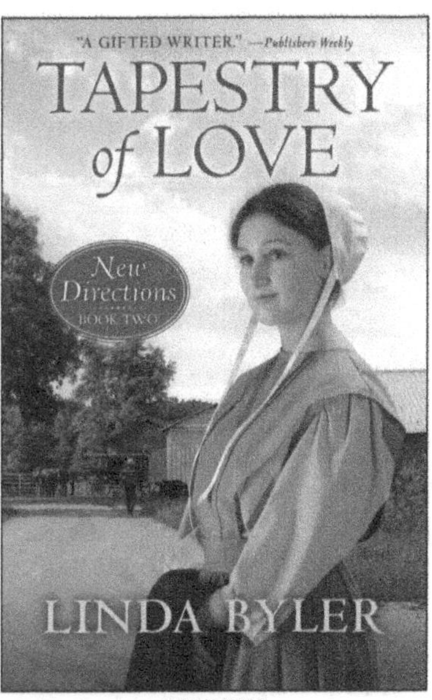

BOOK TWO

BOOK THREE

Stepping Stones Series

BOOK ONE

BOOK TWO

BOOK THREE

Seekers Series

BOOK ONE

BOOK TWO

BOOK THREE

Standalone Novels

THE HEALING

A SECOND CHANCE

HOPE DEFERRED

LOVE IN UNLIKELY PLACES

Buggy Spoke Series for Young Readers

BOOK ONE

BOOK TWO

BOOK THREE

Christmas Novellas

THE CHRISTMAS VISITOR

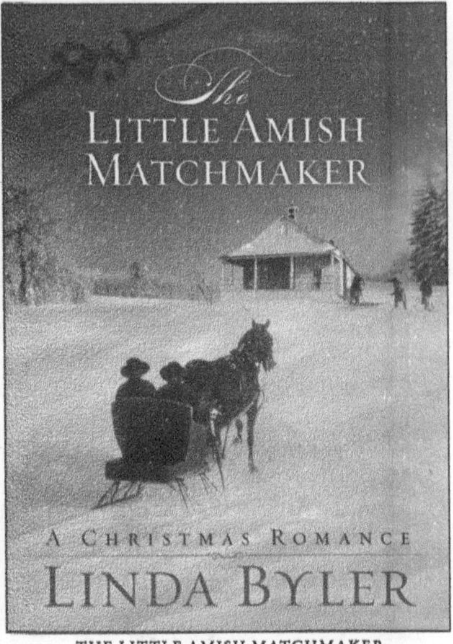

THE LITTLE AMISH MATCHMAKER

MARY'S CHRISTMAS GOODBYE

BECKY MEETS HER MATCH

A DOG FOR CHRISTMAS

A HORSE FOR ELSIE

THE MORE THE MERRIER

A CHRISTMAS ENGAGEMENT

CHRISTMAS EVERY DAY

HONORING CHRISTMAS

LOVE CONQUERS ALL

CHRISTMAS IN WISCONSIN

Christmas Collections

AMISH CHRISTMAS ROMANCE COLLECTION

AMISH ROMANCE AT CHRISTMASTIME